Praise for *Lessons in Faking*

"Athalia and McCarthy deliver peak enemies-to-lovers perfection. They're chaotic, complicated, and completely compelling. *Lessons in Faking* had me flying through the pages and grinning the whole time."

—Hailey Almsted, @haileyalmsted

"That slow burn? Torture, in the best way. I was hanging on every moment until it finally lit up, and wow, it delivered."

—Dana, @thesmallestbookclub

"This fake-dating situationship will have you kicking your feet as you wait to see what happens next between Athalia and McCarthy. A great first installment from Selina Mae!"

—Katie Gia, @thegiacobra

"Oh. My. God. This was so cute and so good. If you love Ali Hazelwood's *Deep End* and Elle Kennedy's college hockey series, this one is for you!"

—MacKenzie Wilcox, @bookskenziereads

"The banter was to die for!! I'm obsessed with Athalia and McCarthy's dynamic. If you love enemies to lovers and fake-dating, then you will fall in love with this book!!!"

—Brianna Whitman, @briannasreadingnook

"I absolutely adored this book. I read it so fast and loved it so much!"

—Abby Roth, @reviewbookswithabby

"The banter?? The tension?? The contracted fake dates that spiral into real feelings?? I was HERE for it."

—Allison, @allisonbookish

"This book had me swooning, crying, laughing, and feeling every emotion."

—Gabriella Tilaj, @gabbydoesreading

"A super cute and funny college romance that's full of yearning, tension, witty banter, and yummy chemistry. Throw in the fake dating trope with a snarky FMC and a charismatic, arrogant MMC, and I am completely SAT!"

—Jess Kaige, @jess.fantasybookshelf

"Fake-dating, spicy study sessions, & the TENSION! Selina Mae is spoiling us with these two!"

—Shay Franklin, @shayreads

LESSONS IN FORGIVING

Also by Selina Mae

Lessons in Faking

LESSONS IN FORGIVING

A NOVEL

SELINA MAE

An imprint of Authors Equity

Authors Equity
1123 Broadway, Suite 1008
New York, New York 10010

Cover design © Jeannine Schmelzer, Bastei Lübbe AG, and © Guter Punkt, Munich
Illustration © fjordwind
Motifs from Shutterstock (© Bobnevv; © Giuseppe_R; Platon Anton; Miloje)
Book design by Scribe Inc.

First published in Germany in 2025 by LYX, an imprint of Bastei Lübbe
First published in the United States in 2026 by LYX, an imprint of Authors Equity

Library of Congress Control Number: 2025945426
Print ISBN 9798893311150
Ebook ISBN 9798893311167

Printed in Canada
First printing

www.lyxbooks.com
www.authorsequity.com

This book contains explicit content. For more detailed information, please see page 403.

Disclaimer: The content warning includes spoilers for the entire book!

We wish you the best possible reading experience.

Love,

Selina & LYX

To those who love hard and fast and never really stop. Thank you.

(P.S. Do not get back with your ex. They're not fictional, and you deserve so much better.)

CHAPTER 1

Then

August: Three years and seven months ago

For the past eighteen years of my life, I'd become an expert at reading my parents. Predicting their whims, knowing when to ask for something and when to keep my mouth shut. When to push a topic and when to drop it.

From the way María Castillo's brows pinched together and the concerned tilt of Juan Castillo's lower lip, I could tell they regretted this. My parents were seconds away from dragging me onto that plane and back to the scorching, familiar Caribbean heat.

They'd lasted a whole two days longer than I'd expected.

"It's . . . big." Despite trying to fit into the English-speaking environment, Mom's accent was thick. She gaped at the high ceilings, eyes raking over the rising rows of seats in the lecture hall. With one last lingering look at the families around us, she turned to me.

Oh yeah. Big-time concern was written all over her face.

"Don't worry, Mami."

I tried not to freak out at the prospect of *her* freaking out, so I waved her off, pretended like I didn't wholeheartedly agree with her.

Dad mirrored the sentiment. "Mi vida," he muttered, trying to swallow his own worries. His hand rested in the small of her back, nudging her out into the hallway. When his eyes found mine, one thing was clear: We were on the same page.

And he was desperate to get Mom there too, trying to convince her of how sure he was I'd find my place here. "Estoy seguro de que nuestra Paulita se integrará—"

But Mom's head swiveled in his direction so fast, he swallowed his Spanish before she'd even said anything. Her withering glare probably helped.

"Coño, Juan. Por favor. *English*!" With one glance down the hallway, she made sure no one had heard the accidental Spanish slip.

Not that anyone cared as much as she did.

But if there was one thing my mom couldn't stand, it was sticking out. If there was another, it would probably be not knowing what her only daughter was doing at any given moment.

Which clearly made the prospect of leaving me in a foreign country more appealing on paper. Proudly telling cousins, aunts, and uncles that her daughter was going to study in America had been fun, but she did not seem to be a fan of what it would actually entail—leaving me behind, alone, in America.

Her brows furrowed, she chewed on her red-painted bottom lip, and I had about two seconds to convince her that I was supposed to be here.

At Hall Beck University. In the United States. About 1,600 miles from the Dominican Republic. *Home.*

Harder than it sounded when I wasn't fully convinced of it myself yet.

"Look," I began, tentatively nudging her into one of the smaller rooms we'd passed on the orientation tour. Gone were the rising rows of chairs and the intimidating podium where professors held hour-long lectures. Entering a simple classroom that would hopefully shake my parents out of their shock-like state, my shoulders sagged with a little bit of relief. "It's not so different from Universidad Tecnológica de Santiago."

That's where I'd probably end up if I didn't sway this situation in my favor. Fast.

Mom shook her head, a disapproving *tsk* passing through her teeth. "Don't lie, Paulita," she said. Looking at the wall of windows and the tablet on each seat, she was probably right when she said, "This is nothing like UTESA." She sighed. "I . . . don't know. Maybe you should come back with us after all. What do you think, Juan?"

Panic. It zipped through my body, white and hot, as she directed a questioning look at Dad. For the life of me, I could not remember a single instance in which he'd denied my mother a single thing. It didn't seem like he was about to start now.

I could see him slip. He was probably already calculating the cost of an extra ticket back to Puerto Plata.

"No!" My intervention kept him from so much as a nod that would set their decision in stone. "Why? Think of how good this school will look on my CV! You've already told Aunt . . . *all of the aunts* about it. And the cousins! Can't forget about the cousins." All twenty-three of them. "What would they think?"

But her head continued shaking, and I was losing momentum here. "No." Her eyes drifted to me again. "I don't care about that." *Lie.* "We just want what's best for you, Paula. I don't know if that's here. I mean . . . have you . . . adjusted?" Concern found its way back into her brown eyes. "Have you made any friends yet?"

I was not surprised by the fact that Mom's only worry was how well I'd fit in—how popular I'd be.

And I did not feel guilty about the lie that flew out of my mouth either.

"Yes!" *I had not.* "Of course." *Hadn't even met my roommates yet.* "Is that what you're worried about, Mami?"

"No."

Yes. Yes. Yes! She was lying too, and I could work with that.

"Oh," I swooned, slowly guiding my parents away from the spot where they'd almost made a decision that would've jeopardized my entire future. Just in case it would remind them of it. "I've met amazing people. They're all so . . . chatty here!"

"Americans do love to talk," Dad agreed gruffly. "Loudly too."

"Really?" Mom wondered. I wasn't quite sure whether she'd asked me or Dad to elaborate, but I took over. Finally, there was a glimmer of hope. Light at the end of the tunnel. She looked relieved, and I could build on that.

If all I needed to fake was an outstanding social life for the next four years, I'd call that a win.

"*Really*," I assured them, throwing all the conviction I could into my gaze. It stayed on them even when we continued making our way out of the room. "We spent all day together yesterday," I lied as I walked backward. "And—"

I couldn't build on my lie when I backed into a solid . . . something. Then, startled, felt myself slip.

I prepared to hit the floor face-first. On impact, my parents would realize I wasn't fit to take care of myself because, well, I'd landed myself in the hospital with a head injury two days into my independence journey, and I'd be forced to agree with them. Mentally, I was already back in the Dominican Republic before I'd even made it to the ground.

I never did.

Instead, I felt a cool hand curl around my wrist, yanking me upright and keeping me there until I managed to find my footing.

I did not face-plant, only stumbled into Dad's chest when the stranger's grip around me loosened. And instead of my parents realizing I was in no condition to take care of myself, I heard an ironic and unfamiliar "Eyes up. Or you might hurt someone."

Followed by Mom's curious voice. "Do you two know

each other?" She sounded . . . excited, and suddenly I did not care who I'd just run into. They would have to do.

I turned just in time to silence him with a look, his lips already parted to give the obvious answer: No.

"Yes!" I blurted, ignoring the confused furrowing of his dark brows. Ignoring how beautifully they contrasted his green eyes. Wincing, I mouthed, *Please*. Then added, *Sorry*.

Turning to my parents, I took a step back to stand beside the brunette stranger, his hair a few shades lighter than my own brown curls. "Of course!" I doubled down cheerily. Too cheerily? "This is . . ."

With the way he winced, I might've *gently* nudged my elbow into his side a little too forcefully. But it must've conveyed my desperation accurately, because he straightened beside me and extended his hand.

"Henry Pressley. Pleasure to finally meet you." His eyes only flicked in my direction for a second before he went on. "I've heard so much about you."

How much could I have potentially told him in the two days we're supposed to have known each other?

I was surprised to hear Dad speak first.

"Pressley?" He repeated the name under his breath, barely loud enough for me to pick up his next words either. Like they weren't intended for the audience he had. "¿Dónde fue que escuché ese nombre?"

Instead of answering where Dad could've heard the name before, Mom lovingly rammed her elbow into his ribs at the second Spanish slip of the day.

"Henry!" she cheered a little louder, smile forced and

eyes glued to the boy. Probably to distract from Dad's Spanish *and* to compensate for his whispering. "No wonder Paula talked so much about you."

I hadn't, obviously. And in any other circumstance, I might've been embarrassed by the revelation, however false. But Henry's appearance had made her forget that I hadn't mentioned anyone until two minutes ago, so it was worth the little color in my cheeks.

"Has she?" His eyes slid to me again before he looked back at my parents. "Only good things, I hope."

"Of course." Mom waved him off, again forgetting I hadn't talked about him at all. She seemed too blinded by the possibility of her daughter actually making a friend. Like she couldn't believe it.

Awesome.

"Pressley!" Dad blurted, only realizing he hadn't used his inside voice when his head snapped up. His eyes widened. "Triste—no! Sorry! Sorry."

It wasn't clear whether he was apologizing to Henry for the outburst or to Mom for the Spanish. His gaze darted between the two so quickly, I couldn't be sure. At last, they settled on the stranger, and a little calmer, though still rattled, he said, "You're Felix Pressley's son. The soccer player."

The shadow that moved across Henry's face was gone as quickly as it had appeared. Like it was nothing, he put on a smile that didn't quite reach his eyes and said, "That's right, sir."

I smiled too, because I knew Dad's favorite thing about Americans was that they regularly called him sir.

"You a fan?" Henry asked.

I'd never had a particular problem with my family's bluntness, but when my dad shook his head and said, "Not really," I wished they had a filter for moments like these. The smile on my face fell.

I expected the same reaction from Henry. But instead of offended gasps, insults thrown, and my little lie revealed, his smile seemed to be genuine. "Yeah." He snickered, sounding relieved more than anything. "Me neither."

And then they bonded.

For a solid fifteen minutes, it was obvious to anyone in our vicinity that my dad knew the guy beside me—or his father—better than I did. But as long as Mom had a smile on her face, seemed delighted by the conversation, and wasn't catching on to my lie, I was happy.

When my parents finally headed outside, the idea of taking me back home with them seemingly forgotten, my sigh was so loud that it carried through the corridor. "You might've just accidentally saved my ass, *Henry*."

"Well, *Paula*." I could hear the grin in his voice. I didn't have to look at him, and in fact, my eyes were still glued to the double doors that just closed behind my parents. "Always happy to help a friend out when she's . . ." He trailed off, hoping I'd fill in the blanks. "When she's what, actually?"

"Oh, you know." I waved him off halfheartedly, my own smile audible. "Just trying to convince her parents she has a raging social life two days into college before they change their minds and make her go to school back home." I realized then that I was speaking about myself in the third person, which was probably weird. Weirder than my explanation.

So I cleared my throat, finally glanced his way, and gave a sheepish shrug when our eyes connected. "No biggie."

"Of course." The amusement in his voice made me hopeful that the whole third-person thing hadn't been as off-putting as I'd feared. "Should've guessed that one myself, actually. My bad."

To really look at him, my head craned upward. He'd tamed his light-brown hair in a casual-enough middle part, white T-shirt tucked into tailored pants and fitting snugly around his biceps. I blinked once.

I'll be damned. Just my luck; Henry Pressley was irrefutably and undeniably . . . hot. Mind-blowingly gorgeous.

When my eyes snapped back up to his dark-green ones, he raised an eyebrow comically. "For what it's worth," he mused, "I think my performance might've changed their minds." He nodded in the direction of their departure, though his gaze stayed fixed on mine. "Hope I'll see you around?"

And I had a feeling I would.

"Here's to hoping."

CHAPTER 2

Now

Two things occurred to me at once:

1. I was chasing my editor out of the building, something I definitely shouldn't be doing.
2. I should, however, really work on my cardio.

"Eddie, please!" Between labored breaths, it was all I got out, hoping I'd catch up to the man responsible for my entire future career before he made it out of the building. "You know I need this," I added. "More than all of them. You know I do."

Instead of looking back at me, realizing I was right (and giving me the damn article), Edward Smith just shook his head. Continued his way down the stairs like he wasn't crushing a piece of my would-be career with every step.

When he started taking two at a time, he muttered,

"I'm sorry, Paula." Halfheartedly, more focused on shoving the large wooden door open to escape to sunny freedom. "Really—"

Which was when I'd fully and intentionally jumped the last four steps to throw myself in front of him. I only winced slightly when he bulldozed into me, and we almost went down on the stony ground in front of the building.

"Jesus Christ." Eddie dusted off his beige sweater once he caught his footing. "Really?" He shook his head in so much disbelief, his blond hair flopped left and right. A deep breath later, and there it was. The finality in his voice I'd hoped to avoid. "Look, I know you want this story," he said, unsure what to do with his hands—whether he should comfortingly pat my shoulder, or keep them swinging at his sides, or scratch his head. He decided on the latter. "But I can't give it to you. It's too important, and after everything that happened last year—"

I could not hear about my failures again, so I quickly cut him off.

"Eddie." A hesitant laugh. "Ed. Look. You don't understand." I swallowed thickly. "I need this article to graduate! *Any* article!"

There was one more assignment to turn in before graduation in a few months, but I couldn't possibly hand in one of the stray horoscopes he'd made me write. That extracurricular project was worth 25 percent of my final grade, and it would've been easy enough a year ago, when I was still getting article after article and I hadn't yet tarnished my journalistic reputation with one stupid mistake. But alas, it wasn't last year anymore, and the piece of writing had to be from the current semester.

Unfortunately, in the last year, Eddie had given me exactly three articles to write. All about what each star sign could expect that month. Absolutely nothing I could submit for grading. If they were to test my ability to go on coffee runs or make exceptional copies, however, I'd pass with flying colors.

"Eddie—" I tried again, which seemed to have been his last straw. He snapped.

"You just don't deserve it!"

While regret immediately registered on his face, it didn't really matter. I could tell he hadn't meant to raise his voice, but his harsh tone still hung between us.

Eddie shook his head again. "I'm sorry, Paula. Really. After everything that's happened, I just can't give this one to you. It's going to Lacy, as discussed."

I think I might've flinched at the insinuation, his harsh words, and that all-too-familiar name before I shook myself out of it. "You're not giving any of them to me, though. None. Nada. Niente. How am I supposed to graduate if you keep every viable topic to write about away from me?"

Eddie pinched the bridge of his nose, eyes closing. When he looked back at me, the trace of regret in his expression was gone, and he looked like a man who had made up his mind. Somehow, I knew it wasn't in my favor.

"Don't worry about that, okay? I'll get you something soon. Just not this one, Paula."

It's the same excuse I'd heard a million times, but it

didn't sting any less. With graduation fast approaching, I wasn't quite sure how much longer he could leave me hanging.

Eddie went back through the massive hardwood doors of the building that held the *Hall Beck Post*'s offices, which brought me back to realization number one.

I just chased my editor out of the building.

Just like that, on a beautiful Friday afternoon, my career died. Over before it even began. I hadn't even made it out of the college paper.

If I couldn't make it at the *HBP*, how was I supposed to succeed in the real world? Among real journalists? What was I supposed to say in job interviews when they'd inevitably ask about the huge gap in publications in my writing résumé?

Oh, that's just Eddie's fault. He rightfully wouldn't give me anything good for a year because I messed up. Really, really badly. He just didn't trust me anymore, but don't worry about it!

My hands curled into fists at my sides before crossing on top of my head, and I halfheartedly started moving again. I took a deep breath and squeezed my eyes shut. On deadline, I'd go back and forth between this building and my place so many times, I could walk it blindly. And I didn't care half as much about how high the risk of running into a lamppost was.

I had bigger things to worry about.

Next week, I'd talk to Eddie again. Explain the situation, make my desperation clear . . . *er.* Although he'd essentially benched me for an entire year, as the *Hall Beck Post*'s head editor, he was obligated to give me something for that extracurricular project. And I wanted it soon, before deadlines might be too tight to—

"Eyes up."

The familiar words made the blood in my veins run cold. I froze, hoping and praying I might've misheard, but—

"Or you might hurt someone."

If I'd been paying any attention to where I was going, I would've seen Henry before I heard him.

My stomach lurched with recognition. I missed a step, almost face-planted on the pebbled road right in front of my ex-boyfriend, and only caught my footing in time to see our paths cross. I hoped he didn't see the embarrassing color in my cheeks as we passed each other; at least Henry didn't turn to look at me again. No smile. No *Hi, how have you been? I miss you, Paula.*

Just that teasing tone like the last time we'd spoken wasn't almost a year ago. My stomach turned at the rich lull in his voice.

Pull yourself together, estúpida.

My best friend took the *No Contact* between me and my ex very seriously, and I took her very seriously, meaning I'd made it almost an entire year without running into him on campus. The Fine Arts and Communications building was the last place I'd expected that streak to end. However childish it sounded, this was *my* little corner of campus. He could have the rest if he wanted to.

The business school. The athletic center named after

his dad. The library and cafeteria, if needed. Just not the *Hall Beck Post*—or the building its office was in.

Every fiber of my being knew I shouldn't turn around—screamed and fought against the urge—but I still did it anyway. *What is he doing here?*

Henry stood in front of the same building I'd run out of minutes ago, seemingly contemplating the same question. He threw his head back, hands disappearing in brown hair that looked lighter now that the sun danced through it.

That was my cue to leave, right? *Before* he could spot me still looking at him. I shouldn't be doing that either, and it became much more apparent when he turned, our gazes met across a two-hundred-foot distance, and it was too late to seem cool and disinterested. Suddenly, I wanted to scream *Please take me back!* across the courtyard.

I'm totally over him, by the way.

I kept repeating that to myself. When I turned on the spot and made a run for it. When I tried not to interpret the way my chest still felt tight in his presence.

I'm totally over him.

Dios mío. I could hear Maeve's words before I'd even made it home: *Paula, get yourself together. It's been a year.* Then: *We said no contact for a reason, darling. That includes not longingly staring after him when you happen to pass him on campus.*

My best friend and I had lived together with two other girls (and Pip, my cat) since our first year. So when I got home, I wasn't surprised by the picture of Maeve sprawled across the entire sofa, ginger hair spilling over the cushions, while Laila and Riley lounged on the floor in front of it. Pip snuggled between the two, sleeping peacefully for once.

Behind them, the counter separating the living room and kitchen must've just been cleaned by one of the girls—probably Laila—because it was empty save for the wooden fruit basket.

I hadn't even opened my mouth, barely managed to slip out of my sneakers and oversized leather jacket, when Maeve's eyes jumped in my direction. One look, and she held up her hand, effectively shushing me.

Reminder: I hadn't said anything yet.

"I can tell you have something to share," she said quickly. Her eyes drifted back to the TV. "But not now, P. The girls are about to come back from Casa Amor!"

Maeve was so engrossed in *Love Island*, she didn't even complain when I hurled myself onto the small, teal-colored couch and forced her to scoot over. As I did, one of the pink throw blankets fell off the armrest it had been hanging on to for dear life, and the *whoosh* was enough to make Maeve send a "Shh!" in its direction.

The inevitable cliffhanger came a mere three minutes later. Maeve and Riley groaned loudly, and Laila threw her head against the couch behind her, blond hair almost tangling with my socked feet.

"Alright." Maeve finally sat up to scan me intently. "I sense reluctance from this side of the couch." She gestured at me with a laugh, drawing Riley and Laila out of their cliffhanger conversation.

Surely they'd be my best shot for backup here.

Maeve, with a knowing smile, said, "What don't you want to tell us but will anyway?"

My eyes narrowed at her brown ones. "How do you know?"

"My psychic abilities." Her smile widened. "And the fact that you wouldn't have shut up when I told you to otherwise."

One thing about Maeve Peterson: Her assessments were always scarily accurate, bordering on actual precognition. More than a few times, I had wiped my thoughts clean just in case she really *could* read minds.

"Alright," I said. "You're not . . . wrong. About the reluctance."

"Shocker," Riley snickered. Laila nudged her with a shush, smoothing a hand down her pin-straight hair, the way she always did when too many people suddenly focused on her.

I cleared my throat. "Remember how I'm really bad at making decisions?" The one time I'd made one, it had literally changed the trajectory of my entire life, and I'd been lying to my parents ever since.

Maeve nodded. "Hard to forget, love."

"So, you help me decide which clothes to buy, what movies to watch. Which . . . exes not to call." And there was only one ex I could be referring to.

Alarm spread across my best friend's features like wildfire. Riley dramatically gasped from the floor. "I didn't call anyone!" I clarified quickly.

Maeve blinked at me, less amused than she was a minute ago. "Spit it out, Castillo."

"Well." I swallowed, eyes trailing across our living room to avoid her hard gaze. The TV beside the front door showed a freeze-frame of the *Love Island* intro, our coffee table was covered in magazines, newspapers, and three of the Daphne Martin novels Riley cycled through. An empty glass vase stood on the sideboard to our left, and on the framed print behind it were our house rules written in primary blue:

1. Shoes off!
2. Laugh loudly
3. Cry freely
4. Dance badly

All in all, not much to see—not more than usual, anyway. "I was just leaving the paper, talking to Eddie about . . . my next article—"

"Oh!" Laila squeaked from the floor. "He finally assigned you something that isn't a horoscope?"

And bless her, I knew she didn't mean for it to sound as . . . sad as it did. When I said no, her face fell. I wasn't sure which I hated more: the pity or the disappointment.

"Not yet," I corrected before getting back to the point. "Anyway, you'll never guess who I ran into after we . . . cordially parted ways."

"Ran into?" Riley again.

"*Almost* ran into," I amended.

Maeve, of course, sighed theatrically before I even mentioned a name.

"Oh, Paula," she muttered. "You talked to him, didn't you?" Another sigh. "Remember that *No Contact* rule? Talking most definitely falls under contact—"

"I did not talk to him, thank you very much." The prolonged silence and my friends' expectant looks forced me to elaborate. "Just looked at him. For a little too long. Until he looked back at me, and we kind of had this eye-contact thing going on, but he was so far . . ."

I was trailing off, and Maeve's grimace told me I sounded too excited. "*I* looked away first and bolted."

"Jesus Christ, Paula," she huffed, hands running across her face. Riley and Laila stayed quiet. "For the record," she continued, "longingly staring after Pressley counts as contact. You'll never get over him like this, darling. It's been a year."

Her tone had taken on a comforting note, the small smile screaming *pity*. Again.

"I know, I know. You've already said that!" I groaned. She was about to disagree with me when I realized: "In my head! You've already said it in my head. And I know. And it makes sense. I want to get over him. I am, kind of. But ay Dios mío, Maeve, look at him! It's impossible."

"He is a catch," Riley agreed thoughtfully, twirling a single black box braid around her finger.

"Thank you!" I swept my hand in her direction for emphasis. "There's nothing wrong with admitting he's a . . . catch." Riley gave me a wink when I glanced at her. "And admiring what makes him so catchy. From afar."

Maeve tilted her head, gaze flicking across my face. My

tan skin, brown eyes, and the curls framing them. "No," she said. "There's nothing wrong with that. And I love the guy—don't look at me like that, I do! But look at you. You locked eyes with him once and fell right back in love."

"That's an exaggeration." My gaze cut to Riley, then Laila, feeling the need to clarify. "She's exaggerating," I doubled down.

Riley snickered, "We know, babe." Raising a suggestive brow, she continued innocently twirling one braid between her fingers. Like she wasn't insinuating what she was insinuating.

Laila, her voice as airy as always, jumped in. "Guys," she pleaded, "Paula doesn't need Henry. She's got Jack."

I didn't mean for my face to do that thing, but I scrunched my nose, furrowed my brow, and physically cringed at the mention. I instantly felt bad.

While Maeve and Riley wiggled their eyebrows, I groaned. "Do I?"

"You could!" Riley half gasped, half screamed, the way she always talked when she was still busy laughing. "You have that poor man wrapped around your little finger. No need to shake your head, it's true. If he's coming tomorrow, you'll see."

"Tomorrow?" Maeve asked.

"Blake's thing, remember?" Translation: A party. It was always a party with Riley. "He invited me, and I know I mentioned that I'm dragging every single one of you with me."

She threw a pointed look at Laila, who definitely did

not want to go but would most likely end up there regardless. The fact that her girlfriend would probably show up was half the reason. Looking back at me, Riley added, "I assume Henry will be there too."

I didn't mean to sit up straighter, but Jack was all but forgotten about when I asked, "You think?" I realized too late that I had not even tried to be subtle about it.

"Good God." Maeve sighed, face disappearing behind her hands. "You shouldn't have said that, Rie."

I gasped like she wasn't completely right. "I just asked! I don't care. It'll be fine." My eyes narrowed into a glare directed at my best friend. "I've spent months ignoring him, and I can continue to do so for a few more before graduation. But thank you for your vote of confidence, Maeve."

Her hands shot up in playful surrender. "I love you?" She winced. "I'm sure you'll manage."

And I thought, *Yes. I can manage.*

Pretending to hate the only man I'd ever loved couldn't be that hard, and it was kind of comforting to know I'd probably never see him again after this.

The heart-wrenching kind of comfort.

CHAPTER 3

Then

September: Three years and six months ago

"I'm sorry." My head fell into my hands with a frustrated sigh, and I blew a stray curl away from my face when I looked back up at him.

Henry blinked, all green eyes and long, dark lashes. I hadn't noticed the few faint freckles across his nose when I'd—quite literally—run into him, and I hadn't noticed them when he had sat behind me in our first lecture a few days later either. The same lecture where he'd leaned closer, breath fanning against my ear, and whispered, "I take it your parents think we're best friends, then?"

Which simply referred to the fact that I was still at HBU. It shouldn't have sent goose bumps down my neck, but it did.

Now, sitting on opposite sides of a library table in the middle of the night, the lights dim and our voices hushed, he was close enough for me to make out the slight crookedness of his nose, the faint scar on his jaw that ran down his neck, and those freckles.

"I'm sorry," I repeated. "This has quite literally never happened to me."

His head tilted. "What hasn't?"

I snickered. "I'm going to sound like a dick."

"Try me."

And maybe it was the lack of sleep and abundance of desperation creeping in that made me confess. "I've never really been bad at . . . anything. School related!" I added as soon as his lips quirked at the words. "I mean, I'm great at school. Learning, calculating, understanding. I don't know what I am if not good at those things. So why am I struggling?"

Henry nodded thoughtfully. "You do seem like a girl who's never gotten anything wrong in her life."

He stated it like he thought a lot about the kind of girl I was. Like it might keep him up at night, and he'd considered it so deeply, he was completely sure of his words. "And you just happen to be in the library after hours with a boy who never has either. We'll get there, Paula."

"Humble." I snorted.

"Hey." His hands lifted in mock surrender as he leaned back into his chair. "You said it first."

With a laugh, I agreed, "I did." But I sobered quickly. "I'm sorry, though. You shouldn't be stuck here just because I can't grasp the concept of data science." When he'd offered to help me out, he'd said he could stay until ten.

It was midnight now, and Henry Parker Pressley still sat opposite me, shaking his head like he'd never given himself a time limit at all.

"And financial reporting."

"What?" I asked.

"You can't grasp the concept of data science *or* financial reporting. Or technology and operations management, actually," he added as nonchalantly as one might report the weather. Like he wasn't listing every single one of my faults.

"Why thank you"—my nose scrunched—"for reminding me of all my shortcomings."

"Which means we're in the same boat here, Paula. I could use some more hours with the material too. And they do say the best way to learn is by explaining it to others."

"Who says that?"

Henry ignored my teasing question. "What was it you were good at back in high school? When you were still at home?"

Everything! I wanted to scream. But even though we were alone, this was still a library, and it would've felt wrong.

I'd been great at school. Math. English. The sciences. Grades were what I'd always measured myself by. When I'd gotten an A on a test, Dad would get me a treat from the corner store. In high school, Mom would take me to get a manicure after a good result, and I'd walked around with bright-pink nails for weeks.

When I got a B or a C, there were no treats and no manicures and fewer of the usual loving words from my parents. It was still *Well done!* or *Not bad!* But never *We're so proud of you, Paulita! You'll go so far in life!*

And I didn't think it was intentional, really, but the difference still seemed to stick with me. If I couldn't show off my grades after this first semester—if they weren't good enough—then what?

I sighed. "English, I guess. And Spanish." My best subjects had always been the languages. "I wrote for the school paper."

"And you didn't think to study something related? Business seems like a big leap for someone whose favorite subject was English."

I took a deep breath, head falling back. "I don't think my dad ever considered I'd study anything other than business, to be honest. He's got a little restaurant back in the Dominican Republic, so he thinks he's a businessman—"

"Technically, he is," Henry said.

"Technically, he *is* a businessman," I repeated with a glare I didn't truly mean. "And he always liked when we had things in common, I guess."

My parents began saving for my college fund when they learned that Mom was pregnant. The decision about what I would study had never even been discussed; it had been made before I could talk.

Henry nodded like he understood all too well. "English." He hummed. "So, vocabulary, then. That's doable."

He said it more so to himself, eyes connecting with mine. "We can meet back here tomorrow morning. I've got practice till nine, and we won't have class until four. Gives us seven hours to study data science, financial reporting, and technology and operations management, but like vocabulary. Flashcards and everything. How's that sound?"

I didn't know what made him so . . . eager to help me. But his brows rose, and his tongue flicked across his lips as if he couldn't wait for my answer. As someone who couldn't make her own decisions to save her life, the way he just took over was so . . . relieving. I wanted to lean into whatever he decided more than anything.

My face soured. "I've got work. Eight to three."

The coffee shop doubled as a flower store, and it was fine. The pay wasn't great in a college town, but it was better than nothing, and I was grateful to find something so quickly. I'd only been at HBU a few weeks, and any job that would help me relieve some of my parents' financial burden was good enough.

Even more important now that I felt like I was failing them.

"You work?"

I nodded. "At Daisy's. Jack doesn't like opening by himself, and someone else got sick. So he asked me to cover their shift tomorrow morning. I'm—"

"Jack?"

"Griffin. Jack Griffin. My coworker? He's the barista. I don't know if you've—"

Henry shook his head before I'd asked. "Haven't heard of him, no. Fuck him for making you work on such short notice, though."

I laughed, the sound somewhere between a snort and

a cackle. "Well, he couldn't have known I'd much rather be in the library." *With you*, I didn't add.

Henry was smart and funny in that stoic way that not everyone would appreciate. He was undeniably handsome, and I'd dreamed about him twice in the weeks I'd known him—neither one platonic enough to write off—and there was no way he felt the same way.

He's only being nice because the first time we met, I told him my parents were scared I wouldn't find friends.

The thought brought color to my cheeks that I hoped the dim light hid well enough.

"Would you?" Henry asked, brow rising in amusement. "Rather be here? Poring over books while I just sit there and try not to watch you?"

More color. Much hotter.

I shrugged, trying my hardest to keep my cool instead of blurting, *Gladly!*

"You're surprised by that?" I asked. "My parents think we're best friends, after all. What am I supposed to want more than to spend time with friends?"

Henry couldn't hide the hint of a grin on his lips. When he leaned his forearms on the table between us, casting his face in shadow from the light right above us, something shifted.

Between us. In the way I breathed and the way he looked at me.

"It's cute that you say that." I didn't know why I held my breath until he continued. "But I don't think we're going to be friends, Paula."

CHAPTER 4

Now

I know I should've slowed down after the third tequila shot. In all honesty, I'd probably reached my limit after number two.

But Riley was handing me another one, yelling, laughing, and singing along to the music. Everything about her was so magnetic, her mood so contagious . . . How could I say no? The decision was basically made for me when she gave me the cup.

Plus, I had almost completely forgotten about the man currently standing on the other side of the room.

Henry was propped against the back of the couch when we arrived, arms crossed in that way that made them strain against the confines of his sleeves. His brown hair parted down the middle, and he was talking to someone female who wasn't me.

Which made me remember I shouldn't notice—*didn't*

have any right to notice—who he was or wasn't talking to. I downed that first tequila shot so fast I almost coughed it all back up. Now I tipped my head back with the fourth one, liquor burning down my throat, soothing the unjustified jealousy still burning in the pit of my stomach. *Involuntarily,* I might add.

The girls cheered, and Maeve threw her arm around my shoulder, swaying us to the sound of a mediocre ABBA remix blaring through the frat house.

It will be fine, I told myself.

Although I couldn't count the number of times I'd stumbled, stepped on a foot, or reached for an arm for balance, and although my ex-boyfriend was somewhere in this room—most likely heavily flirting with a girl whose name I didn't know—I'd be fine. Right?

I had my girls, my cat . . . and before I got the chance to ponder how pathetic I sounded, Riley handed me an empty cup just in time. She filled it to the brim with some kind of alcohol concoction that could probably kill someone, and we all drank it anyway.

I was just looking for a clock on the wall the next time my eyes involuntarily searched the room. And surely, the way my stomach dropped was because I couldn't find the time, not because I couldn't find him. Henry was nowhere to be seen.

Not that I wanted to. *See him*, I mean.

"Girls," I . . . panted? *Dios mío*, was the alcohol catching up with me that quickly? "I'm just gonna go to the bathroom."

Laila jumped into Mom Mode, concern riddling her tone, blue eyes wide in worry. "Do you need us? Are you going to throw up?"

She was the only one who had refused the second shot, instead opting for a sweet mixer that would allow her to wake up without a pounding headache tomorrow. I was already way past that point.

I shook my head, and unfortunately, the world began spinning around me. "No." *Maybe.* "Peeing."

Apparently, I couldn't muster more than one-word answers.

Although it put a steep staircase between me and release (in whichever form it came), I heroically climbed it to avoid the line that had formed in front of the much busier guest bathroom downstairs. At the top, I let go of the banister reluctantly and reached for the opposite wall for the support I definitely needed. Pretty sure I was feeling the world spinning on its axis at that moment, which reminded me that we were, in fact, on a ball orbiting in space. Spinning with it. I never quite understood how that worked, and now the thought made me feel sick.

"Fuck," I groaned again, resting my forehead against my arm on the wall for . . . more support? With my eyes closed, I noticed less of that spinning globe we were all trapped on doing its thing.

Out of the void around me, someone asked if I was alright. I nodded as fast as I could, already muttering multiple variations of yes against the wall that were only answered with an amused snort. Then the beginning of a laugh that just sounded so, so, *so* . . . familiar.

My eyes snapped open.

Holding steady eye contact with the wall, my forehead still pressed against it to avoid looking at Henry. Right next to me.

I could feel his presence now.

A single, cautious glance out of the corner of my eye confirmed he stood with his hands in his pockets, leaning against the wall as he waited. For the bathroom door to open or for me to acknowledge him, I wasn't sure.

I huffed into my arm, eyes closing again in frustration. And maybe some relief that he hadn't left with the beautiful brunette after all. But as much as I tried to ignore him, I felt Henry's gaze raking up and down my body, taking in the dress I wore. My bare legs.

It was driving me mad.

"Mierda," I cursed between gritted teeth, finally turning toward him. "*What?*"

Henry seemed as taken aback by my tone as I was.

I hadn't expected whatever emotions were simmering in the pit of my stomach to make it to the surface either, but now that they were out, it felt kind of . . . great. And this was good! Wasn't it?

If I focused on how much I hated him rather than how good he looked tonight. If I reminded myself of all the reasons I *should* hate him instead of the fact that we hadn't been this close to each other since our breakup, then maybe this could work.

Henry's ego was big enough on its own. I didn't need to inflate it more by making the fact I hadn't quite moved on (yet) obvious, when he clearly had (e.g., beautiful brunette from earlier). I think I might've flinched at the reminder.

When I doubled down, I surprised myself again. "Spit it out, Henry."

"Nothing," he said smoothly. "Simply concerned you might fall down the stairs just by standing too close to them."

I wanted to roll my eyes at the (accurate) observation, throw some remark his way that proved him wrong and showed that I wasn't half as drunk as I actually was.

Unfortunately, as if on cue, when I let go of the wall I'd been holding on to for support, I swayed. Probably just a step or two—I wasn't sure because I caught my footing quickly, kind of proving him wrong? Somehow?

A proud smile sneaked onto my lips when I looked at him again. *See*, I wanted to say. *I can stand upright.*

Which was when I noticed his hand around my wrist.

A second ticked by, then another. My eyes slowly drifted to where he held me, right above my pulse point, and I hoped to God he couldn't feel it kicking into overdrive underneath his touch.

I hadn't found my footing at all. Henry had simply caught me.

Our gazes locked for a moment, but whatever he was searching for in my eyes, he didn't find. He cleared his throat, cautiously letting go of my arm to make sure I could stand on my own two feet without falling over like a baby giraffe. *Great.*

"Are you sure you're fine, Paula?"

I scoffed. "Yes. Thank—" *Angry,* I remembered. I was supposed to be angry. Or at least not pleasant. "No." There would be no such thing as gratitude. I was failing Operation No Contact badly enough already. "Not *thank you.* In fact . . ." *In fact what?* "Nothing at all."

Before I could stop rambling, the door to the bathroom unlocked, and a girl rushed out, leaving it empty for the next person. Which was Henry. "Would you just get in there, p—?"

"Don't say *please.*" Henry was clearly holding back a smile when he interrupted me. "You might regret your manners, Paula." Before I could say *Don't say my name like that, it's doing things to me!* he stepped aside, gestured to the bathroom. "It seems you need to get in there more urgently."

*

He was right. The second I locked the door behind me, I hurled into the bowl. I was very glad the lid was up, then even more glad I'd made it this far—that I hadn't puked on Henry's shoes. I stayed on the floor for . . . a while. And as I hung there (head over the toilet, surroundings spinning, contemplating the last twenty minutes), I decided not to tell my friends about this encounter.

Which wasn't the easy way out. I loved oversharing. Though if Maeve considered even looking at Henry a breach of our No Contact Agreement (NCA), talking to him—*touching him!*—was a federal offense.

When I left the bathroom, Henry was gone. Either he'd considered his odds downstairs better or he just didn't want to see me again.

The painful thump in my chest propelled me downstairs, where Maeve patiently held my drink, covering the top with her palm. My best friend eyed me curiously, gaze flicking between me and the staircase. And I knew that look. Psychic Maeve was back, and my plan not to tell her about what had just happened became significantly less likely to succeed. The redhead gave me a conspiratorial smile.

"What took you so long?" she asked.

She knows was my first thought. She'd probably seen Henry come downstairs and put two and two together. Maeve inconspicuously swayed to the music.

I shrugged. "I threw up."

Laila bumped my shoulder with her own, mouth open in a soundless gasp. "You should've said something!" she squeaked. "Girls should never have to throw up alone! Who held your hair, Paula?" She looked genuinely concerned, maybe even distressed, and I couldn't help giggling.

"Yeah, Paula," Maeve said. "Who could've possibly been up there to hold your hair?"

There it was.

I decided to ignore her knowing smile and instead turned back to Laila.

"I'm sorry, Lil," I said, one hand on my heart, the other on her shoulder. "Next time, you can hold my hair."

She huffed, though a smile replaced the frown from a second earlier. "Good."

One last time, Maeve's attention drifted to the staircase before she seemed to drop her suspicions. For now, she didn't have much of a choice because Riley dragged us onto the makeshift dance floor a second later.

CHAPTER 5

Now

Sunday wasn't great. As expected, it passed by in a blur of painkillers and memories of Henry's hand around my wrist, briefly interrupted when I chugged water or had a greasy breakfast at 3:00 p.m.

Monday was when the real fun began.

The clacking sounds of fingers hammering against keyboards, the whirring of our no-good printer, and a strong scent of coffee hit me when I got to the office. That I-desperately-wanted-to-sit-at-my-desk-and-write-something-meaningful-again feeling hit. *I need to talk to Eddie.* He'd either give me an article or kick me off the *Hall Beck Post* for annoying him too much, but at least then, no one could say I hadn't tried hard enough.

My entire future in the hands of a PhD student a few years older than me . . .

A few heads emerged from behind their screens to greet

me with soundless smiles. Riley—who thought signing up for the *Post* might make a good addition to her event management degree—waved from where she was preparing what was likely her fourth coffee of the day. Alfie, who probably hadn't expected the desk next to him to be occupied today, gave me a surprised look from the farthest corner of the office we'd both been banished to. Lacy—*I-get-every-article-I-want* Lacy—acknowledged me with a brief nod, too focused on the words on her screen to speak.

Despite what happened last year, a weird sense of belonging rushed through me whenever I walked into the office. Whether I was writing about the stars' predictions, going on coffee runs, or loudly arguing with the printer until it did what I'd asked of it, I could almost pretend everything was fine. Normal.

The people in this office still thought of me as a respectable journalist, even if I'd messed up one of Eddie's most important articles. Alfie had made about a hundred mistakes in his one semester at the paper, and he'd reassured me that *"mistakes come with being human."*

I'd probably worry less about mistakes if my degree wasn't directly linked to them. Especially if, like Alfie, I was still able to snag an article here and there because my media-conglomerate dad's sizable donations basically funded the damn place.

Unfortunately, my parents weren't in a position to donate. So I was mostly stuck with coffee and printers. Plus the respect of my fellow journalists-to-be. Whatever that was worth.

"Paula!" The fact that it had taken Lacy five minutes to acknowledge my presence most likely meant she'd been too busy with the article I had begged Eddie for last week.

That should be me.

She was getting most front-page articles these days, and she seemed to handle the daily deadlines like they were nothing. Like she probably submitted them early and still managed an everything-shower and a blowout in the mornings.

Whenever I looked at Lacy for a little too long, noticed a few too many things about her, I couldn't help but wonder how I ever thought I'd compare. To her easy smiles and perfect blond waves. To the fact that Eddie had found his star writer in her.

I could hardly remember the time when *I'd* been that star writer.

"You don't know how glad I am to see you. What are you up to?" she wondered.

But at least people still loved me here.

Lacy waved me off before I could say, *Looking for Eddie? Begging for the life that you stole from me?*

"Would you mind grabbing me a coffee from the machine downstairs? I am swamped with this"—she gestured to her computer screen—"and I have to hand it in for editing in an hour." Lacy winced at her own request, then smiled like she knew she'd get away with it regardless.

Maybe I should clarify some things: My peers' love and respect went as far as their love for coffee that wasn't filtered.

"Oh! Did you bring another batch of your vegan chocolate chip cookies, by the way?" Lacy asked. "The sugar really got my brain going the other day."

Unfiltered coffee *and* baked goods.

I huffed, catching Riley's eye roll in my periphery. "Sorry, Lacy." I turned back to face her, and I wished I could say her round, piercing blue eyes were only half as mesmerizing after almost four years. "No cookies today."

She pouted. "How about that coffee, though?"

And those coffee runs had become so common, I didn't have to ask how she'd like it. Two cream, one sugar. "Sure."

Lacy exhaled loudly with relief. "You're an angel," she said, then disappeared behind her screen again. I wasn't surprised.

The only thing surprising was finding Eddie in the door when I turned.

"Actually." He cleared his throat, clearly having followed our brief conversation. "Paula, would you mind?"

He gestured into the hallway, and I honest to God thought Edward Smith was ushering me along for Lacy's coffee. But instead, he said, "I'd like to talk to you about something. Sorry, Lacy!" he added across his shoulder, not at all apologetic when he gave her a last, lingering look. "And get that article done. Fifty-seven minutes. Ticktock." He tapped the watch on his wrist and then disappeared through the door, expecting me to follow.

We walked the hall aimlessly. Past the rec room, the

media labs, and when we passed his office—its door, as always, slightly ajar—I started to worry. Usually, serious conversations with Eddie happened in that office.

After the article last year, he'd taken me there, told me I'd misquoted, and revealed that my source had filed a complaint with the Society of Professional Journalists' ethics committee. Which, unfortunately, couldn't be scratched out of my record until that same source withdrew it or the claim was disproven. The burden of proof wasn't on the complainant.

"I've been thinking," Eddie finally said, mercifully dragging me out of my own head and away from his office, down the stairs.

It occurred to me halfway toward the exit. Eddie was walking me out. He was literally walking me out of the building, about to send me on my way with a *Good luck!* followed by a *Let me know if you ever make it out there!* Maybe the way I'd thrown myself in front of him last week really had been the straw that broke the camel's back.

Jesus Christ, I was about to get fired. From a job that didn't even pay me.

My breath hitched in my throat. "Me too. Actually." The words just shot out. It was a bad attempt to avoid or, at the very least, delay that outcome. "About the *Post*. And me." Reaching the massive doors leading outside, I dared a glance at the man beside me when he held one open for me.

His blond hair. The small, crooked mouth. Brown eyes, perfectly curved nose. Round cheeks. At just twenty-seven—two years into his English PhD—Eddie did not look like a man who was about to crush my dreams.

Those small lips were tilted up. Just slightly, right in the corners. That was a good sign. Then again, the rest of his body looked tense. Like he wasn't quite sure what to do either.

I began rambling. "I'm sorry for last week. And last year. I think if you gave me another shot—"

Eddie shook his head quickly. That weird tilt of his lips finally developed into a smile. Maybe he was more sadistic than I thought, and he *was* actually enjoying this.

"Why don't I start?" he suggested. "I know what you want to say. Trust me, it'll be unnecessary by the time I'm done."

Something inside of me shattered. The hope I'd still had left or my heart or whatever plan of the future I'd envisioned over the past years. Everything I'd worked toward. All those fake exam results I'd sent to my parents. All that lying and deceiving had led me here. *Dios*, I should've stuck with my business degree.

Eddie nodded toward the other end of the park bench he sat on. Pulse racing, I obliged his request to sit.

"I'm wondering, Paula," he began. I think I winced even before he said the next words. "You into sports?"

Huh? Was this really the best time to discuss favorite sports teams?

But I decided to go with it for the sake of my maybe-future, regardless.

"Watching? Sure," I said carefully. "I'm not really the

exercising type, though." Which was when it dawned on me, and oh my God—"Please don't suggest I join some sports club instead of the *Post*."

Apparently, this was where the pleading began. Where else could this conversation be going, if not—

"*What?*"

Or maybe . . . not?

"I'm not—Why would you—? What?" Eddie asked again, seemingly more confused than I was. "What do you think this is? If I wanted to kick you out, I would've done it when you messed up! Your degree is tied to the *Post* now, Paula. Even if I wanted to, *which I don't*, I couldn't get rid of you for something that happened last year." His eyes narrowed, like he'd thought that was obvious too. "Jesus, is this what you've been so worried about?"

Something untangled in my chest at the words. Relief spread into every part of me, so all-consuming I could only nod.

"I have no intention of letting you go," he clarified. "I just . . . have a project for you."

Slumping over at the confirmation, I buried my face in my hands. "Fuck!" I groaned, and I did not care that I'd just cursed in front of my superior. "I think I almost had a heart attack, Ed. Don't ever do that to me again."

"Do *what*, exactly?"

I could feel my pulse returning to its natural rhythm and the cloud of anxiety in my head clearing as I processed his words. "Ominously taking me away from the group.

Not telling me where we're going or what we're doing. Walking me out of the building. Only—" I interrupted myself with a pained laugh. "Only for you to say—"

No intention of letting you go. I just . . . have a project for you.

It clicked then. I straightened so fast, I think I pulled a muscle on my way up.

"A project?" I knew I wasn't playing this one cool. I did not even attempt it. "*The* project?"

One I could hand in for that extracurricular grade? The only thing missing for my degree?

"Yes," he said.

"The kind that needs research and writing and gets printed eventually?"

Eddie huffed, nodding solemnly. Clearly, he was not excited about the prospect. Me, on the other hand? I was through the roof without even knowing what he was putting me on. *Progress.* That was all that mattered.

"Yes," Eddie repeated. Sighed again. "But I don't know how much you'll like it once I tell you—"

"Nonsense!" There was literally nothing in the world I wouldn't write.

If he wanted me to, I'd write a killer article about this year's grass growth on campus. And I'd make it interesting. Front-page worthy. I'd talk to landscapers and the gardening team. Make sure to get accurate quotes. "Of course, I'll be careful with sources. I'll double-check—triple-check! The whole shebang. I've got it covered."

"Yeah . . ." He trailed off. "Listen, Paula. That's not what

I'm concerned about. Sources won't be a problem with this one. If you think about it, there'll only be one, really."

The smile on my face dimmed. Slightly.

"One source?" I asked. "What kind of article only needs one source?"

"Well." Eddie took a deep breath, like he was preparing for something unpleasant. His eyes diverted. "Maybe a couple more, but not many. It's more of a profile than an article, you know?"

My brow furrowed as I watched him fidget with the zipper of his jacket. "Sounds like a sweet gig to me." Which was why I couldn't explain the miserable expression on his face. "Don't worry. I can do a profile. On who?"

"Henry Pressley."

CHAPTER 6

Then

October: Three years and five months ago

It took me a while to come to terms with the fact that a business admin degree just wasn't for me.

Despite Henry's vigorous efforts, despite his impromptu flashcard business-vocabulary tests during my shifts at Daisy's, and despite diving headfirst into assigned *and* unassigned reading about concepts I couldn't care less about every afternoon, my heart was not in it. My brain clearly wasn't either.

I should've called my parents to tell them. Discuss the opportunity to change majors to something that was a little more creative and a little less numbers focused. Something I could actually see myself doing for the rest of my life after graduation.

Instead, I'd been staring at my screen for the past ten minutes, unable to move. The fan of my laptop was getting louder with every second my mail app was open, and although I was concerned about the possibility of an explosion, I still didn't move.

I was physically unable to stop rereading that email.

> Congratulations! You've successfully transferred from HBU Business School to HBU's Fine Arts & Communications Campus.
>
> Old: Bachelor of Arts—Business Administration
>
> New: Bachelor of Arts—Journalism
>
> Please talk to your assigned advisor to get settled as soon as possible. We wish you the very best and cannot wait to see what you accomplish one day!
>
> —Hall Beck University

The exact reason why I didn't trust myself to make decisions was staring right back at me. Impulsive, stupid, and irreversible.

Like the one time I went skinny-dipping to try and fit in with the cool kids—who had proceeded to run off into the night *with* my clothes. Then, too scared and way too self-conscious about the curves no one else had developed yet, I refused to get out of the water and had almost been eaten by a shark.

Okay, maybe not eaten, but its fin definitely grazed me. In dark, open water, it was almost the same thing. *Then*, like that wasn't enough, I stepped on an urchin and had to ask the nearest stranger on a beach in Puerto Plata to call an ambulance. They'd taken me to the hospital in nothing but an abandoned towel that barely reached my thighs.

So I was no stranger to impulsively stupid decisions with irreversible consequences, and I'd made one last decision that night: Avoid making any more.

I'm also a Libra.

My parents had decided I'd go to college in the United States. My parents had decided I'd study business. My parents had decided that living in a shared house was cheaper and safer than sharing a room with a stranger.

Then I started rolling with my housemates' dinner plans ("Whatever is fine, really"). My housemates had quickly decided we'd all be best friends, and I'd gone along with that too. Was really, really happy with it, even. They'd become friends with the neighbors on the same soccer team as Henry, and so I did too. I'd started going to my best friends when I needed help with an outfit or couldn't decide what to do with my hair, so not making decisions had always been easy.

I seemed to draw strong-willed, decisive people to me like moths to a flame. Maeve was that way. Henry was too.

And yet.

I read through that cursed email one last time, then forced my laptop shut. The missing sound of its fan was eerie, though the silence only lingered for a second. I'd spent about two months in this house, and I could already tell by the sound of her footsteps that Maeve was the one who'd burst into my room before I'd even looked up to check.

From the doorway, she assessed me, gaze narrowed. Probably noticed the way I slumped against the wall beside my bed, how my breathing was labored, and how Pip was not calmly napping on my pillow but pacing the room like she always did when I was on edge.

I was sure she picked up on the signs, but instead of pointing any of them out and then guessing the cause of them with scary accuracy, she looked at the wall behind me and said, "We should really paint that in the orange you liked so much."

I blinked at her. "What orange?"

Maeve rolled her eyes as she leaned against the doorframe, her arms crossed. "When we went to pick out a rug last month, we walked past the paints. You pointed to an orange and said, 'This would look nice on a wall.'"

I did not remember that. At all. But then again, I had just officially changed majors, and there wasn't enough space in my head to remember much else.

With a groan, I fell into my white sheets. "I did something," I confessed, voice whiny. I might start crying.

I could hear Maeve shift around the room, but I could not see her. My eyes were squeezed shut tightly.

"I know, honey," she cooed. Gentle concern had replaced the previous amusement, and she scooted onto the bed beside me. "What is it?"

I blindly pointed to the laptop at the foot of the bed. In the silence that followed, she probably read the email. The one that had literally changed the course of my entire life. A reply to a form I'd desperately filled out the week before, when I'd been struggling with programming languages I had not expected to be on the syllabus. After our first test, on which I'd gotten a C-minus.

The first C-minus in my entire life. Which was when I'd realized I was really struggling.

However, I had not struggled to write that change-of-major essay. At one in the morning, I'd sent it off and expected to never hear back from them.

About a month ago, I'd applied to the college paper as some kind of counterweight to the endless numbers I'd been dealing with in most of my classes. Also because I'd missed writing. Helping out at the *Hall Beck Post* fixed that. Writing about the weather and taking a stab at horoscopes had been so much fun that the only reason I went back to the library to study was for the evenings I knew Henry would join me.

Fast-forward a few weeks, and I was *majoring* in journalism now.

I groaned once more.

"Paula!" Maeve gasped, and I think for the first time, I'd taken her by surprise. "Holy shit. I'm so proud of you."

Not the words I'd expected from her.

Slowly, my head emerged from the depths of pillow and blanket and whatever else I'd buried myself in to look at her. *Really* look at her. Hoping, or expecting, to find a trace of humor or ridicule in her expression, but I came up empty. She beamed at me, and her freckled arms were around me before I could try to find anything suspicious about her reaction.

I almost smiled myself because *Holy shit, I did that!* Until she asked, still giddy, "What did your parents say?"

I stiffened. And she understood immediately.

"Oh my God. You didn't tell them."

*

Meanwhile, Henry insisted that he was not surprised. Not about what I thought had been my spur-of-the-moment decision to change majors. Not about the fact that I hadn't told my parents either.

When I'd gone to see him after his home game the next day, I'd gotten there just as Dylan McCarthy Williams delivered HBU's winning shot into the other net.

I'd like to say I'd watched the rest of the game intently, but really, I was watching Henry. My eyes followed him when he had possession, and probably more so when he did not. Because it meant he might look back at me too.

Twenty minutes later, when I surprised him outside the locker room and told him about what I'd done in a fit of rambling, excitement, and fear, he only smiled. The corner of his lip curled just slightly, and his gaze flicked down and back up my frame in what could've been silent praise. Not for my outfit—wide blue jeans, graphic tee, a black oversized leather jacket . . . definitely nothing to write home about—but perhaps for me?

Which was when he'd said it. "I'm not surprised."

I couldn't help the amused snort that came out of me as I walked beside him. "You're not?" I asked teasingly. He just sounded *so* sure.

I could feel the way he studied my profile, no sense of shame in how long his green eyes lingered on me. Like I was the last few minutes of the World Cup final, and he couldn't bear the thought of accidentally missing something.

A hint of citrus and pinewood I'd come to know as the scent of Henry's cologne lingered in the air, mixing with the smell of the rain from last night. The dark sky seemed to promise more of that today, so I was relieved to spot his car in the lot behind the soccer field.

"Not even the tiniest bit, Paula. When you're confused, you scrunch your nose, and it's basically scrunched for however long we study for. When you're frustrated, there's this sound you make. Something between a huff and a groan and a sigh, and I've heard you make it so many times, I dream of it sometimes."

I didn't know why that confession brought heat to my cheeks. Or why I couldn't keep my lips from pulling up. I think I was smiling. At the floor. Looking anywhere but at him, because God forbid he found out I'd dreamed about the sounds he might make too.

"You were confused and frustrated, and you're not used to that. So, if anything, I'm surprised you lasted as long as you did." Henry shrugged, unlocked his car, and held the passenger door open before he'd even asked if I wanted a ride home. I got in with a glare, finally looking at him.

"I dare you to call me too dumb for your major again, Henry Pressley," I muttered when he got behind the wheel, trying hard to keep my amusement at bay and hoping it wasn't audible in my tone.

But Henry and I both knew my accusation wasn't at all what he'd said. He hit the nail on the head. Read me like he'd known me for years.

"Or what?" he asked.

I snorted, finally breaking when I could tell he was way past the point of believing I was sincerely hurt.

"Or I might just change back to business admin specifically to ruin your life."

He shook his head. "You couldn't ruin my life even if you wanted to."

"I'll egg your apartment. Your car." I thought for a moment. "I'll egg *you*."

His head finally turned in my direction, hair damp from the quick shower after the game. Our gazes locked for one, two, three seconds, and I think I might've been holding my breath. "You're vegan."

My eyes narrowed. "You might just be worth breaking my morals for."

He chuckled. Between one laugh and the next, he said, "Charming, Paula. You're a charm."

CHAPTER 7

Now

I can't do a profile.

Not on him.

"It's a pretty good deal, Paula. Great for your extracurricular project. Even better if you still plan on going into sports journalism after graduation. I heard you're into soccer, anyway? The thing is practically made for you."

Eddie had been trying to rationalize my stern *Nos* away for a while now. I'd taken up pacing like a madwoman in front of the park bench he sat on.

"I can't." And I didn't care how pathetic it sounded. "You know I can't." My gaze slid to him, pity meeting me in his eyes.

Lately, it seemed that's all I found in anyone's.

I wondered whether that was what I'd see once I told my parents about this mess. That I'd thrown away their dream for me, then ruined my own because of a man, of all things.

"Look," Eddie said tentatively, getting up. "I know you guys have history. I know you don't like to talk about what happened, and I honored that when I didn't ask about his involvement in what happened with your last article."

The one that had messed it all up. Me and Henry. Me and the *Post*.

Standing opposite me, Eddie's hands were on my shoulders, and I wasn't sure if he was going for reassuring or intimidating. I wasn't sure if he knew either. "But we're a small paper, and it's inevitable that some of you will report on friends, classmates, boyfriends—"

"Ex-boyfriends."

"You know what I mean."

And I did. At the bottom of every issue, there was a disclaimer in the fine print reminding us—and our readers—of that exact possibility:

> The *Hall Beck Post* is a small paper, and as student journalists, that means we're often covering our classmates, teachers, friends, former roommates, and various people we've had relationships with. We try to avoid doing so as much as possible, and when it's unavoidable, we make a parenthetical notation in the text of any preexisting or past relationship.

But I didn't want a parenthetical notation reminding the entire school that Henry had dumped me a year ago.

"I need you on this, Paula. There's no way around it."

My head shook again, kind of like a little kid who was about to throw a tantrum.

"It's this or nothing," Eddie doubled down. "And since I can't *and won't* allow the latter, you're going to have to do this." His already small lips thinned into a straight line. "I wish there was another way. I really do."

That sentiment, at least, seemed genuine. Like he wanted someone else on this as desperately as I did.

"So why me?"

Eddie shrugged. "Look. The HBU soccer team wants this article about Pressley. The school's marketing team wants this article. The *Post* does too. Forget about why and how, Paula. Think about what! What could come from it. What it might do for you. It'll put you on the radar."

Again, I added silently. *It would put me on the radar again.*

"Between you and me." My editor lowered his voice when someone passed us. "A bigger magazine has already expressed interest. If you do a good job, they might pick up the story. Consider the optics! For you. For the *Post*."

Gnawing on my bottom lip, I ignored the metallic taste in my mouth. Even with the chirping of the birds, the wind rustling through the newly green trees, and the distant chatter filling my ears, the silence between us felt deafening.

"For your sake," Eddie huffed. "I'm going to pretend you have a choice in this. Sleep on it, then come see me in the morning." Before he left, he added, "But don't think the decision hasn't already been made for you."

Lunacy, I thought as Eddie went back inside, and I slumped onto the wooden bench. Cruelty. A really, really bad joke. From him. From the universe.

It could've been anything, but not real life.

I'd probably be able to write an article on my ex. A profile, though? One-on-one time. Shadowing. Once again being wound up in Henry's routine and scheduling my days by how well my plans fit into his . . . It sounded like a nightmare.

And yet I couldn't let him be the reason I passed on an opportunity like this either.

I groaned when I realized Eddie was right. If there was external interest, this could be huge for anyone involved. And perfectly timed to throw me back on the radar—just in time for graduation—when all that mattered were the kind of job offers and freelance gigs that would keep me afloat and my parents off my back.

But out of everything Eddie could've given me, did it have to be this?

*

"You cried," Maeve noted as soon as I'd appeared in the door to her room, lowering the book in her hands.

If there was one sign that Maeve had her life together, it was her room. Not a single piece of rogue clothing was scattered across her floor, the makeup on her vanity was neatly organized, and the white walls were filled with framed motivational quotes in different shades of pink and sketches of her favorite designers.

"Did I?" The mascara had already smudged under my eyes, but I wiped at them anyway. "I don't know what to do, Maeve."

Her lips quirked in sympathy, furrowed brow relaxing. "That's nothing new." Beckoning me over with a pat on her bed, she scooted to one side. "Come here, honey. What is it?" The southern drawl in her tone always became heavier with concern.

"I don't know," I groaned, stomping over to let myself fall on top of her white bedding. Before she could say anything, I added, "I mean, I do."

"Yeah, you do."

"Eddie finally gave me something I can write the extracurricular about. An article. An amazing article, really." Which, in itself, was good news. The best of news.

"Paula! That's incredible!" Confusion laced into her tone. "Isn't it?"

"So incredible," I agreed truthfully. As my head gently fell against her metal bed frame, I let out an ironic huff. "The best. It comes with all these opportunities. A chance of being picked up by bigger press and all that. Eddie thinks it could put me on the radar—put the *Post* on the radar. He's ecstatic." I snorted. "Or at least his equivalent of that."

Maeve nudged me again, and when I finally looked at her, my eyes still a little red and puffy, she was very clearly trying to figure out the *but* in this. I suspected not even my psychic best friend could figure that one out.

She considered me for another second. "And what does Henry have to do with that?"

Never mind.

"How—?"

"Paula," she sighed as if I should know better. "You're proudly presenting your Henry-scowl. Don't expect me not to pick up on it."

I gasped. Mostly in faked outrage. "I'm not—" I tried to argue.

"You were wearing it on Saturday too, by the way. When you came back from hurling your guts out. You're an awful liar." I really wanted to laugh at that—my failed attempt to hide anything from her—but even the amusement in her tone did little to take the edge off.

I shook my head quickly, waving her off. "Completely different thing." I forced the memories of Henry's hand around my wrist—of his face so close, his expensive cologne lingering—out of my mind.

Those only made my predicament clearer. "It's on him," I said to snap out of it.

"What? The fact that you haven't gotten a single good article in a year? Yeah, that's on him." She snickered in annoyance. "We've been blaming him for just as long. So?"

"No," I whined, although she was right. Kind of. Not really. "That's not what I mean. It's *on* him," I repeated. "The article. It's a profile. About Henry Pressley."

If I weren't so caught up in this, I'd enjoy watching Maeve be surprised by something. It did not happen often. "For real?"

"For real."

"Oh my God." Her brown eyes flicked up to mine, the

furrow in her brow deepening. "It's like a cruel joke. Eddie doesn't give you anything for a year, and when he finally does, it's *this*?"

I was so glad she shared my sentiment. It *was* a cruel joke! Only that my life had become the punch line, and it wasn't a very good one.

"But . . ." Maeve continued slowly, features softening, "what do you mean *you don't know what to do*? What's there to consider?"

"Well." My arms flailed around wildly. Apparently, it did nothing to explain. "You know. It means spending time with him, traveling around. Being really close. Like, really, really close." Her expression didn't shift at all. So I doubled down. "For several weeks. I don't know if—"

"If *what*?" she cut in harshly. "If that's worth it? If your career and your dreams are worth that?" Her head tilted slightly, and I was once again faced with pity. "Come on, Paula. You don't mean that."

But I did! Didn't I?

"I kind of thought you wouldn't want me to do it," I confessed. "You know, with the whole *No Contact* thing." That had been her idea, after all. And I knew it'd be easier to say no if Maeve thought the article was a terrible idea too.

She only laughed airily. "Paula," she said. "We don't sacrifice our dreams for men. They're never worth it."

I sat up. "But—"

"You're getting a second shot here! Not everyone has the chance for do-overs."

I knew she was right; I just didn't want to come to terms

with it yet. "But this will be a lot of contact, Maeve. Kind of defeats the whole purpose of *No Contact*. Right?"

Her lip twitched a little higher. "Henry shouldn't even be a part of this equation. He's just a subject. Like any other. You do what's necessary, write a killer article, and then you move on." She squeezed my hand tightly. Just once before letting go again.

A nervous laugh slipped past my lips. *Treat Henry like any other subject.* I wasn't quite sure I could. Because I knew him, and I knew us, and most of all, I knew myself.

And I missed him terribly.

I shook my head quickly. "You're right," I conceded. "God, you're right. Of course you are." I smiled, not quite sure if I was trying to convince her or myself. "I should be excited about this, not anxious about him. Fuck Henry."

Maeve raised an eyebrow. "Not literally, though."

CHAPTER 8

Now

Clutching my phone between ear and shoulder, rushing out of the *HBP*—past Eddie's office and two floors up—I realized I'd definitely be late. Without looking at the time, I knew. "I'm good, Mami. Sí." I exhaled into the phone.

If I could just get my mother off the line, maybe I'd actually be able to read the documents in my hands. Maybe if she hadn't called an hour ago, barely taking a break between sentences since, I could've adequately prepared for Henry's first interview.

Sure, her endless monologues were currently distracting me from the nerves I couldn't afford to show, but at what cost? She'd robbed me of the one hour I'd set aside to prepare questions.

I'd called Eddie two minutes after my conversation with Maeve, mostly to make sure I didn't have time to change my mind again. *I can't do it. I have to do it. Do I really? I shouldn't even care who the profile is on. But I do care.*

"Are you busy, Paulita?" Mom asked through the phone she surely had on speaker with all the background noise it was picking up. Clattering dishes, animated conversations, cicadas, the ocean. "You sound like you're busy."

"Well—"

"Is it school?" She cut in before I had the chance to gracefully exit the conversation with a *Why yes, I'm very busy. Talk to you later!* When I saw my destination at the end of the corridor, my steps slowed. "How is school? You know, your cousin Sofia dropped out just last week. My God, can you believe it?"

The line went silent just for a moment, like she was thinking. Then, panicked, she asked, "You haven't dropped out, have you?"

"Ay Dios mío, Mami, no." I came to a screeching halt outside the room I'd been looking for, maneuvering the papers from my hand under my arm.

Knowing Henry and his rigid schedules, he was already inside, just a closed door separating us. A glance at my phone told me it was two minutes past.

"Listen. School's good, I'm actually"—I hesitated, but only for a second—"on the way to speak to my professor about an upcoming tax law exam?" I sounded less sure than I intended. "Gotta go!"

"Good, good." Mom sighed. "Our little American businesswoman. We're so proud of you, Paulita."

"Te quiero, Mom. Bye!"

Hanging up, I exhaled forcefully, an involuntary physical reaction that followed every conversation with her. I glanced at the screen to ensure I'd ended the call.

Little American Businesswoman.

I'd laugh if it wasn't so unnerving.

It had been almost four years, and I still hadn't told my parents about changing my major. Honestly, I'm not quite sure how I'd gotten away with lying about the degree I'd been working toward for that long. It kind of just happened.

Sure, I loved journalism, and I did not regret spending the past three and a half years perfecting it instead of learning how to commit legal tax fraud. But I still hated lying to my parents.

To everyone back in the Dominican Republic, I was Paulita, their Little American Businesswoman. Here at HBU, I was Paula, that failed journalist who used to date Henry Pressley. I didn't know which was worse.

I gave myself one deep breath to get into character. *Ex-girlfriend who didn't still care and actually kind of despised Henry.* It had worked last time, right?

Silently counting to three, I pulled the door open.

Usually, my interviews were in classrooms with multiple rows of desks, big windows, and plants that were at least my size in the corners. Bright and spacious. Eddie had organized this room for us, and it was . . . not at all that. Best described as somewhat of an expanded broom closet, or perhaps a luxury storage space, it was too small and too dark for today's sunny weather.

Henry leaned against the wall by the only window with

his arms crossed in front of his chest in *that* way. Whatever he saw in the courtyard must've been interesting enough to keep his attention. His gaze didn't shift when he said, "I thought you might not come."

I couldn't interpret the tone in his voice. Relief? Disappointment? Annoyance?

The door closed behind me, and I cleared my throat. "Hope you haven't been waiting for long," I said, trying to force as much confidence into my voice as I could. "I would've been on time if it weren't for—" Turning back to him with my best shot at a polite smile, I realized he was still not looking at me. My tone dropped, and so did my lips. "No matter."

With a straight face, I sat on the chair closest to the door. To avoid eye contact, I rummaged through my tote bag for pen and paper.

"Was that María?"

But hearing my mom's name come out of his mouth caught me so off guard, I froze. Something about it felt too familiar. Like we were still part of each other's lives. "On the phone, I mean."

His voice continued to rumble through my brain without any sense of reason. Deep, silky, with the tiniest hint of a British accent leftover from his childhood in Chelsea.

I focused on my bag, unable to meet the gaze I could now clearly feel on me. After a few more seconds of silence that I couldn't find a way to break, he added, "Sorry. Didn't mean to eavesdrop."

"Oh." *Say something*, I begged myself. *Anything*. "Yeah,

my mom. Still haven't told her about the whole journalism thing." I was well on my way to oversharing, and I almost sighed in relief when Henry spoke quickly enough to stop me.

"About that," he said, a hint of amusement in his voice. I could hear him make his way over to the other side of the table. I could feel him take a seat opposite me. I could not see him because I was still staring into my bag. "We're focused on project management, business simulation, and thesis writing this semester. Tax law was last." Henry cleared his throat. "In case they happen to ask again."

They being my parents. This conversation showed he still knew them way too well.

I finally drew my eyes away from the contents of my bag to meet his. As expected, green and big, they reflected the humor that had previously been prominent in his tone.

Like a mantra, I repeated the role I was supposed to play in my head: *Ex-girlfriend who didn't still care and actually kind of despised him.*

"Why don't we get started?"

Although I offered an innocent smile, I'd never been good at hiding my thoughts and feelings. Maeve had said they were written all over my face, free for anyone to read. She'd also said it was her favorite thing about me. Right now, with the way Henry scrutinized that smile, I wished I'd taken Riley up on her offer to *poker-face* me.

"Of course." He paired the words with a courtesy nod. *So far, so good.*

Eddie had shared his expectations for the profile

as soon as I'd . . . officially agreed to do it. Character instead of just a list of Henry's accomplishments. *Anyone could Google those*, he'd said. They wanted childhood, family life, personality, with a side of stats and soccer. More importantly, they wanted me to focus on the Henry beneath that carefully crafted mask. The one he hadn't even fully let go of months into our relationship, by the way.

Someone should've told Edward Smith that asking Henry's ex-girlfriend to pry for personal details probably wouldn't result in the *Post* running the information he'd hoped for. But it was too late for that.

My phone sat on the table between us. "I'll be recording our conversation," I informed him unnecessarily. "So make sure not to say anything you don't want to read in an article later on."

Henry cocked an eyebrow, a teasing smile hanging in the corner of his lips. "I thought your job was to get exactly those kinds of things out of me." His tone was less question, more challenge.

I leveled the man opposite me with a look that screamed professionalism. I needed to in order to keep myself from letting every word he said affect me.

I can do this.

I was the journalist here. I was the one in control, and I needed to start acting that way. Henry was just another subject. *Fake it till you make it.* Right?

That finally helped me find my footing. "Don't worry," I said. "If there's something I want to know, I'll get it willingly, and on the record." I paired the words with my sweetest smile.

Henry shifted in his seat, sweeping a hand through his middle part. When his head tilted slightly, he matched my smile with one of his own. Blinked once. Leaned forward. "I'd expect nothing less from you."

He was the one to press start on the recording.

I tried not to let that get to me. Surely, it's what he was trying to do: get to me. Controlling the room by controlling the effect he had on me. After all, one could not separate Henry Parker Pressley from his need to be in control.

"Let's start with . . ." My eyes fell on the blank page in my lap. The same page that was meant to hold all my prep—talking points, questions—was virtually empty. The only writing on it said "Henry Pressley, 1st; 15th of March." Thanks, Mom.

Alright, then. Improv it was.

I cleared my throat. "Start with . . . your name."

I wasn't great at improvising, by the way.

Henry raised his eyebrows. "Seriously?"

"Yes." I leveled him with a glare. "I'm taking this very seriously. Aren't you?"

I was overcompensating for that blank page in front of me and the fact that I hadn't taken this seriously enough at all. I suspected Henry knew too.

But he just nodded, smirked. "I am."

"Good."

A second ticked by.

"I just think it's funny how . . ." He hesitated, which was

a first. The one thing Henry Parker Pressley didn't do, on or off the field, was hesitate.

And it piqued my interest. "How what?"

His eyes flicked to my phone resting between us, seconds of the recording running by: 00:55, 00:56, 00:57. He shook his head. "Forget about it."

But I couldn't, wouldn't—and really, didn't *want* to. My job was to pry, wasn't it?

"Oh no," I said. "Don't hold back on my account. What's so funny?"

In the seconds of silence that lingered, when his gaze swept across my face, I could tell he was trying to figure out my game plan. So was I.

The analytical expression washed off his face a moment later, like he'd figured me out before I'd done so myself. He shrugged, and it felt as if he knew he'd won without having to say a word.

"I just think it's funny," he repeated. "How you're pretending you don't know my name when it was loud and clear that you did most nights."

And there it was.

His winning hand. He could tell by the violent blush across my cheeks. I could tell by the simmering flame ignited low in my belly. "Way back when, of course." Now the challenging tone was back. He was dangling it like a carrot from a stick, like he knew it would make me want to bite back, throw professionalism out the window. I swallowed the urge.

Instead, I plastered on that same smile and vowed to

make use of Riley's How to Fake Facial Expressions 101 course as soon as I got home.

"Just for the sake of it, why don't you?" I halfheartedly gestured toward the recording, then settled into my chair, notebook and pen in hand. "Maybe I've been mispronouncing it."

Henry's eyes followed my hand, then settled back on me when he leaned halfway across the desk. "Let the record show," he said, gaze fixed on me, mouth by my phone. "My name is Henry Parker Pressley. Twenty-two years old. Defender for the Hall Beck soccer team." He raised his eyebrows, then asked mockingly, "Like that?"

I nodded curtly, eyes twitching into a glare. "Perfect. Thank you so much." Irony dripped from my voice.

He was playing me like a fiddle, and I couldn't have that. "Tell me, *Henry*." I emphasized his name, and something in his smug expression twitched, if only for a fraction of a second. I took it as a small win. "What made you get into soccer?"

It was the easiest question I could think of. Safe terrain. A way to get the ball rolling and our solely professional relationship off the ground.

And it worked beautifully.

Our previous tension seemed to be forgotten. "Most people think it was Felix." His dad, whom he rarely referred to as such. "Makes sense, right? Pro player without a life outside the game. People thought it kind of just rubbed off on me. I did too, for a while." In the silence that lingered, he gathered his thoughts, rearranged them in his head to craft the narrative he wanted out in the world. I knew that calculating look on his face.

"I think it was actually my sister. Athalia." His eyes darted toward mine at the mention of her, his smile growing. "Big pain in the ass when we were growing up. More of one now, probably. She used to hate soccer so much; I think I started training just to get under her skin. To force her to my games. We were eight."

As he talked, he had a distracted look on his face, eyes glazed over with a mixture of glee, and joy, and pride. It was his soccer face. He'd always looked like an excited little schoolboy when he talked about it.

Although he'd had a jump start with Felix Pressley's legacy, not everyone who dreamed of going pro would end up making it. Actually, only about 1.4 percent did. Henry had every right to be proud of himself, even with the advantages that came with his last name.

Knowing that a Major League Soccer team had drafted him and that I was to write a profile about him that a bigger press had already expressed interest in made me feel that way too.

Proud.

*

I was right, by the way. That single question did get the ball rolling and held him over for the majority of our time. Apart from obvious follow-up questions to his answers, I hadn't said a word.

"After that, I had a few college choices, but HBU was

the best, and I'd already met Coach Hepburn once or twice. It felt good to know I'd join his team. Like I was meant to be there." No mention of his parents or the fact that they'd both studied here. That *that* might have made his decision easier.

"We'll see if he has as high an opinion of you," I challenged lightheartedly, watching my voice rip him out of whatever soccer trance he'd previously been in. Blinking rapidly, his gaze found mine.

"Most definitely not," he said. My lips almost twitched at the humor in his tone.

A buzz on the table kept me from answering, and we broke our eye contact simultaneously to look. Minutes still ticked by on the screen, though it wasn't the 50:27, 50:28, or 50:29 that caught my attention.

JACK, Thursday, 4:57 PM
> Still on for tonight?

Yes, my phone was turned toward me, but I had no doubt Henry could read the text, even if it was upside down.

"Big plans?" he asked, but he sounded more amused than he looked.

I turned the recording off and threw the phone in my bag, where it could no longer wreak havoc. The light, *almost* comfortable air we'd been working toward for the past fifty minutes was gone. So fast, it gave me whiplash.

"Something like that." Actually, nothing like it. I'd probably end up canceling on Jack because I had to transcribe those fifty minutes of audio he had just brutally interrupted. But I'd be damned if I told Henry that.

If he could flirt with a beautiful brunette, I could very well be texting potentials.

"Did you already get our schedule from Eddie?" I asked to move things on, throwing the rest of my equipment into my tote like I'd gotten an emergency call.

Henry stood as soon as he realized I couldn't wait to get out of here. He'd always been great at reading the room. "No," he said, the sound incredibly close to his usual grumble. "I don't think I've ever even heard you say the word *schedule* before."

Granted, he wasn't wrong. Still. "I told you," I snickered, scraping my chair back and getting out of it hastily. "I'm taking this very seriously." He opened the door for me, and I stepped through like it was second nature.

In the four years I'd known Henry, I don't think I'd opened a single door in his presence. I didn't even question the gesture, just silently appreciated it. He fell into step beside me.

"I'll email the *schedule*"—I stressed the word, and he had to keep his lips from twitching—"to you by tonight."

It made me realize that I had beautifully method-acted my way into the role of ex-girlfriend who didn't still care and actually kind of despised him.

"Tomorrow is fine. Don't let me spoil your fun with—"

"Henry!" We both turned toward the call. Really, though, I immediately recognized the voice that regularly ordered me on coffee runs.

"Lacy," we said in unison, which made me turn to Henry with the obvious question written all over my face.

I had no idea the two knew each other. They hadn't a year ago. Despite their first-name basis, the crease between Henry's brows pleased me more than it should.

Clutching the strap of her messenger bag, Lacy came to a halt by his side. "Back again already," she mused. "To what do we owe the pleasure?" She pushed some of her blond, freshly blown-out hair behind one ear. Her head tilted slightly when she looked up at him, and I wasn't quite sure whether she ignored me on purpose or genuinely blanked me out.

Henry's brow lifted as if it was obvious. When he pointed at me, and Lacy's gaze followed his gesture, I could see her awareness latch onto me in real time. Her eyes widened just a little as she put two and two together. It took another second before all the dots were connected.

"Oh!" She shook herself out of her surprise to see me. "Paula! Hi."

Her tone was perfectly friendly, but the pointed look didn't match the attitude. Just as quick, it was gone again, and she looked back at Henry with a smile. "The profile. Of course." She nodded. "Such a shame I have too much on my plate already. We would've made a great team, don't you think?"

The revelation wasn't necessarily shocking. Of course the only reason I'd gotten this opportunity was because Lacy Halloway had *too much on her plate.*

Still, it kind of stung. Getting her leftovers. Being

second, third—perhaps *fourth*—choice. Even after a year on the metaphorical writing bench, I never got used to it.

"Sure," Henry said roughly, pulling me out of my thoughts. "You're saying this was supposed to be your thing? The profile?" His follow-up question seemed to catch her off guard, but she nodded grandly.

"Oh, yeah," she said as if it should've been obvious. Maybe it was. "Edward basically begged me to do it."

This was quickly turning into one of the worst conversations of my life. Didn't matter that I'd just somewhat survived an interview with my ex-boyfriend with little to no preparation. A sixty-second conversation with Lacy had flushed it all down the toilet.

"It really is a shame," she said again. Her eyes swept across his frame once, not very subtly.

Mierda.

"So fun catching up with you!" I basically beamed, my smile so fake it hurt. Almost as much as leaving them by themselves. "But I've gotta go."

Henry's eyes were already on me when I turned to him. "Big plans. Remember?"

A shadow moved across his face. "How could I forget?"

And I felt his gaze on me until I'd disappeared down the stairs.

CHAPTER 9

Now

> HENRY:
> I just think it's funny how you're pretending you don't know my name when it was loud and clear that you did most nights. Way back when, of course.

If I hadn't been continuously jumping back to that line, I'd have been done transcribing the interview a long time ago. But it felt physically impossible not to scroll back to the top of the document, read his words, and blush like he was still in the room with me.

But the reality was that I'd canceled my plans with Jack minutes after I'd come home and had been glued to my screen ever since. The only company I'd kept was the black pile of fluff currently residing in my lap, which, yes, kept me from typing at my usual lightning speed but was in no way the main reason for how long transcribing had taken.

That was all me.

And my inability to treat Henry like any other subject, the way Maeve had suggested. How could I, when he was saying things like that?

Who says things like that?

I deleted the paragraph before saving the document and sending it over to my editor. Eddie had requested to take a look at the first few interviews to get a feel for the *dynamic*. He could've just flat-out told me he didn't trust me, and I'd have been fine with that too. If I wanted to write, which I desperately did, I had to be okay with being treated like a clumsy toddler sitting in front of a keyboard for the very first time.

With a frustrated groan, I shut my laptop. Pip gave a pleased meow. She snuggled deeper into the blanket draped across my legs, clearly satisfied she no longer had to hear Henry's voice.

She'd never been his biggest fan, and apparently, even his voice on a recording seemed to bug her. "I know," I cooed, scratching her chin with a sigh. "You were right from day one."

I should've taken her hisses around him as the warnings they were. Instead, I just ended up at his place more than my own. Which, at the time, I didn't mind. Maybe even welcomed.

His apartment was godly, and even now—almost a year later—I still miss his silky sheets and the comfortable mattress that had cost more than most things in my room combined. For a second, I wondered if he still shared the loft with Heather and Reuben.

None of my business, I reminded myself. Shaking my head, a dry laugh escaped me.

If I couldn't stop Henry from making guest appearances in my head, the least I could do was make them productive. Not think about how much I missed his bed or the things we'd done in it.

I just think it's funny how you're pretending you don't know my name when it was loud and clear that you did most nights.

Get it together, Paula.

Right. Productive! Focus on a profile that would (hopefully) put Henry Pressley on the radar of mainstream press and social media fan pages and, in return, do the same for HBU and our soccer team. Show the world that he wasn't just his father's son, born into wealth and privilege and a pro soccer career. How hard could that be?

Very, I decided. Because in the three years I'd known Henry, he had barely let me scratch the surface. I could count the number of times he'd mentioned his parents or their accident on one hand.

Another frustrated sound escaped me right as my phone rang. "Eddie (HBP)" flashed on my phone's screen, only making my groan louder. Maybe after reading that joke of a first interview, he'd assign me something else for the extracurricular.

Only when the call was about to go to voicemail did I pick up.

"Paula. Good," Eddie chose as his opening line, sounding somewhat surprised to have reached me. "You had about half a ring left before you would've lost me," he said, and for him, that was almost a joke.

"Sorry." I tried my best to match his surprisingly chipper mood. "Just . . ." I glanced toward my cat—on my lap, purring contentedly—then took in my dark room. I hadn't even noticed how late it had gotten. "Super busy over here." *Obviously.*

"Ah," Eddie said. "Is this a bad time? Lacy mentioned you had big plans. Honestly, I'm kind of surprised you still managed to get that transcript to me today. I thought I'd have to hassle you about it tomorrow, and we both know how much I hate that. Anyways—"

I wasn't even listening anymore. He'd lost me about three sentences ago.

"Lacy?" I cut him off bluntly, and if the circumstances were different, I'd probably feel bad about it. Right now, though, it was worth figuring out what my name was doing in Lacy's mouth. "Lacy said what?" I asked. It took a lot to keep the edge from my voice.

"Not much. Just that she thought you were busy tonight. Mentioned big plans?" *Of course.* "Something wrong with that?"

I blinked back my confusion. "Nothing."

I did just tell him I was *super busy* myself. Something else I'd love to tell him: Lacy had no business telling him mine. "Absolutely nothing. The connection was just . . . bad for a second."

"Anyways. What an interview, huh?"

My stomach dropped. Obviously, he wasn't calling to

chitchat about what Lacy may or may not have said, but my short-lived annoyance with her had made me forget the actual reason for the call.

What an interview.

"That bad?" I didn't really have to ask. I knew.

"Well." Eddie cleared his throat. "No, not *that* bad." I think he might've winced as he said it. "You just seem a little stiff. Quiet. Right?"

I sighed into the speaker, leaning back in my chair. The movement earned me a complaint from Pip, who quickly decided my lap was no longer suitable for her needs and made herself scarce. Stretching at the newfound freedom, I listened to Eddie.

"It's fine, Paula." His voice took on a soothing note, which kind of surprised me. "I've basically shelved you for a year. I don't expect you to return to top form immediately."

But I wanted to, I realized. *Spring back into top form right away.* If this was supposed to be my calling, if I'd given up everything to be a journalist, shouldn't it come easily? Shouldn't I be a natural?

"These are minor things. We'll fix them in a heartbeat, alright? We'll schedule more interviews. You can go through the questions with me beforehand if you want. You'll get back into it. Promise."

Deflated, I just nodded, not caring that he couldn't even see.

Only time would tell.

CHAPTER 10

Then

March: Three years ago

Once a month, the girls and I drank cheap wine, played cards, blasted loud music throughout the house, and called it Game Night.

Laila brought the tradition from home, where she'd do the same with her mom and without the cheap wine. We only had *that* courtesy of Riley's fake ID.

This month, we also had company.

"Uno!" Blake practically screamed across the table, holding the last black card in his hand up like a trophy. His huge smile revealed a set of perfect white teeth that contrasted with his dark skin.

Behind him, Dylan and Caden cheered with matching laughs, whooping like he'd just won them the NCAA championship and not like he'd *almost* won a game of Uno against their neighbors.

"Look at you guys," Riley cooed from the opposite side of the dining table. Among us girls, she was the only one who still had a chance to win. Laila, Maeve, and I had had over twelve cards each and had ceremoniously given up. We stood behind Riley like her emotional support wall. "You're acting like you've already won."

She placed a matching +2 on the pile of cards. "Uno."

Blake's eyes lifted in sync with the corner of his full lips. With a smirk, he placed a blue +2 on top of it. "Uno. Uno."

The boys behind him—who had abandoned their own game—grew louder, which I hadn't thought possible. They high-fived each other over what they believed was an easy win.

"Boys will be boys," I sighed, and Riley placed another +2 on top of Blake's, winning the game.

He froze. Caden stopped celebrating first, and Dylan quickly followed suit. For a second, they gawked at the last card. Then the complaints flew across the table.

"Hey! He already won!"

"That's not how the game works!"

"It was over! You can't just apply house rules!"

Maeve shook her head, proud smile on her face when she placed her hands on Riley's shoulders. "Nu-uh," she tsked. "It's our house. Which means our house rules. You lose."

Caden and Dylan, who hadn't played in over seven rounds, seemed more wounded by Blake's loss than he was. Caden drove a hand across his bleach-blond buzzcut in clear distress, Dylan sank into the neighboring chair with a groan, and Blake just . . . sat there.

“Congrats, Rie,” he said with a smile on his face that almost made it seem like he was content with the outcome.

“I usually take my apologies in cash.” She winked at him, and I knew Riley was only half joking. Her last boyfriend had cheated on her, and she’d gotten a grand out of it. For emotional damages.

Blake huffed. “What would I apologize for?”

“Underestimating my Uno skills. Thinking I’d lose. Thinking you’re better than me.”

I wish I could’ve heard his reply, but my phone rang, and I’d been waiting for that all evening. Given how fast I jumped for it, everyone else could probably tell.

Dylan’s eyes flicked from the vibrating device up to me. “Boyfriend calling?” he asked mockingly.

I knew he was talking about Henry. And I knew he’d said it the way he did because the two weren’t . . . each other’s biggest fans. To put it lightly.

“He’s not—”

But Maeve interrupted me with an endearing eye roll. “Not yet,” she corrected, leveling Dylan with a look. *The* look. To emphasize her point, she nodded over at the vase in the living room that Henry had been supplying with fresh flowers on a weekly basis. “Give it another week.”

I glared at her, finally grabbed my still-vibrating phone, and then glared at Dylan. Who was grinning widely, by the way, like he was in on some secret now. “And no,” I snickered. “Not Henry. It’s—Eddie!” I said by way of greeting, already halfway up the stairs by the end of my sentence.

Enthusiasm was an understatement. The smile on my lips was so wide, my cheeks hurt. “What did they say?”

I had expected the news earlier, right after his meeting about my third real article for the *Post*: “Mental Health in Times of Crisis (Finals Week).” Waiting seven hours to hear from Eddie had not contributed to mine.

He snorted on the other end of the line, and I closed my bedroom door behind me. Maeve had given me fairy lights to hang across the room, and they were the only lights on.

“I’m fine, thank you for asking, Paula,” Eddie joked. Which was rare. The man barely even laughed. And now I’d gotten an amused snort and a joke. All in the span of seconds. Good sign, right?

I couldn’t help gnawing on my bottom lip, not sure what else to do, with nerves and anxiety threatening to burst at the seams. Mom had tried countless times to get rid of my habit—unsuccessfully.

“Please, Eddie,” I begged, throwing myself onto the bed. “I’m dying here. Don’t do this to me. What did they say?”

“Alright, alright. I’m sorry,” he snickered. “It’s just so fun when you guys doubt me and I prove you wrong.”

“*Ed—*” I almost complained again, but then his words settled. My eyes widened.

Because for him to be right, for my doubt to be proven wrong . . . That meant that—

“They loved it, Paula.”

They loved it.

An actual news outlet *loved* something I’d written. Just like that, changing majors seemed worth it.

If I was actually good at this—good enough to do it for more than a student-only readership—maybe my parents wouldn't be too disappointed, too mad. Maybe instead of that truckload of *chanclas* I'd been worrying about, it would only be one. Maybe two.

"And they—?" I couldn't even say it.

"Yes. They'd like to publish it."

CHAPTER 11

Now

I arrived overprepared and extra-early to our next interview, but somehow Henry still beat me. He sat at one of the tables in Daisy's, the coffee shop where I occasionally still picked up shifts.

He looked too large in his chair, almost comically so. Long legs extended to one side of the small white table, he'd left a spot on the bench empty. For me, presumably.

I took a deep breath, appreciating one last moment before he'd notice me, and stepped through the door. *Ex-girlfriend who didn't still care and actually kind of despised him*, I reminded myself. The bell above the door chimed. Henry turned with a smile like he knew it was me.

The same smile he'd given me when I walked into his apartment without a knock and stood in front of him, demanding a kiss, a hug, or just general attention. The same smile he'd given me from the field once he spotted me on the sideline, knowing we'd get exactly thirteen minutes alone in the locker room between his teammates heading out and the janitor locking up for the day. The same one he'd give me after we hadn't seen each other for a while, because he'd become busier with soccer and I'd become much busier with the paper after that first article sold.

That's how much I could see in his smile, which is probably why it tugged on my heartstrings.

"Paula!" I thought he said, but his lips weren't moving, and his voice was usually a pitch deeper. My eyes flickered behind the counter and almost doubled in size.

"Jack," I said by way of greeting, forcing myself to walk up to him instead of sitting at that small table. I held up a finger in Henry's direction, beckoning him to give me a second I didn't even want to give myself. "Didn't know you were working today," I admitted.

Jack laughed. He drew a hand through his strawberry-blond hair, then messed the front of it up to frame his face.

"We used to cover this exact shift together," he reminded me. "But it's been a while, hasn't it? What's got you so busy that you can't help dear old me out anymore?"

I physically fought the urge to look at Henry. When my head moved to turn in his direction, I managed to shake it instead. "The *Post*." A happy sigh accompanied the words, like I was finally doing what I'd been supposed to all along. "I don't think I'll be able to cover shifts anytime soon. Could you tell Daisy when you see her?"

Jack's eyebrows rose with surprise. He was just as aware

of the fallout caused by my last article for the *HBP*, and neither of us thought I'd ever write for them again.

"Paula." He was smiling again. He did that a lot in my presence. "That's awesome. Of course I'll let her know." His eyes shifted behind me when the door announced another customer, and he cleared his throat. "Can I get you anything, then?"

I shook my head, remembering Henry. "That's alright, I'm here for—" My hand swept in his direction before I could stop myself. When Jack's gaze followed, I cut myself off.

He had never been Henry's biggest fan. Not while we were dating, and especially not after we broke up. Even less so after Jack had kissed me, and I—in a whirlwind of nerves, pity, and heartache—told him I wasn't over my ex.

That was six months ago. And to give credit where credit was due, Jack had been diligently waiting for me to do just that: get over my ex.

Seeing Henry now, he probably wasn't thrilled. So I scurried away with a "Gotta go!"

Henry's eyes flicked to the smartwatch around his wrist, then back up to me. "Only two minutes."

I immediately stopped caring about Jack behind the counter, watching us like a hawk as he took another order. "How do you do it?" I asked, shrugging out of my jacket. "I really tried to be on time today. Between training, school, and . . . everything else you've got going on, how are you still earlier than me?"

Henry leaned into his chair, crossed his arms in front of his chest lazily, and watched me unpack my equipment.

The early spring sun peeked through the window, streaking his brown hair with temporary highlights and making him squint. He shrugged.

"I've been getting better at prioritizing," he said. "But that's off the record. If anyone asks, I've *always* been great at it."

I wasn't sure if the problem in our relationship had been prioritization generally or just prioritizing the wrong things.

"*If anyone asks*," I mirrored. "I won't attest to that." Pressing the record button on my phone, I placed it on the table between us. "And everything's on the record going forward."

Once again, Eddie had been right. Scheduling the second interview in a less formal place was doing wonders already. It's like I really was getting my footing and asserting myself as a journalist. I felt lighter. More confident.

Maybe it was just the full notepad of questions staring back at me like a lifeline, but I'd like to believe I was getting used to conversing with Henry as if I wasn't one right word of his away from falling back in love with him.

His green eyes flicked from the phone back up to meet mine. "I wanted to talk to you about that . . . *schedule* you sent, actually."

The air quotes around the word confirmed he did not think it was a schedule at all. Just because it didn't have set dates yet? *Please.*

"Can't imagine why," I lied. The corner of his lip twitched before he could catch it.

"Paula. It tells me nothing."

"It tells you *some* things."

His head shook, half amused, half exasperated. He was

grinning now. Widely. "Not the things I need to know. Like when, and where, and who." His brows rose with his—unfortunately valid—point. "'Interviewing friends' isn't really all that specific."

"Because we haven't spoken about when and where and who yet," I countered. "I'm sure you wouldn't want me to ask McCarthy for his opinion, would you?"

Admittedly, bringing up his biggest rival on and off the field was a low blow, and it did nothing to defuse the tension quickly building. He was eager to match my attitude.

He grimaced. "Don't you just know me so well, Charm?"

The nickname slipped out, I know it did. He wouldn't have willingly brought up every single memory attached to it. But before I could linger too much on the good ones, I stirred in the opposite direction of that feeling.

"Clearly not well enough, or I'd be in your head, knowing when you're free and where you'll be at all times so that I could get a finished schedule to you without discussing it first."

I was hungry, and I was taking it out on this conversation. On him.

So much for professionalism.

"That would be the dream." Henry's eyebrows rose at my tone. "But since that's very unlikely, why don't I just email you the times I'm free and the best days for you to stick around?" Now his lips twitched into a satisfied smirk. I hated that I didn't hate it. I hated that I kind of . . . liked it. Missed it. "You know. Like I had planned to."

My cheeks were bright pink when I nodded. "Perfect."

The situation was anything but. I felt even worse once

I remembered I'd have to transcribe the entire exchange later tonight. Though, while we were already on topic, I figured I might as well get the rest of those pesky organizational details out of the way.

"I'd love to talk to Coach Hepburn, of course. What about teammates, though? Anyone come to mind who could give some insight?"

Henry nodded. The force of his unwavering and focused gaze suddenly made our surroundings that much more interesting. No need to look into those green eyes when I could check out the pastries in the display case behind him. I wondered if any of the vegan ones were still available. "Sure," Henry said.

I purposely did not look his way, and like the universe was giving me an out, the bell above the door chimed, offering something else I could focus on that wasn't Henry. "I'll send the names over with the rest. What about—?"

"Athalia." His sister's name slipped past my lips when I didn't really mean it to.

"Yes! That's what I was about to ask. Are you gonna talk to her?"

My head shook, eyes finally snapping back to him. "No." *Wait, he asked a different question.* "I mean, yes. Would love to. But I meant *Athalia* as in she's just walked through the door."

Henry followed my subtle nod in her direction, looking across his shoulder to find her at the register.

"Oh." He glanced at the watch around his wrist. "Makes sense. It's eleven on a Saturday. She does this sometimes."

He raised his voice with the next words, making sure

his sister could pick up on them a few feet away. "Probably just woke up instead of getting an early start on the thesis she has to hand in next week." A pointed tone edged into his voice, and although they were twins, Henry slipped into big-brother mode. I didn't remember him doing much of that when we were together.

When she found him in his seat, Athalia gave her brother a wide, teasing smile, as if she knew he had a point and was ignoring it on purpose.

As far as I had been able to tell, the twins hadn't been particularly close. I only knew Athalia because her best friend was dating one of mine, not because Henry had introduced us. That would've meant opening up. To her and to me. It would've also meant showing me parts of his life he couldn't control. *Unthinkable.*

Her gaze slid to me, and she almost dropped the coffee Jack had just handed her. Henry turned with an eye roll.

She mouthed a *What?* in my direction so dramatically, I almost laughed. In the few seconds of silent conversation between us, I'd tried my best to let my expression convey *No, I'm not dating your brother. Again.*

Miraculously, she must've understood. Her hands raised in mock surrender, in sync with the smirk on her lips. With a wink, she paid and left.

I focused on the man in front of me again. He spoke before I could start asking the first of many wonderfully prepared questions.

"You know, she asks about you an unsettling number of times," Henry said, driving a hand through his hair casually.

Somehow, it looked better after the fact. *How was it fair that I had to stand in front of a mirror for hours to get my hair decent; meanwhile, men could just . . . ruffle a hand through their own and look great?*

"One might think she misses us together more than I do."

Which made me wonder: Since when had they been close enough to talk about things as personal as our relationship?

"Oh," I offered. Then managed to squeeze at least one question into our allocated time slot. Henry was a busy man, now more than ever. "How are you guys, anyway?"

"We're like we've always been." He said it so quickly, the answer must've been prepared. Like people asked him about their relationship a lot, and he got used to saying exactly that before moving on with no further comment.

Except now, his brows drew together, and he scrunched his nose in thought. "Better, actually. We're much better. Even if she's still . . . hanging out with McCarthy, and I try not to tear him apart every time I see him."

Which is every day, I added in my head.

I snickered. "Hanging out? Someone's in denial," I added in a singsong voice, kind of hoping he would snap at me so I could stop enjoying our conversation on a personal level. Dangerous territory.

"I call it self-preservation." Unfortunately, he did not snap the words at me. "I'm better off not thinking about them together. *He's* better off that way, definitely."

I barked a laugh. I couldn't help it. "I wish I could've been there to see your reaction. Maeve said she would've paid good money for it. The rest of the girls too." My nose crinkled in further amusement, and it seemed he couldn't hold it off any better than I did.

The corners of his lips turned upward, and behind them, his tongue traced along his teeth in an attempt to keep himself from smiling. It failed miserably.

"How is she? All of them, actually?"

I didn't mean to go on a tangent about my friends. Really, I was here to talk about *him*. Though with graduation looming, I couldn't help it. I bragged about that major fashion house internship Maeve had lined up in New York and Riley's junior role at one of the biggest event planners, which she'd accepted just last week. Laila wanted to open her own animal shelter, for God's sake! They were all making it big out there, and I was just so, *so* proud.

"Laila and Wren, though, huh?" Henry muttered absentmindedly, a smile playing on his face.

"The world is so small."

Henry nodded, elbows propped on the table between us. He seemed pleased. "In a good way. It's refreshing to see Wren smile every now and then, and nobody gets it done better than Laila Levison."

I hummed in approval, and my eyes drifted onto my phone for the first time in a while: 45:16, 45:17, 45:18. The seconds ticked by like my heart hadn't just stopped. *Forty-five minutes?* It couldn't have been that long. There were literally five useful minutes in the entire exchange.

"Mierda," I cursed. "I'm supposed to be the one asking questions, Henry. You're supposed to do the talking. No one is asking for a cover profile on Paula Castillo, shunned college journalist."

Henry huffed, the epitome of calm, cool, and collected. "What if I just prefer listening to you?" he asked as if it didn't mean anything.

I tried desperately to come up with a response that wouldn't embarrass me and failed miserably. In the silence that lingered, I came to the conclusion that he was making this difficult for the sheer sake of his own amusement.

"And they should," he added.

"What?"

"They should want to write a profile on Paula Castillo, *unjustifiably* shunned college journalist."

I laughed, mostly to override that feeling wreaking havoc in my stomach. "And who would read that?"

"I would."

He could not keep having this effect on me. I tried not to nervously giggle, instead clearing my throat with a finality that would hopefully stop him from . . . doing whatever it is he was doing. Flirting, maybe. For whatever reason.

Henry mirrored me. "Alright, Paula Castillo," he said. "What do you want to know, then? We have about ten minutes left."

My eyes jumped between him and my questions, an incredulous look on my face. "Go on," he urged. "We'll make them count."

I took a deep breath, then nodded once. "Ready for a speed run?" I wiggled my notes in the air between us.

"Ready as I'll ever be."

CHAPTER 12

Now

There was a significant difference between my best friend and me. When my alarm went off at six on a Saturday morning, I reluctantly forced myself out of bed. Maeve, on the other hand, had just returned from her morning run. "You have to be possessed," I grumbled begrudgingly, watching her close the front door.

For the first time in my life, I regretted not liking coffee. Still, I forced another sip down my throat. "Ah," I winced, leaning against our kitchen counter for support. "Battery acid."

Maeve laughed as if it wasn't still the middle of the night. She took a sip from the water bottle previously strapped to her waist and shook her head. "This"—she gestured at herself—"is normal. But seeing you up at the crack of dawn, drinking *coffee* leads me to believe you're the one not in your right mind."

I groaned, and it took all the energy I could muster this early in the morning. "I feel dead. Do I look dead?"

"Yes." She didn't even look at me. Taking off her running shoes, she asked, "What are you up to?"

My nose twitched at the thought. "The gym."

Maeve whipped her head in my direction, scrutinizing me as if I'd just told her I'm going to the moon. "Henry's profile?" she guessed. Correctly, of course. Then, unnecessarily, she added, "Like that?"

I glanced at my sweatpants and the oversized T-shirt I'd thrown on in desperation ten minutes ago. I hadn't been able to find the energy in me to care what I looked like, even if it was my ex-boyfriend I was meeting.

"It's gym appropriate," I said matter-of-factly.

"Honey." Maeve shot me a look of pretend pity. "You wouldn't know gym appropriate if it was an eighteen-wheeler and ran you over."

"I'm not the one working out," I clarified. "There's no need to make my outfit a whole . . . thing."

But Maeve was not convinced. She was moving now. Toward me, with a look of determination I knew all too well.

"Your outfit will always be a *thing*, Paula. Whether you want it to be or not, it's the first thing people notice." I rolled my eyes at the monologue I knew all too well. "Plus," she said, standing in front of me, "now that you're forced to break the NCA and spend time with Henry, the least you can do is look sexy while doing so. Make him regret it, right?"

Taking my hand in hers, she dragged me back up the stairs. I was too tired to fight her on it, and when she pushed me onto her bed to go through her closet, I was actually kind of glad. I think I might've fallen asleep in the ten seconds she left me unattended.

Don't force a tired girl into bed if you're not willing to live with the consequences.

"Paula!" Her screech should've been my cue to open my eyes again. I did not.

I mumbled, only half sure I made any sound at all, "Hm?"

"It's 6:40. Get! Up!"

It wasn't the clothes she hurled at my head that got me to sit up and open my eyes. It was the fact that I was supposed to have left ten minutes ago.

"It's *what*?" I asked, so panicked, Maeve furrowed her brow. Struggling to climb out of bed for the second time today, I ignored the shorts and shirt she'd thrown my way. "I have to go—"

"It's 6:35, to be exact." Which made me exhale so loudly, with so much relief, I wouldn't be surprised if it woke Riley and Laila down the hall. I could make up those five minutes easily enough. I'd allowed for an extra ten for my walk to the gym anyway.

"And you're not leaving anywhere without"—she grabbed the clothes she'd picked out for me and shoved them into my chest—"putting these on."

I had no choice but to accept.

And really, who was I to deny a fashion major her

opportunity to dress someone for an occasion? Even if that occasion was . . . the gym. I changed out of the baggy sweatpants and traded an oversized T-shirt for a cropped, long-sleeved compression shirt.

Maeve seemed pleased with her work. Nodding, she said, "It'll be warm enough for that by the time you get out of the gym." Like she knew the exact time that would be. "And take this." When she threw the white T-shirt at me, I actually caught it. *Is this what coffee does?* "For a change of clothes," she added as an afterthought.

"Again," I stressed, "I'm not the one working out. Why would I—?" But she was already pushing me out of her room. Halfway down the stairs, the doorbell rang.

I needed about one second to guess who it could be. Maeve only needed half a second, though, and rushed past me without so much as a glance for permission.

My heart dropped into the bottom of my stomach when she coolly said, "Henry."

What was he doing here?

"Some things never change, do they?" she asked, referring to his punctuality.

I managed to reach them just in time to see her fake smile fall into a straight line. "Never mind," she said, shaking her head as if she'd just remembered something. "A lot of things *have*."

Henry's eyes flicked to mine, and I couldn't do anything but give him an apologetic smile by way of greeting. In Maeve's direction I mouthed a simple *What the fuck?*

When I looked back at Henry, the beginning of a scowl

on his face blew away like dandelion seeds on a summer breeze.

"Good to see you too, Maeve," he said, and it actually sounded sincere. "Heard about that internship you landed. Congrats, really." Sincerity, again.

Without waiting for a reply, Henry gestured for me to follow him to the Audi parked on our curb, which I didn't get to without a confused glare from my best friend. She was probably wondering how Henry knew anything about her internship when all we were supposed to talk about was him.

I didn't want to explain that, so I hurried to catch up with the brunette waiting by his black SUV. "*What* are you doing here?"

He held the passenger door open like I should know the answer. Maybe I already did. "You've been late twice now. And you think I'll believe the interview at seven in the morning is going to be the one you're on time for?"

I wished he wouldn't show how much he still knew me every time we spoke. I'd been well on my way to *being* late, but I tried to defend myself anyway. "I was just about to leave!"

"Of course."

I rolled my eyes, slipping happily into the passenger seat. Henry closed the door behind me and leisurely walked to the other side, key swinging on his finger.

I'd avoided looking at him in Maeve's presence simply to prevent her from seeing how dangerously close I was to falling into old habits again. Now that our front door had closed, I was catching up on what I'd missed on the porch.

My eyes just *flickered* across the gray short-sleeved shirt that exposed his toned arms and clung to his body like a second skin. Something in my stomach tightened at the sight.

I made sure to divert my gaze when he got into the driver's seat.

The engine roared below us. "So Maeve still obviously loves me," he deadpanned, and I couldn't help my amused snort.

"You've always been great at reading people," I agreed as we got rolling.

The gym was a ten-minute drive from my place. When Henry used to spend the night, he'd jog there, calling it his *pre-workout workout.*

"No pre-workout run today?" I decided against recording on a drive as short as this one, but I could still use the time.

"I wasn't sure if you'd be able to keep up." The challenge in his tone underlined his smirk. I glared at him.

"Very funny." I wanted to smile. I did not.

"Unless anything's changed?"

"Nope."

Maybe coffee *was* a godsend after all. I couldn't even remember being tired.

With my newfound energy, I added, "I'm still the passenger princess I've always been." I could tell he wanted to say something else, which was why I cut him off. "*But,*" I stressed, "this isn't about me, Pressley. I totally see through your tactic now."

"Got me," he admitted, one hand raised in defeat, the

other on the steering wheel. "So it really is all about me today, huh?"

"All about you, baby," I said in a singsong voice, nodding grandly and very enthusiastically. To the point where I'd only realized my mistake after it made it past my lips.

Baby.

Not something you called your ex-boyfriend. Not even in a mocking voice and high on caffeine.

"Sorry," I blurted. All that earned me was a hearty chuckle from the man beside me, whose eyes I was avoiding vigorously now. "Coffee," I offered as an explanation.

Like when you did something incredibly embarrassing but all you had to say was "Sorry, third tequila shot" and everyone understood? That's what this felt like.

"No!" Henry gasped.

Someone else might've described the sound of his laugh as delicious. As all-consuming and warm. Not me, though. Definitely not me. "Paula Castillo," he went on, "you didn't drink coffee, did you? For me?"

He'd said it as if I'd just sacrificed my firstborn. But remembering the taste, the reaction was justified. "I'm honored. Truly," he added as he turned into the parking lot of the HBU athletic center. The one literally named after his dad.

"I know," I played along. "You owe me. Big time."

Stopping the car, he turned just in time for me to see something shift in his expression. A half smile still hung in the corner of his lips when he said, "I imagine I'll owe you much more once we get through today."

CHAPTER 13

Now

"No." My eyes flicked from the treadmill back to Henry. "Not in a million years. No."

Nothing—not even the way his face lit up or the way his laugh rang through the empty gym—would get me onto that thing. My anti-workout stance was so firm that this was the first time I'd ever been *inside* a gym.

"Oh, come on," he pleaded, getting onto the next machine over. After a single tap, he was strolling in place at a leisurely pace.

Turning to look at me, he walked backward. "You're already wearing workout clothes. You might as well get one in." His eyes traced my frame so quickly, anyone else might have missed his gaze dropping. But I wasn't anyone. "It would be an outfit wasted."

"No way."

"Paula," he teased. My stomach dropped at the way my

name sounded on his lips. "You want to write about me, you gotta get a feel for what it's like to *be* me. Right?"

"I didn't *want* to write about you." And despite myself, my gaze drifted to the treadmill next to his wearily. "I was forced. Blackmailed, actually."

It's this or nothing.

I could hear the grin in his next words. "Oh, really?" He turned to the front of the treadmill again and quickened his pace.

Goddamn it. Maeve had been right. I was clearly possessed, because a hesitant moment later, I was standing on that forsaken thing, and it started moving beneath me.

"Yes. Really." My eyes sliced to Henry, narrowed in annoyance. "You owe me answers to five deeply personal questions for this, Pressley."

At the very least, that way I could get something out of it.

"One."

"Hah!" *Outrageous.* "Three."

"Two," he proposed.

"Three." To press my point, my finger hovered over the red "End Workout" button on the screen. He dropped the negotiations with a slow nod, but judging by his smile, I wasn't quite sure I'd actually won.

Holding his hand out across the empty space between our treadmills, we shook on it, and I ignored the way one innocent touch scorched through my veins. Shot up my spine.

"By the way, for a business student, you are incredibly bad at negotiating."

"For a journalist—" he began in the same tone, laced with irony and sarcasm.

"Don't even think about finishing that sentence." My threat hid behind a wide grin I had no control over. It kind of defeated the purpose, but Henry still listened.

He powered up his treadmill. His walk turned into a light jog, and another minute later, he was running beside me at an impressive mile pace of five minutes.

I enjoyed my leisurely walk. That's all he was getting.

Every time my eyes involuntarily drifted in his direction, he was a little more flushed. I tried to ignore how his shirt came off after mile two. Then when the treadmill came to a stop and he theatrically collapsed on top of it, I tried to ignore everything else about him too.

His chest rose and fell rapidly. Sweat clung to his muscled chest, abs, and arms. His hair curled at the nape of his neck.

None of the words in my head were in the Bible.

As perfectly practiced in the past fifteen minutes, I diverted my eyes quickly. "Yeah," I nodded, ordering my own treadmill to a halt before sitting on the edge of it. "I feel the same."

Henry panted a laugh. "Walks can be very demanding," he agreed.

But I wasn't here for a workout or to ogle my ex-boyfriend after his, so I signaled to my phone and pressed the record button. "This is what you usually do? Fifteen minutes of . . . a light jog?" I couldn't help the sarcasm, and it earned me another deep rumble of a laugh.

"Yeah," he said, loudly inhaling, exhaling.

Please stop panting, I pleaded in my head. *It's really distracting.*

"A light jog," he said pointedly. "Followed by forty-five minutes to an hour of weight training, then another half an hour of cooldown in the offseason. Well—" He cut himself off, unsure. His eyes flicked to me before he thought about it, then said, "For about a year now, anyway. I changed it up around that time, put more of my focus on running."

"How come?"

"It helps me relax."

Which was about the most absurd idea to someone like me, who wound down with a good movie or a bubble bath, not a five-minute-mile run.

"Plus," he added, "around that time, other . . . forms of cardio fell out of my routine. So I had to substitute."

"Other forms of—?" I caught myself just in time.

Other forms of cardio. For about a year now.

When he looked back at me—still sprawled across his treadmill and shirtless, by the way—I knew we were talking about the same thing.

"Surely—" I cut myself off again. *Surely you're still participating in* other forms of cardio, I wanted to say. But that wasn't where this conversation should go. Even if I really wanted it to.

So instead of asking how many girls he'd slept with since we'd broken up—and if he would be so kind as to share both first and last names as well as social media handles—I said, "That makes sense." And moved on.

Like any self-respecting journalist would.

Henry talked me through his workout split, sets, and reps as he performed his exercises, then explained why he chose each one. Just watching him was exhausting, but he got through the entire thing and still had a smile on his face.

It was past nine by the time we walked out into the parking lot.

Like Maeve had said, it was warm enough for leggings and the oversized T-shirt I'd changed into after *my* very demanding workout.

"I'm usually a little quicker," Henry said, eyes drifting away from his watch.

"Oh." *My fault, obviously.* "Sorry. Did I mess up your schedule?" I didn't think even a natural disaster would make him divert from his holy agenda of the day, but maybe . . .

Henry gasped, clutching his chest. "I'm offended. *Really,*" he stressed. "You should know me better than to suspect something so criminal." Clearly overplaying his part, he really wouldn't divert from his schedule for anything.

He'd planned for the extra time. Of course he had.

"What's next?" I asked, watching Henry open the passenger door. He waited for me to climb in before I guessed, "A protein-heavy breakfast?"

Maybe his schedule was still buried somewhere deep in the back of my mind, because after he shut my door and jogged to the other side of the car to open his, he sported a wide smile.

"So you do know me," he drawled as he slid behind the wheel.

He was clearly pleased by the fact, but in the few seconds between getting in and starting the car, his mood sobered. "If you don't want to come to my place, though . . ." With a glance at me, he turned the key in the ignition and got the car rolling. "If you're uncomfortable or, I don't know, it's too weird or personal for you, I'd completely understand. I can pick you up after."

For the first time since I'd started interviewing him for the piece, it seemed that Henry grasped the position I was in. It was the first time he'd acknowledged that we'd broken up at all. Sure, he'd made a teasing comment here and there, but never an *Are you okay?* or *I'm sorry.*

Probably because he wasn't sorry. Which was fair enough.

"Is it for you?" I asked. My gaze was stuck on the passing buildings. "Weird, I mean. Or too personal. Both?"

Henry laughed as softly as my tone had been. "Never."

I could feel his attention flicker to me, but I didn't meet his gaze. My eyes stayed glued to the window, scared of what he might see if I looked at him now. The raw emotion, the vulnerability.

"I just want you to be comfortable. I never considered what this might—" He hesitated. "After everything. You know? Sorry about that."

I scoffed, finally turning toward him when that strange, hollow feeling in my chest turned into something else. I wasn't quite sure what it was until I spoke.

"For what? Breaking up with me?" I could hear the disdain in my tone.

Henry's brows rose in mild surprise. He knew better than to look at me this time.

"That too," he said. "Obviously that." His voice gained conviction. "But I just meant . . . I should've considered how you might feel, having to spend so much time with me. And I didn't until now." It sounded like he'd been working up the courage to say that.

I considered him for a moment—took in his disheveled hair, his tense expression—and decided he was being sincere.

"Well." I exhaled, shaking off any lingering petty feelings. *Professionalism.* "It's not your fault we're stuck doing this profile together, is it?"

Henry shot me a glance, surprised by the hint of a smile on my lips. I was too. But he returned it with a single nod.

"So," he said. "Your place or mine?"

I rolled my eyes with an amused huff.

"I'm all in if you are, Henry Pressley."

He mirrored the sentiment when he said, "I was thinking protein pancakes?"

"Definitely all in, then."

CHAPTER 14

Then

September: Two years and six months ago

"I only have a couple of minutes, Mami," I muttered by way of greeting. Halfheartedly, I tried to fold the newspaper I'd been skimming with one hand, holding my phone in the other and clutching last week's edition of the *Hall Beck Post* under my arm. Rounding another corner, I spotted the red brick of Henry's block. My heart skipped a beat.

It had been a week since we'd seen each other. And you'd think after a couple of months together, the need to spend as much time together as possible would ease up. Unfortunately, whenever I wasn't with Henry, I was thinking about being with him. If he wasn't there when I fell asleep, I always considered getting up in the middle of the night to change that.

Wanting to spend every second together wasn't ideal when I had exams to prepare for, papers to research, and articles to write. Plus, he had games to play and practice to attend on top of studying.

"Paulita, thank God you picked up!" Her accent slipped halfway through the sentence, and she sounded more Dominican than I had heard in a while. I was on high alert right away.

"What is it?" I checked both directions before I crossed the street to Henry's side, still determined to cut this conversation short. I had exactly an hour and a half before I needed to be back at Daisy's for the closing shift. Henry had a rare spare hour between class and a strategy meeting for their game next weekend. It was the first time our schedules had somewhat aligned since last week.

So yes, I was rushing. Running, almost, until I pressed the intercom of Henry's building. "Mom? What is it? I've got to—"

"There's this article. With your name on it, Paula."

I think someone buzzed me up. The low hum of it reverberated in my very bones, begging me to push the door open, get in the elevator, and forget that my mom had just said the word *article* and my name in the same sentence. "What?"

It was inevitable, wasn't it? Did I really think publishing articles under my real name for six months would escape my entire extended family's attention? When the articles all went online?

I'd never been the lucky kind.

"An article, Dios mío. Someone is publishing nonsense under your name!"

I should've latched onto the fact that they thought it wasn't me writing them. That they suspected someone had stolen the name and identity of Paula Castillo to write about mental health, student life, and their university's sports highlights.

Instead, I felt another word much deeper. Not with my head but with my heart. Which ached in a way I didn't know it could. "Nonsense?"

Faintly, I could hear one of Henry's roommates over the intercom. Probably Heather wondering if the mysterious visitor was someone she knew or just a delivery they'd forgotten about. I wasn't aware enough to tell her.

All I could hear was the word *nonsense* in my mom's voice echoing in my head over and over until she broke the loop by saying, "Yes!" She sounded outraged on my behalf. "Your cousin found it online. On some website. *Buzzweb—Newsbuzz*? I can't remember now, but—"

I didn't feel the need to correct her, and she went on too quickly for me to say anything, anyway. But at least that gave me enough time to find my footing. I might need a few more seconds to make whatever lie I was about to sell believable. I just had to come up with one.

"We've got to do something about this . . . this impersonator! Did you know about this?" she asked.

"No," I said.

My mind raced, eyes flickering through the street, hoping to find an excuse behind Henry's parked car. I didn't notice the tall brunette boy stepping out of the elevator, frantically scanning until he found me pacing up and down the sidewalk. He was watching me from the building's doorway when I finally saw him. I flinched. Stopped abruptly.

"Why didn't you come up?" Henry asked, oblivious to the phone by my ear.

My head shook quickly, finger lifting to my lips. But it was way too late for that.

"Are you with someone?" Mom's tone leveled, like just the thought of her daughter's social life eased all her worries.

I finally saw an end to the conversation. "Yes," I said, eyes on Henry. "I'm with . . . friends, Mom. Don't worry about the article. You wouldn't believe how common my name is!" I didn't believe it either. "Lots of Latinas whose parents had good taste. Te quiero. I've gotta go. Call you later!"

I hung up before she could protest but knew she wouldn't have. Mom might be concerned about Paula Castillo writing articles under her daughter's name, which could harm my career prospects, but she was far more worried about my social life.

"I didn't know Paula Castillo was that common of a name." Henry raised his brows in that amused way of his, interpreting my sigh perfectly. Opening his arms, it took barely two seconds before I slung mine around his torso.

He planted a kiss on the top of my head, and my face pressed into the T-shirt that smelled of citrus and linen, the way all his freshly washed clothes did. It felt like safety, care, love. After my mom unknowingly chipped away at them all, this was needed. *He* was needed. "They found your articles?" Henry asked into my hair.

I nodded and didn't complain when he threw me over his shoulder to carry me up to his apartment like a sack of flour.

CHAPTER 15

Now

I'd been so excited by the prospect of pancakes that the possibility they might not be vegan only occurred to me when they were stacked on a plate between Henry and me.

And I didn't want to be *that* person.

The batter had been meal-prepped—of course it had—so I hadn't seen him make it. I couldn't have given the bowl a subtle whiff for any residual eggy scent because I'd been feverishly scribbling down the information I hadn't recorded while he was preparing breakfast.

When I was still a frequent visitor in this apartment, I knew he'd always had cartons of oat milk, and his pancake recipe was vegan. But that was a year ago.

Henry's fork stopped midway to his mouth, and he narrowed his eyes. "You're not eating. Why?"

"I—" My eyes flicked to the pancakes on the plate in front of me, the blueberries on one side and the maple syrup on the other. I'd rather lie and say I wasn't hungry than bother anyone with my personal food preferences, but I *was* hungry, and I didn't think I could go another few hours without turning into a hangry Godzilla. "Are they—?"

"Yes." Before I'd even finished posing the question, Henry answered it. "They are."

I blinked at him. "Vegan?"

"Yes." He rolled his eyes, smiling. "I knew you'd probably be coming around. So . . ." Trailing off, he gestured to the stack of pancakes, half of the original pile already on his plate. The other half was now on its way to mine. Smothering them in maple syrup, I tried not to swoon at how thoughtful the whole thing was.

I cleared my throat. "Thanks for that." Instead of sounding composed, I just felt awkward. A little rude. So I put my metaphorical journalist glasses back on. "You haven't secretly taken up a plant-based diet, then?" I asked, amusement edging into my tone.

He shook his head in answer, swallowing before he sighed, "I know, I know." His hands raised in mock surrender. "I'm an awful person. I'd love to try it for a month, though. Just to see how it would affect my body." He shrugged sheepishly. "Didn't really want to risk it right before the draft, though."

"Fair enough," I muttered through a full mouth. "I probably get about ten grams of protein a day. Turns out, instant ramen isn't very nutritious."

"Who would've thought."

"I know, right?"

When I looked down, failing miserably at hiding my smile, with gut-clenching clarity I realized something fatal. I was enjoying this—*him*—way too much.

And I couldn't have that.

To think of literally anything else, my eyes roamed the familiar apartment. Its modern white furniture hadn't changed. As usual, there wasn't a single thing out of its designated space. There were actual coffee-table books *on* the coffee table. The remote lay in front of the TV. Keys on the sideboard by the door and jackets on the rack beside it. It was just so Henry.

"Do you still live with them?" I asked absentmindedly, only now noticing the unusual quiet. Heather and Reuben had never been known to be *quiet.*

"No." It kind of surprised me. "I know," he said. "It's weird without them, right? Calm. But I prefer that to sharing my space with two people who can't keep their hands off each other. Only a matter of time before I walked in on them. They moved out a month ago."

"No!" I gasped. "I didn't know they were . . . I thought Reuben would die before making a move."

Henry laughed. "He probably would have. Heather did."

"Figures," I huffed. "Good for her, though." Looking around once more, I added, "And you, I guess. Three bedrooms, huge living space, a kitchen to die for. And you've got it all to yourself."

"It gets pretty lonely."

"No bachelor pad, then?"

"What?"

My head shot in his direction. "What?"

By his smug expression, I realized that yes, I really must've said that out loud.

"Not quite a bachelor pad, no," he said. The first thing his words did was calm that unwarranted jealousy in the back of my mind.

I tried to convince myself that the burning of my cheeks was natural. "You know . . ." I tried to say casually. I probably failed.

"Do I?"

"Just saying because people might expect you to enjoy those single years at college before going off into the big league." *Excellent save, if I do say so myself.*

"People?" Henry's brows rose.

"People who probably want to know what you do when you're not lightly jogging, lifting weights, or . . . letting goals through the HBU defense." If there was one thing Henry didn't do, it was let things through their defense.

"*They'd* want to know?"

"Mm-hmm," I mumbled around the bite I'd taken to do anything other than look at him. "I'm sure they would."

Henry snickered in amusement, leaning back into his chair on the other side of the dining table. "But you obviously have no interest in that?"

"No!" But it was too quick. I settled back and took a second before elaborating. "Why would I?"

Henry didn't say anything else, just looked at me. I

suspected he knew I was currently melting under his gaze, and he enjoyed that too.

"It's not like you care . . ." I had no idea what would come out of my mouth next. "What or . . . who I do, I mean."

Which was no one, by the way. Although Jack had kindly offered twice, and it's not like he wasn't good enough. He was fine, probably more than fine. He just wasn't . . .

My eyes trailed to Henry again, his pink lips, his brown hair parted down the middle, and the way he was looking at me so unapologetically. Thoroughly.

I rambled on, scared the silence that lingered had become too long, too deafening. "I mean, it's been ages! So I don't care either. Obviously." And then, of course, I topped it all off with a nervous laugh. "You're being ridiculous."

Henry blinked slowly, then brought his glass of orange juice to his lips. He took a sip without breaking our eye contact.

"You're right," he said grandly, placing it back on the table. "I'm the one being ridiculous."

"Are you saying it's *me*?"

"Oh God, Paula. What would give you that idea?"

I huffed at his words, head shaking when I relaxed back into my chair. *Just . . . pretend that never happened.*

"What's next on your agenda?" I asked, watching him get up to take our plates into the kitchen. I followed him with the maple syrup and empty blueberry bowl.

"Shower." He quickly checked the time on his wrist.

"Right about now. We'll get to the field by eleven thirty, and I'll just be kicking around until three."

By kicking around, he meant going about carefully crafted routines he didn't want to bother explaining to me.

"Practice is until five, and . . ." This was where he hesitated. "The boys are going out to celebrate . . . something. Honestly, I'm not even sure myself." He seemed amused as he considered his teammates. "Obviously, you're free to go home. Partying isn't really part of my usual routine. So . . ." He shrugged, trailing off.

So.

I really did need to take some notes on today's material and maybe start transcribing some of the audio as well. But only an hour ago, I'd claimed to be all in. And where would I be able to get better stuff than with Henry and his team on a night out?

I said what any sensible journalist would: "All in, remember?"

CHAPTER 16

Now

"All in?" Maeve repeated, basically screeching the words. "What does that even mean? All in on *what*?"

"The article!" I shot her a glare through the mirror, scrunching the rest of the mousse into my curls. "Obviously."

"Is it?" She threw her red corset top at my head and missed by only a few inches. "And does Henry know that? *All in* could mean any number of things. It could mean *everything*, actually."

"Of course he does." I checked the time on my phone absentmindedly. With another fifteen minutes until he'd pick me up, I noticed the text notification below the time and groaned, then turned the screen to Maeve so she could read it.

Her brown eyes flickered across the message before she said, "You need to put that boy out of his misery, babe." Glancing back at Jack's text, I felt a twinge of guilt.

JACK, Saturday, 8:19 PM
> Already got plans later?

"I'm bad at that," I confessed to her. "And he's nice. I like him. Just not . . . like that."

"Well." She snorted, red hair bouncing when she shook her head. "It just so happens that you're a gorgeous angel and he *does* like you like that. Let him down gently so he can move on!"

I stared at my phone, not even bothering to lift my gaze. "Now?"

"Obviously not."

Sometimes I wondered how she dealt with me. Other times I wondered how I'd deal *without* her once we went our separate ways after graduation. "Tell him you're busy, which you are, and then get dressed. You have about ten minutes before the love of your life is standing on our doorstep."

My head snapped in her direction. "He's not the—" I cut myself off when I caught her teasing expression. "You're a child, Maeve Peterson."

But I changed anyway.

When the doorbell rang through the house ten minutes later, I certainly wasn't surprised by Henry's punctuality. I flew down the stairs to avoid another Maeve-Henry incident and waved goodbye to Laila and Riley on the couch. Pip was sleeping slap-bang in the middle of them, enjoying Laila's belly scratches.

"Don't do anything I would do!" Riley called after me,

but I'd already slipped into my sneakers and was halfway out the door by then.

With my eagerness to keep the girls from interacting with Henry (because that had gone so terribly well this morning), I almost ran into him myself. I screeched to a halt just in time, and my hands merely grazed his chest to steady myself.

I didn't want to dwell on how he'd felt under my touch, how the brief contact made me remember every time he'd been at my mercy or I'd been at his.

"Eyes up, remember?" His voice sounded smug. I'd already slammed the door shut behind me, so I was essentially trapped.

Henry did not attempt to take a step back, and he was everywhere. In the soft gust that fanned against my nose when he huffed, the air that smelled like him: expensive, elegant. Like pinewood, citrus, and bad ideas.

"What's the rush?" he asked.

I looked up to find his green eyes gleaming with amusement. I narrowed my own, hoping the glare would be more prominent than the light blush of my cheeks.

"Usually, once someone rings, they take a few steps back to wait a safe distance away from the door. Have you ever heard of that?"

He finally did take that step back, even though I didn't really want him to. "Never," he insisted. Throwing a glance over his shoulder as he walked toward his car, he arched a brow. "Are you *sure* they do that?"

"Positive."

Henry's black polo was casually tucked into tailored pants in the same color. The belt around his waist and the watch around his wrist were his only accessories. Walking after him, I gave myself a single second to marvel at how great his ass looked in those pants, then moved on to think about more mundane things.

Like how the year had finally moved along enough to make the light breeze feel like a warm hug. Or that I could still hear birds singing in the trees. That we'd both left our homes without jackets.

The simple things.

But I couldn't help that my eyes dipped lower again, really just for a second. Which didn't matter much—it was still one too many, and when my gaze snapped back up, Henry was already waiting for me to get in the car. Our eyes connected, and there was a knowing gleam in his.

I slipped past him to get into the passenger seat, but what I really wanted to do was turn around and hide in my bedroom for the rest of the night. Die of mortification.

He closed the door behind me, strolled to the other side, and I braced myself for the comments I knew were coming. He didn't say anything when he got in, started the car, and began driving. But it didn't take long for him to break.

"It is my best *ass*et," he said.

"Wow." I sighed theatrically, though there was no point in denying it. "You managed a whole two minutes without bringing that up." I shook my head with a snicker, glancing at him. "And you look about five seconds away from bursting if you don't let all of your terrible puns out."

"I have nothing else to add," he said. "Your attempt at subtlety just felt a bit half-*ass*ed."

"I've changed my mind," I whined. "I want to go home."

Henry huffed in amusement, eyes on me for a brief moment. "Too late, Charm."

*

I know, I know. I shouldn't drink on the job. But the more time I spent with the HBU soccer team in a dingy bar, the less I considered it a job.

Just something that could enhance my work with meticulous details. Like the fact that Henry's drink of choice would've been a Negroni, but he'd opted for water tonight. Or that he knew the bartender so well, he'd been off talking to him for twenty minutes.

Dylan had practically thrown himself on the empty seat once Henry got up, and not because he'd been so eager to talk to me. The wide grin on his face told me he was well aware of how Henry would feel about it.

You'd think once the guy you hated started dating your sister, you might reconsider your feelings about him. You'd think perhaps the two boys would make up for *her* sake, at least.

From what social media had told me in my endless hours of online research (falling down the rabbit hole of his sister's profiles for clues about the past year I hadn't been part of), Dylan treated Athalia in a way any brother would approve of. Not Henry, though. To him, Dylan was still enemy number one.

And he was sitting right next to me. Michael, the team's captain, was on my other side.

"Paula!" Michael sighed, resting his head on my shoulder. "We've missed you terribly." A drop of alcohol in his system, and he lived up to his dirty-blond hair and turned into a golden retriever. He was six beers deep, and the boys only drank in the offseason, so his tolerance wasn't great.

I patted his head clumsily. "Yeah? Are you sure it's me you missed and not just my protein cookies?"

"Definitely the latter," Dylan chimed in from my other side, most likely because he hadn't missed out on me much.

Dylan and I could still see each other through our respective living room windows if we chose to. Besides Caden and Blake, who must've been around here somewhere, he was the only one on the soccer team I'd still regularly seen once HBU games became off-limits.

By our third semester, I'd asked for sugar or flour when ours had run out so often that he started getting them for us at the store. And after Henry and I broke up, there was no one better to shit-talk my ex-boyfriend with than his sworn enemy. Despite Dylan's bad jokes and his occasional arrogance, when I'd told him what had happened, he'd given me an earnest hug and told me it would be okay. Not soon, but eventually.

Still, I whipped my hand across Dylan's dark hair teasingly, meeting his brown eyes with a glare. "No one asked you, McCarthy." Then, laughing, I turned back to Mike with big eyes and an exaggerated pout. "What is it you were saying? About missing me?" I bumped his shoulder with my own, then sipped the beer in my hand.

"I did miss you," he said, then hesitated. "But those cookies—I'm sorry! They're just so good."

"Fuck you both," I laughed. The two high-fived each other, and with an amused eye roll, I got up.

"Are you getting another drink?" Mike asked, and the pleading look in his eyes combined with the half-empty beer on the table told me he was about to ask if I'd bring him one too. He didn't usually drink, but the season was over, and it had been his last for Hall Beck University.

"Food," I corrected. Mike's face fell in disappointment.

Already up, Dylan told me, "Athalia loves their nachos," and sent me on my way with that piece of information.

As I pushed through to the bar at the other end of the room, I recognized a few faces in the crowd. Not just Henry's teammates, whom I'd gotten to know plenty during our time together, but other HBU students. Valentina Rhodes, from my academic research class. Steven, who worked at the library on weekends. And happened to be good friends with—

"Paula."

I froze mid-step. For a split second, I seriously contemplated making a run for the exit. But I needed Henry if I wanted to leave, and Maeve had deleted his number after my second drunk call nine months ago. I was ashamed to admit it, but that was the only reason I turned to face the man behind me.

"Jack!" I cheered in greeting.

The six-foot blond did not look pleased to see me. Not even surprised, for that matter. His eyes slid up and down my frame like he was assessing a prized possession he hadn't seen in a while.

"What are you doing here?" he slurred, his voice so loud I unintentionally flinched as he leaned closer. Which he had to do—*lean closer and speak loudly.* I wouldn't have heard him otherwise.

I gestured for him to follow me the few missing steps to the bar to lean against it. Jack came to a halt by my side. "Do you know what this thing here is?" I asked instead of answering his question, sweeping my hand across the crowd.

"You're here. Shouldn't you know?"

Alrighty, still grumpy. *Noted.*

"So are you," I challenged, leveling him with a playful glare. It seemed to work, because something relaxed in his demeanor, and he sighed when he sagged against the bar. He ruffled a hand through his hair.

"All I know is that, about three hours ago, I asked if you wanted to come here, and you blew me off." Before I could argue that he had never said *this* was where he'd wanted to take me, he asked, "How often have you done that? Lied about being busy?"

My eyes were darting through the crowd so I wouldn't have to see the emotions settling over his features. I'd take watching the couple making out on the stairs over having to see someone disappointed in me any day.

"I didn't lie," I said.

I could see how it looked like I had. If the roles were reversed, I'd be just as suspicious. Only that he wasn't my boyfriend; he was barely even a friend, and not someone I owed anything to.

Put that boy out of his misery.

Maeve's words echoed in my head when Jack laughed dryly. "How so?" he demanded. "You told me you're working tonight. Didn't you? I should've known when I didn't see your name on Daisy's schedule—"

"I am!" I finally found it within me to turn and look him in the eyes. "This"—I gestured to the soccer team—"is work."

Jack's gaze trailed after my hand, and when his eyes found mine again, his expression shifted. His brows rose in what might've been regret.

I'll never get to know what he'd been about to say, though, because his eyes fell on something behind me, and every single trace of guilt drained from Jack's face. The sweet boy I'd known for almost four years now—the one I'd shared opening and closing shifts with, the guy I'd politely rejected after we'd kissed once, and the one I remained on friendly terms with regardless—was gone.

"Hey, I was looking for you." It seemed Henry only noticed my company when he stood right behind me, his hand gently placed on my shoulder to announce his presence.

A knowing look crossed Jack's eyes, and we were back to square one. Disdain, annoyance.

I hadn't dared look at Henry yet, but my entire body

vibrated with the feeling of his hand on my bare shoulder, with the way the lingering scent of beer was taken over by his cologne. Pinewood, citrus, and bad ideas.

Something in Jack's gaze hardened, as if he had just made a decision and was about to set it in stone.

"Work," he said, grimacing. "I didn't know screwing your ex counted as work these days."

Henry took a single step to stand beside me, and I could feel him tense up. His hand dropped from my shoulder. I knew he wanted to say something—many things, probably. But he didn't.

Jack did. "Last time I checked, prostitution was illegal in all fifty states."

Henry let out a deep sound that felt like a threat all in itself. Still, he kept himself from butting in. Just lingered.

Honestly, it took me a moment to realize Jack had just called me a slut. Essentially because I hadn't slept with him, and now I never would.

To a man, what could've been sluttier than that?

The guilt I'd been carrying around—felt every time he'd texted, I'd seen him, or he'd made a move I had regretfully rejected—died. Despite Maeve's suggestion, I hadn't been stringing him along, not really. After we'd kissed that one time a few months ago, I'd been clear that nothing more would happen between us. I'd communicated honestly and without room for misunderstanding. If he'd stayed around anyway, how was it my fault for trying to be his friend?

Clearly, there was nothing *friendly* between us. He'd just called me a slut.

"In all fifty states?" I clarified harshly. I wasn't quite sure where the confidence came from—maybe the three beers?—but I'd roll with it. "And why'd you have to check that?"

"Oh, fuck you, Paula." Jack shook his head as if he couldn't believe I was talking back. Like he hadn't expected it from the girl who'd always put his feelings before her own comfort. "Don't start now! You've always been such a prude—"

"I'm not a nun, you know!" The loud music drowned out the fact that I snapped at him. The fierceness in my voice still took me by surprise.

"I do *not* know, actually," he said, fuming. Because his eyes stayed on me, he couldn't see the way Henry's hand balled into a fist, twitched. I felt it because his knuckles brushed mine. "That's the problem, Paula! One day you kiss me, the next you're like fucking Mother Teresa or someth—"

I exploded. "Just because I didn't want to sleep with *you* doesn't mean I don't want to sleep with h—anyone else!"

And I could tell it stung by the way he didn't immediately fire a comeback. Meanwhile, I tried to *un-notice* that Henry was looking at me now.

Jack snorted in fake amusement, eyes flickering between me and the pissed-off man beside me. They settled on Henry.

For a long moment, they just looked at each other. Then Jack said, "You know what you're getting yourself into. Good luck, man." He pushed himself off the bar to brush past us. I'm sure the way his shoulder bumped Henry's wasn't a coincidence. Then again, neither was the way Henry grabbed him just before he was out of reach. His green eyes shot to Jack's. I thought he might still punch him.

But all he said was "Watch your mouth." There was an eerie calm in Henry's tone. He held his gaze for another moment, then pushed the blond along and spat his last name as an unkind goodbye. "*Griffin.*"

In less than a second, Henry's attention was on me. The silence between us stretched, though it didn't feel quite deafening with the music blaring. I wasn't sure what to say, even less sure of what *he* might say. He could latch onto all kinds of things from that conversation: *You kissed him?* or *Did you just almost say you wanted to sleep with me?*

I think I was holding my breath.

"Has no one ever punched that guy in the face?" His words were so vastly different from what I'd imagined, the whiplash made me laugh. Genuinely burst out laughing. *Cackle.*

"You didn't," I remarked, failing to swallow the rest of my amusement.

He matched my smile. "But I really wanted to."

And yet. "Why didn't you?"

Henry shrugged. "You can handle yourself." His tone had dropped, and despite the rowdy bar scene around us, I could pick up the softness in it. The fact that I could hear him at all was a miracle. It was like my ears filtered the pitch of his voice and drowned everything else out.

"Next time you need me to beat someone up for you,

give me a call, Paula," Henry added playfully. He wasn't joking. "But I know you're capable of doing that just fine. Case in point." His hand waved to the exit, which Jack was approaching now. Taking the last step, there wasn't a lingering look back before he slipped through the door. "Are you okay, though?"

My eyes slid back to Henry. "Of course," I said, even if I wasn't quite sure. "Turns out he's an asshole! Not surprised; few men aren't."

If Henry hadn't broken up with me when I'd needed him most, I'd probably have gone as far as saying he was one of those few.

CHAPTER 17

Now

Once Jack left, I remembered why I joined Henry on his night out in the first place and actually got some decent material. Most likely because the Jack incident sobered me up enough to focus on the bigger picture again.

I needed to impress.

This profile had to show Eddie that he'd made a mistake—which he admitted to rarely—by benching me for a year. More than that, it had to show whichever bigger press had expressed interest that they were right to do so.

Which meant that two days later, I was vigorously working on it at the *HBP* office. Given how much time I'd been spending with Henry, I had enough conversations with him and his friends that I hadn't recorded but still needed to be written down. Easy stuff.

Who would've thought that the real challenge was transcribing our post-run gym interview? Eddie had been happy enough with the stuff I'd shared after my butchered first attempt, so I no longer needed to send him all my interviews. But I did have to transcribe them for when I began drafting the profile regardless.

I was locked in, focused. My headphones were blocking out any distracting noise, which was usually very prominent at the *Post*. And yet I couldn't concentrate.

PAULA:
This is what you usually do? Fifteen minutes of a light jog?

HENRY:
Yeah. A light jog. Followed by forty-five minutes to an hour of weight training, then another half an hour of cooldown in the offseason. Well, for about a year now, anyway. I changed it up around that time, put more of my focus on running.

The transcript made it sound like a normal, coherent conversation, but through my headphones, Henry's words were paired with his heavy breathing, panting. I could almost *see* the way his chest heaved, the way his throat worked.

Before I could get the next words down, Riley snatched one of the headphones out of my ear and plugged it into her own. With her hands on my desk, she leaned forward to get a better look at my screen.

I jumped. I gasped. And the moment I needed to recover

was enough time for Riley's eyes to triple in size. Her head snapped in my direction.

What is this? she mouthed, shellshocked by what she thought she'd discovered. By the sheen of red on her dark skin, none of her thoughts were holy.

Another one of Henry's huffs rang through the recording, and I finally turned the thing off.

"Paula!" she gasped. "I did not think you were the kind to—" Her eyes scanned my transcript again, hoping to find clues that would support her theory. "To get him off for information—"

"Dios mío!" I screeched. She'd already said enough for me to glance around the office, scared someone had overheard her. When no heads turned our way and no one peeked out from behind their screen, I swiveled back around. "No. No, of course not!"

Riley's perfectly trimmed eyebrow rose.

"Why is he all hot and bothered, then?" She wiggled the little earpiece between us like a friendly reminder.

"He's not—" I hesitated. It felt wrong to say it out loud. "*That.* He's out of breath. Because we were at the gym." *Running five-minute miles.* "And this was right after his cardio—"

"Cardio. Of course."

Exhausted, I fell back into my chair, arms slack at my sides and hoping a bolt of lightning would take me out.

Riley suppressed a chuckle. "Hey, I'm not judging, girl." Grabbing the chair from one desk over, she sat and rolled back to me. "You gotta do what you gotta do."

My eyes sliced to hers with a glare. "I'm not sleeping with him!" I cried.

Too loudly.

The office fell quiet. Although everyone was trying to be inconspicuous, I could see a few heads turn our way and a few more curious faces pop up from behind computers.

"I did not sleep with a subject," I amended, calmer. "Now, if we could all just go back to ten seconds ago, when conversations were very animated. Thank you."

I turned to Riley again, and the look on my face made her wince.

Sorry, she mouthed. "I was joking!" She raised her voice, notifying the rest of the office of her nonexistent sense of humor. Just for me, she added, "Mostly," before her attention went back to the open document on my screen.

"Don't get me wrong, Paula," she sighed after reading a few lines. "I love that Ed finally got over what happened last year. I just don't understand why he had to give you *this*."

Yes, working on something again was nice, but no, it didn't have to be this.

"I mean, just ethically speaking," she said. "You're not even supposed to get close to your subjects like that. It's in *The New York Times*' guidelines! Does Eddie think he's better than *The New York Times*?"

"Probably. And it's not like I didn't ask. I literally said, '*Why do I have to do this?*' And he just . . . went on a different tangent."

Before Riley could form a reply, Alfie's cheery voice

announced that he'd decided to join this conversation. Which completed our usual *Post* trio.

"I know why!" he said from a neighboring desk. With his chair, he rolled to ours and huddled between Riley and me. One of his red hairs tickled my nose—that's how close he was.

"You don't," Riley decided. I wasn't convinced either.

"I know *something*," Alfie amended. "Maybe. I was leaving when Pressley was in Ed's office, the door open like always. Just before he assigned the profile to you."

Oh?

"Your talents are wasted with horoscopes," I marveled in amusement. "Do go on, investigative journalist."

With a contented grin, Alfie looked around the room as if he might find someone in it who shouldn't be. His smile faded just before his head snapped to the door. "Follow me," he said very vaguely and got out of his chair.

We both did.

Alfie led us to the stairs, taking two at a time toward the exit. "I was, like, ninety percent sure Eddie was *this* close to kicking Paula out of the paper. You know, with the way he didn't even give you that lame article last month, and then you tried talking him into it? I thought after a year of benching you, he finally had enough."

I vividly remembered chasing my editor out of the building, begging and pleading for something to work on. I nodded as we stepped into the afternoon sun.

"So I went to look for him. Because really, if he's starting to clean out the crew, I'm next. Which was terrifying." His dad basically owned the *Hall Beck Post*, so I didn't think Alfie was going anywhere. But perhaps he knew his father better than that.

"Anyway, he must've just gotten back from an errand or something. He was kind of out of breath when he asked Pressley into his office." *My fault*, I realized. "Which is when I decided to hide behind a wall and listen. I was like, *What's Paula's ex doing here? And can I give Henry a piece of my mind while we're at it?*" Alfie glanced at me, a little sheepish. "I didn't do that."

"Obviously," Riley added helpfully.

"Well." He shrugged. "Long story short, all I heard was Eddie asking, *'Are you sure?'* Like a million times. Let me tell you, whatever it was, Pressley was very sure of it." Alfie stifled a laugh. "He said something about you, started with your name." His eyes were on me again. "He was all *'Paula should . . .'*"

Alfie's impression of Henry was just a swoony, deep voice. It kind of worked.

"And I wish I could tell you what he said next, but Miss Lacy thought hiding behind a wall and spying on our editor was suspicious, or so she said. When she saw me, she told me to stop. Threatened to tell on me, that little snitch. I would've told her to screw herself if I hadn't thought I was minutes away from being kicked out. Promise!"

Computing the information took me a second, and all I could latch onto were his last words. "Alfie," I said, bumping my shoulder against his. "You don't need to justify that. At all."

It was enough that he'd stayed and tried to listen. Who'd willingly go head-to-head with Lacy Halloway?

Riley nodded grandly. "You tried!" she encouraged. "It's all anyone can do." Then her expression darkened. "Why is it somehow always Lacy, though? *How?*"

"She's obviously the reason I didn't just tell you inside," Alfie said. "Her desk is right in the middle of the office, where she can pick up gossip from every corner." The way he lowered his voice even further as he said it, Alfie sounded like he was sharing his greatest conspiracy theory with us.

The idea that Lacy somehow always knew everything wasn't an exaggeration. It might as well be printed in next week's issue; that's how much of a fact it was. Which also meant she knew what had happened in that office of Eddie's after she sent Alfie away for eavesdropping. She most likely stayed to do the exact same thing.

So she knew whether Henry had been sure of wanting me on this profile. She knew if he'd said *"Paula should have this"* or if it had gone a little more like *"Paula should not even be close to my profile."*

After he broke up with me, I doubted Henry had wanted me anywhere near him, his story literally in my hands.

CHAPTER 18

Now

I hadn't been to an HBU game since our breakup. And now I didn't know what to wear.

It used to be easy because Henry would jokingly tell me I wasn't invited if I wasn't wearing his jersey, and I'd obviously oblige. Fishing through my closet now, I found all my tops to be lacking . . . something.

Specifically, his name on the back.

I was still in sweatpants and a baby tee when the doorbell rang, and I cursed Henry. If he wouldn't insist on showing up early everywhere, I'd still have some time to look like I hadn't woken up ten minutes ago. Rushing downstairs, I threw a glare at my cat that told her to behave, and she blinked back at me like I'd lost it.

This time, Henry stood on the porch with a respectable distance between himself and the door. He seemed proud of the fact. "Is this what you say they do?" he asked by way of greeting, gesturing at the gap between us.

"Wow," I gushed. "You pick things up fast."

He pretended to bow as a thanks before I added, "Let me just get my stuff and we can go. Come in."

The vase that always held his weekly flower deliveries was empty, probably a little dusty, and the photo wall no longer had any pictures of the two of us up. I wondered if he felt that same *pang* in his chest when he realized. I wondered if he noticed at all. The thought finally propelled me forward.

"One second," I repeated, then rushed up the stairs, taking them two steps at a time. A decision I immediately regretted when my breath was heavy enough to suggest *I* had just run that five-minute mile.

I snatched the tote bag from my bed—pre-packed and everything—and threw a last glance in the mirror. It felt stupid to change now, when he'd already seen me and would most definitely notice a different outfit on me.

Ex-girlfriend who didn't still care and actually kind of despised him. That's the vibe I was still going for.

I tried to remember that as I forced myself back downstairs, expecting Henry to be standing where I had left him by the door, evaluating our house and the changes it had undergone since last year. He was not.

My heart dropped into my stomach at the thought of him leaving. Maybe he'd given up after discovering something he didn't want to see, or he never cared enough about whether I'd be with him or not. It seemed uncharacteristic of Henry, but how well did I really still know him?

"Paula?" came hesitantly from the kitchen behind me. "A little help here?" A second later, I heard the intimidating hiss of my cat and realized she was no longer on the couch. Instead, Pip was standing by Henry's feet, fur raised and back arched, emitting another threatening sound.

Muscular, six-foot-one Henry looked terrified. He pressed himself against the kitchen counter, and Pip pushed him farther into it. The scene reminded me of all the times she'd tried to take his eyes out. He was probably right to feel as scared as he did.

Pip was a stray, and we'd always figured she must've had a bad history with men. She despised every single one. Even Dad, who'd been the one to insist on taking her in five years ago, despite her hissing, growling, and scratching. Mom had agreed as long as I promised to take the black cat with me once I went to college.

With a snicker, I lifted Pip into my arms. "Dios." I sighed, shaking my head as I created some distance between the two. Henry let go of a relieved breath. "What is your problem?" I muttered to her in Spanish, gesturing for him to make his escape before I released the wild . . . eight-pound beast. I didn't have to tell him twice.

With Henry on his way to the car, I silenced my cat with a glare, holding her at arm's length in front of me. "That man has been nothing but kind to you," I chided. Pip growled in annoyance, then started fussing in my grip. "Behave," I warned before letting her go. She couldn't get up the stairs fast enough, and I felt the same way about catching up with Henry.

"I'm sorry," I groaned once he slid behind the wheel.

"Pip will make sure you end up alone, you know," Henry said before he turned the key in the ignition. "What have I ever done to that cat?"

"Exist," I stated matter-of-factly. "It's not personal. You're just a man."

Henry snorted. "I'll apologize for that next time I see her. How dare I?"

"Next time?" My brows rose teasingly.

An exasperated look played on his face when he looked at me. "*Right.*" He attempted to roll his *R*, but just like when I'd tried to teach him some Spanish, he failed miserably. It sounded choppy and rough, and I still somehow adored it. "You let her know how sorry I am, then."

"She will not accept it," I informed him. "But I'll try my best to change her mind." Which was impossible. My cat was as stubborn as they came.

For a moment, there was nothing but the radio filling the air between us. "You look good, by the way."

His words took me so off guard, there was nothing I could've done about my laugh. "It's sweatpants and a shirt, Henry."

His gaze swept across me once—very quickly but not very subtly. "I can see that."

"So," I stressed, "you can't mean that."

"I do." His tone nonchalant, he went on. "Although I preferred my name and number on you."

My eyes snapped to him, watching carefully, curiously. Honestly, a little confusedly. But I stayed quiet, just observing his focus on the road, like he hadn't said anything at all.

Or like the thought was so normal to him, so common, he forgot it shouldn't be.

*

"Are you guys sure this isn't . . . weird?" Sitting between exposed six-packs and developed calves, it kind of seemed that way.

The energy felt different in the locker room. The air thrummed with excitement; anticipation seemed to reverberate off the walls. The boys laughed at bad jokes, chugged more water, and discussed strategy; some huddled in a corner, performing their pregame rituals.

Which was what I was here for: Henry's pregame ritual.

"It's not weird unless you make it weird," Dylan snickered from the other corner, sending me a look that soundlessly added, *And you are.*

"McCarthy," Henry barked from beside me, always annoyance in his tone when he spoke to him. Or about him. "No one asked you."

"She quite literally did."

Henry ignored him and turned to me instead. "It's not weird," he promised, sending another glare to make a point. His hand settled on my shoulder in a gesture that was meant to be reassuring.

It was, kind of.

Only that instead of the quiet calm that was supposed

to flood through me, it ignited a fire that slowly made its way to my cheeks.

He's touching your neck, not kissing it.

Although it's not like he hadn't done that in here too.

With his eyes resting on me once more, I tried not to look at his hand on my shoulder. Cool, calm, and collected.

Ex-girlfriend who didn't still care and actually kind of despised him.

But his gaze found its way to his hand on me anyway. He lingered for another moment—one I enjoyed—then drew back like my skin was a hot stove he hadn't noticed he was touching. "Ask literally anyone else," he added quickly.

Those close enough to hear gave wild nods or shouted in agreement. Which was enough to soothe the awkward feeling low in my belly.

"Alright." I cleared my throat, still trying to shake off the aftermath of Henry's very . . . appropriate touch. "So . . . you just do what you usually do. Pretend I'm not even here."

"Got it, boss." With a little salute, Henry walked back to his gym bag on the other end of the bench.

I was unprepared for what followed. Should've just asked about his ritual instead of being there to see it.

In one smooth motion, Henry grabbed the back of his black polo and pulled it over his head, leaving his upper body for all the world to see. Primarily: me. Nobody else was even glancing in his direction. Why would they?

They hadn't had the pleasure of their fingers trailing down his pecks, watching—memorizing—how he tensed the farther they wandered south. Their tongues hadn't traced along the toned crevices of his stomach. Hadn't elicited deep groans by doing so. So they didn't miss it.

I did.

The realization hit me like a bolt of lightning might, scattering the thoughts of his sounds and the images of us into oblivion. My eyes snapped away from his chest just as he pulled his jersey on, and in my hurry to look away, my gaze crossed Dylan's. Who must've witnessed the whole thing.

His lips pulled upward with another knowing smirk, and as if that wasn't enough, he winked before going to tie his shoes.

He'd been right. I *was* making this weird.

Focus, damn it.

So in the least creepy way I could, I observed the team, their dynamics and quirks, and wrote it all into my Henry document. I noted Dylan counting to four out loud and how often Henry's eyes flicked toward me.

Twenty-three times.

With ten minutes to spare, the HBU soccer team dispersed from their huddle with hollers and shouts, and I noted that if I ever needed a motivational speech, Coach Hepburn was just the guy for it.

"So, was this as insightful and exciting as you thought it would be?" Henry settled beside me as most of his teammates made their way onto the pitch. He retied his shoes.

"Glorious," I agreed. "Even though when Dylan started counting out loud, I thought he might've actually lost it for a second."

"Well, he has," Henry stated matter-of-factly. "But you should've noticed that way before he started counting."

I snorted a laugh, but Henry just shrugged before he clarified. "It's his thing, though. Counting to four." He threw me a sheepish look, then moved on to tie his other shoe. Very slowly. As curtly as he possibly could, he explained, "Four sisters. So he counts to four."

I'd known about his sisters, but not that he basically dedicated every single game to them.

My bottom lip quivered as I tilted my head. "That's adorable." I didn't know what else to call it.

I hadn't detected any particular thing Henry did today, but if he *had* a ritual, it wouldn't be half as cute. Probably more like solving related equations in his mind or calculating a win using the stats and numbers of his opponents.

"Do *you* have a thing?" I asked anyway, because at the end of the day, I was writing a profile on Henry Pressley, not Dylan McCarthy Williams.

Henry thought, making sure whatever answer he'd be giving was deliberate and calculated. Depending on the information you'd want to get out of him, this could be every journalist's dream or nightmare.

"On the record or off the record?" he asked. There was no phone recording our conversation, but his eyes flicked to my open laptop sitting beside me.

"On the record, of course."

"I look at the opposing players way before the game, try to remember their strengths and weaknesses. A few minutes before kickoff, I usually let all that just blast through my brain until I feel I'm in their heads instead of my own. It works most of the time."

My urge to shout *I knew it!* wasn't as pressing as the question burning on my tongue.

"And off the record?"

I didn't know why I held my breath, but when his eyes batted open and their piercing green connected with mine, it almost knocked the wind out of me.

"You."

The word seemed to echo through the room, and in that moment, my world became significantly smaller. It felt like there was nothing else outside those doors. Like there was only him and me and the dingy smell of a boys' locker room.

The way it used to be.

Me? I wanted to ask, but it felt impossible to form even a one-word sentence.

"For a long time, it was you," he went on. The past tense shouldn't have stung. "And even after . . . everything." He shrugged, unsure. "*You* worked so well. With the draft coming up, I was kind of scared I'd mess up if I didn't think of . . . well. Of you. So I continued, and just—" His eyes danced through the room like he'd rather be anywhere else, but the words still left his mouth. "Never stopped."

There were a thousand things I wanted to say and do.

Kiss him, for one. Climb him like a tree and touch him until he made those agreeable sounds I'd been thinking about earlier. I wanted to tell him that I appreciated his words, that I felt honored. Honestly, that I was probably about two seconds away from falling in love with him if he kept this up. *Again.*

I didn't do any of that.

The door swung open before I could react at all, and Coach Hepburn reminded me that we were, in fact, not the last two people on earth and that Henry had a game to get to. "Pressley!" he shouted into our little bubble and burst it.

I tried to convey as much of what I'd wanted to say in the few seconds when we locked eyes, but it didn't feel like enough by a long shot.

At least they won the game.

CHAPTER 19

Then

March: Two years ago

Henry's dining table was big enough to hold my printed-out research and his entire assortment of planners and calendars. Somewhere between the endless papers, I tried to compare my halfheartedly kept Google calendar on my phone to his passion project of a schedule.

The vase in the middle of it all held the bouquet of peonies I'd been eyeing during my shift at Daisy's, which doubled as a flower shop. I wasn't quite sure how Henry had managed to buy them from the neighboring register without me noticing, but he had.

I focused back on the mess of scheduling.

"Saturday?" I asked.

Henry trailed his finger over the calendar until it reached the Saturday I suggested. His head shook, and my heart sank a little. But I wasn't necessarily surprised.

"Can't. Away game, so we'll be gone all weekend." He continued to study the schedule. "What about Wednesday?" *A week from now.*

Hope shimmered in the green of his eyes when he looked back up. I wanted to agree just to make them shine with something other than disappointment.

"Editorial meeting at the *Post*." Like every Wednesday.

I didn't blame him for the fact that he kept forgetting about my plans when I could barely keep up with them myself. Despite his vigorous need for planning and control, he had more than enough on his plate. He did not need to keep track of mine too. I doubted there would be space in his calendar for my schedule anyway.

"They usually go late," I reminded him. "And you need to be in bed by ten, right? With practice in the morning?"

Henry groaned. "I want to see you, Charm. Why is it so hard to see you?" He drove a hand across his face before it disappeared into his hair, messing his neat middle part up as he let out another frustrated huff.

This was becoming a more frequent problem: managing our time together.

One NCAA championship season ending meant the next one was just around the corner. Others might've given themselves a few months off after the high season of college soccer, but not Henry. To him, losing in the quarterfinals only meant more training, more workouts, and more strategy meetings.

And that, of course, meant seeing less of his girlfriend.

Henry's priorities had always been crystal clear. I don't

think I had ever met a person as sure of the things they'd wanted and as determined to make them happen. I'd never been under the impression a girl would get between that, and I never *wanted* to get between that. But trying to plan my days around him was exhausting, especially when mine were pretty busy too.

After selling another one of my articles to an external outlet, Eddie hadn't hesitated to drown me in more work, hoping whatever I'd make out of it would draw more attention to the *Post.* He'd given me a month for my latest assignment, a cover story on the impact of college sports, which required deeper research, more detailed interviews, and a well-developed story. This was big and demanded the time necessary to make it big.

I wish my priorities were as clear as Henry's. But I missed him, and I knew, after two weeks in which we only saw each other when he came by Daisy's for his morning coffee, that if we were going to see more of one another, it would be because I made time. I took a deep breath, and when I watched him get up and walk around the table to my side with a pout, I asked, "Where's the game? Could I join?"

His eyes widened like he hadn't expected the suggestion. Like I wasn't here because I'd canceled karaoke night with the girls. Like changing my plans hadn't become a key part of making this relationship work.

Henry drew me off the chair and into his chest, our hands interlacing. "Would you?" And it almost sounded like he was holding his breath, keeping the grin threatening to spread across his lips at bay. "I promise I'll make it up to you."

And I couldn't help it. Seeing the corner of his lip tilt into a devious smile just as his fingers trailed up my arms and disappeared into my hair. I'd made the decision right then and there. I'd still have enough time to write the article anyway.

"How?" I asked, arms crossing behind his neck. I barely noticed the way he led me backward, presumably to his room.

He snickered, the sound tinting my cheeks and turning my legs to jelly. "A house in the Hamptons?" he joked. I think.

I hummed as if considering, then shook my head with a smile. "Seems unlikely. What else do you have to offer me besides a house in the Hamptons, Henry?"

He rolled his eyes when he sat back on his bed, and I had about three seconds before he pulled me onto his lap, my legs on either side of him, leveling our eyes. "We had one. My parents sold it, though."

Whenever he mentioned his parents, it didn't seem like he cared much about what had happened to them at all. Like they were still sitting somewhere in a penthouse on the Upper East Side or a big-shot office on Wall Street. Not like they were buried six feet below ground.

They weren't a frequent topic, and whenever they did come up, I still wasn't sure how to react to his nonchalance. If I should treat them like any other subject or tell him how sorry I was for his loss.

"Why?" I asked. "Why'd they sell it?"

Henry shrugged. "Doesn't matter," he said, apparently having moved on. His hands trailed down the contours of my body and settled on my waist. He pressed a single kiss to my neck, the touch barely a peck, and looked up at me. "Let's focus on what you want from me, Paula. Anything."

And I thought he could really mean that.

Anything.

Anything but time he can't compromise on.

CHAPTER 20

Now

Eddie had asked me to meet at his office in a way that wasn't really a request but a demand, and it usually meant something serious was going on.

That suspicion was confirmed when I arrived and found his door closed. Which hadn't even been the case when he'd told me, about a year ago, that he couldn't give me another article until the mess I'd created had been dealt with. The fact that Henry was propped against the wall beside it hardly made the situation better.

"Didn't know you'd be here," I admitted by way of greeting, eyes still on the closed door.

His gaze followed. "Is that a good or a bad thing?"

I thought, leaning against the opposite wall, *I'm not quite sure myself.*

"The closed door, I mean," he added.

"Oh." Of course he didn't mean his own presence.

"Most definitely bad," I offered plainly. "Makes it worse that I don't know what it's about. You?"

"No idea."

My mind raced through possible scenarios that required Henry and me and Eddie's closed office door. I tried to remember whether I failed to deliver on deadline or sent the wrong document. Perhaps I'd forgotten to delete an inappropriate comment from one of the earlier transcripts.

Which reminded me of Riley's joke in the office last week and Alfie's conspiracy theory that Lacy picked up gossip from every corner. I wouldn't be surprised if I found her on the other side of that door with Eddie. I could perfectly picture her waiting to snitch on me for something I hadn't done.

"If he asks if we hooked up, just deny it. Don't ask any questions."

Henry's brows shot up, intrigued and confused at the same time. "Wouldn't that be the truth? Or did I miss something I shouldn't have?"

I sighed at the way he tried to hide his smile. "No, didn't miss anything."

Henry huffed. "A shame."

We were interrupted before I'd processed his words.

I hadn't expected a smile on Edward Smith's face when he finally opened the door. "Paula, Henry," he said. "Thanks for coming in on such short notice."

He gestured into his office, and Henry and I exchanged a single glance before following him inside.

I tried to imagine how getting Henry here on such short

notice must've gone for him. Eddie's flushed cheeks. Henry trying to explain he had to eat dinner at the exact time his schedule outlined or he would combust.

It seemed I'd been about to get my answer when Henry began, "I won't have much time. This really was quite last—" But he stopped when his eyes fell on a fourth person in the room I only noticed when he did.

Not Lacy. A middle-aged man, maybe in his late thirties? Skin dark and head bald. He stood next to Eddie's desk, hand extended for me to shake first before diverting his attention to Henry, who did not appreciate whatever kind of surprise this was.

"Pressley," the man greeted him. "Good to see you again, son. We haven't heard from you in a while." The casual hug paired with a pat on the back suggested they weren't strangers.

At my confused look, Eddie just gestured for me to take one of the empty chairs.

"Marty." Henry's brows drew together. "I didn't know you were in town." His shoulders sagged as he relaxed slightly, but the edge in his voice lingered. "What's up?"

"Sit," Marty offered, tone warm and comforting. Hesitantly, Henry did. "First of all," Marty continued, "it's so nice to meet you, Miss Castillo. Marty Meyers," he added in introduction, like the name should mean something to me. "I cannot tell you how much I loved your article in *The New York Times* a few years ago."

It was only one year and four months ago, to be exact. And a guest essay, not an article.

That was when my career seemed to be on an endless upward trajectory. It was like being strapped into a roller coaster, driving higher and higher, nervous and excited. Only that I'd forgotten that every roller coaster eventually comes back down. Mine plunged dramatically into the pit I was still trying to work my way out of now.

This profile was the first light I'd seen from the bottom in months.

"You will do wonders with this profile, I'm sure. Plus, the Blue Eagles could use some extra buzz around their players. It's perfect timing."

It wasn't often I remembered I'm actually good at what I was doing. This was the first reminder in months, maybe a year. I smiled so widely, my cheeks hurt.

"Thank you so much," I said, and I meant it.

Marty settled into his chair with a warm smile that somehow conveyed superiority and authority simultaneously. "Which is why your editor and I think it would be a great idea for you to join Pressley when he flies down."

Henry tensed beside me.

"What?" His tone was a little too insulted for my liking.

Henry cleared his throat, and I could tell he was trying his best to stay calm, not letting the apparent change of plan get to his head. "I feel like there should've been a third party consulted on that," he said flatly, stoic mask twitching just once. "Don't you think?" Before anyone could answer, Henry muttered, "Before bringing the idea to her."

I could hear him loud and clear, though.

"That's what we're doing now." Marty's eyes were fixed on Henry, unrelenting.

"Sorry," I said, awkwardly chuckling. It drew the two men out of their competitive staring. "I just—*who* thinks *what* is a good idea?"

"The New York Blue Eagles," Marty said, like I should know what was going on. "Henry's team. Officially, once he finally signs the remaining contracts."

His tone insinuated there was something he wasn't saying. Henry's deep breath told me he knew what it was. "Which is why he's flying down. To New York." Marty seemed to consider his next words, then his gaze settled on me again. "Hopefully with you in tow."

Eddie jumped in and explained the situation. "You're joining Henry for his weekend in New York." He made sure it wasn't a question. I was going whether I wanted to or not. Whether Henry wanted me to or not.

Eddie cleared his throat. "You won't have to worry about anything. I spoke to Alfie's—Mr. Dunbridge, and the paper will be happy to cover your expenses over the next three days."

Happy was probably an overstatement.

Henry's head fell back with a deep sigh, like he, too, had given up. Clearly, he wasn't a fan of the idea. Of *me*. Which must've at least partly been due to the fact I'd be throwing off his entire plan. And so spontaneously—

"Wait," I thought out loud, Eddie's words only now really sinking in. "*The next three days?* As in, we're leaving tomorrow?"

"The flight's at nine," Henry offered unhelpfully, with about as much enthusiasm in his voice as I'd brought along to do the entire profile.

"It'll be great. You'll get to see the amenities, be in the stadium. Henry in our colors. You get me?" Marty looked back at me. "We're not trying to tell you *what* to write." He winked, which made the entire statement seem meaningless. "Like Mr. Smith said, it's fully arranged. All you have to do is say yes. Your choice."

One glance at Eddie told me it wasn't. And anyway, what was it I'd vowed?

My throat worked, and I kept my eyes away from Henry, if only to ignore how little he wanted me in New York with him and how much it hurt.

"I'm in." *All in.*

Henry seemed about ten seconds away from spontaneous combustion as he got out of his chair and left without another word.

"I'd love to talk more," Marty said, already following his newest defender. "But it seems my client is running away from me."

And gone.

Which left me with Eddie to deal with. "Fantastic choice," he said. The smile on his face told me it hadn't been mine.

"Was it?" I laughed dryly.

"Trust me, Paula." And it almost seemed sincere, the way his eyes met mine. "It'll make your profile better. Where else will you see him in his element like that? When else are you going to get a close-up look at the MLS draft like that?"

I knew he was right.

"But—"

"As for Henry," he cut me off, "he knows what he signed up for, and he was very sure he wanted it."

"The profile, yes! But not—"

"You." The word reverberated off the walls. "He was very sure he wanted this profile and everything else that comes with it."

A second ticked by in which I'd searched for the right response and failed miserably at finding it. "Now"—Eddie gestured to the exit, an easy smile back on his lips—"I think you have some packing to do. I'll email you everything you need."

CHAPTER 21

Now

"I can't do this," I repeated, continuing to throw things into my overnight bag like I maybe *could* do this.

Without Eddie's easy smiles and bossy attitude, it was hard to keep my doubts at bay. *Maybe I shouldn't be intruding the way I am. Maybe I shouldn't go all in on a man who dumped me.*

Spending an entire weekend in a city you didn't know, with an ex you shouldn't *get* to know again, didn't seem like a great idea. Add the fact that said ex did not want me in said city, and . . . yeah. Doubts. Many of them.

Not that my editor wanted to hear about them. Nor did Henry's manager. All they saw was what this trip could do for my article or their team's PR. The Major League Soccer draft had always been a bit of a mystery to me, and when I'd prepared for this profile, I couldn't find many articles talking about the process or giving a behind-the-scenes look.

So as someone who enjoyed soccer a fair amount, I'd been excited. An exclusive look behind the curtain! Awesome.

But did it have to be by my ex-boyfriend's side? As his plus-one?

I groaned, letting myself fall to the floor I'd been sitting on: Maeve's cue, apparently. She jumped into motion.

"She's losing momentum!" the redhead reported, moving from my bed to heave me back into a seated position. I did nothing to help her with that.

"Do you need me to repeat it?" Laila asked from the chair by my desk. She whirled around to face us.

Although I faintly shook my head, Maeve was adamant when she said, "STAT!"

"Paula." Suddenly, Laila was kneeling in front of me, holding my hand as if I were about to undergo open-heart surgery and she hadn't said goodbye yet.

I wanted to grab her by the shoulders, shake her so hard her white-blond hair ruffled with the motion, and tell her, *I'm not dying!* But realistically, who could do that to someone with a face as sweet as Laila's? Never mind the fact that I *did* feel like I was dying.

She smiled at me. "You're about to get an all-expenses-paid weekend away for doing the thing you love," she reminded me for the second time in the hour we'd all been holed up in my room. "If that doesn't tell you you're a darn good journalist and that you're going to write something just as amazing about this, I don't know what will." Maeve bumped my shoulder in agreement, still holding my entire body weight up.

"Listen to sweet little Laila," she said, so close to my ear it felt a little hypnotic.

"I am." It was more of a groan than an answer, but at least I began throwing things into my bag again. Which was Maeve's sign to let go.

"And if that doesn't work," Riley perked up, giving me a look from where she let her head dangle off the edge of my bed, braids sprawling across the floor, "just remember you're not only getting paid to do what you love but also getting to experience the most expensive city in the world with a man who can afford it." Henry was filthy rich, yes. But—

"New York isn't the most expensive city in the world. Zurich is," I corrected.

Riley shook her head, and for a moment, it seemed she might lose consciousness. She turned upright and flopped onto her stomach.

"They're tied," she said. "Plus, that wasn't actually my point." She leveled me with a look while the blood rushed from her head back to her feet. "Henry's hot and rich, and you're about to spend three whole days with him."

"He's also her ex-boyfriend," Maeve argued, getting comfortable against the foot of my bed. "For good reason. So whatever it is you're trying to do here, missy, stop it."

Maeve couldn't see when Riley gave me a suggestive wink.

"Just trying to come up with all the reasons why Paula should get on that plane tomorrow," Riley said innocently, batting her perfectly winged eyes at the group. At that,

Maeve turned to give her a look. "And even though Paula thinks Henry is one of the reasons she shouldn't." Her brows rose when she looked back at me. "I think he's the main reason she should."

"After the fact that her career depends on it," Laila added quickly, then gave me a thumbs-up.

"Yes." I perked up. "Most definitely after that."

I'd prioritized him once before, and it had not turned out well for me. Like almost-being-kicked-out-of-the-paper-and-not-getting-an-actual-project-for-an-entire-year kind of bad.

*

Despite my roommates' encouraging words and Maeve's insistence that we watch my go-to comfort movie, I didn't sleep. At five, my alarm rang, but I was already awake.

The only positive? My night wasn't long enough to grieve the sleep I'd missed out on. That didn't mean I wasn't tired, though. Or grumpy. I think Henry noticed when the first words I said to him were in the coffee shop line, after airport security. It became glaringly obvious when he asked for my order.

"Coffee," I grunted. Then as an afterthought, I added, "Black."

"You will hate it," he warned.

"I'll need it if you don't want me to drool on your shoulder for an hour straight."

Henry huffed in amusement. "I'd survive," he said before turning to order our drinks anyway. He seemed to have adjusted to the idea of my presence on this trip fairly well, which was a relief.

Equipped with a coffee so dark I could smell the bad taste, we marched toward our gate. I scowled at my first sip. Somehow it tasted worse than what I'd had a few weeks ago.

Henry watched me in amusement. "Long night?" he asked.

I smacked my lips in disgust, grimacing. "More like too short." I regretted the cup in my hand. "Do people really drink this for enjoyment?" My eyes drifted to him for confirmation.

Henry wiggled the cup in his hands. "Apparently." To make his point, he took a big sip. Voluntarily! He didn't even look *that* tired.

Alright, he didn't look tired at all.

"You're a black coffee drinker." The realization hit like lightning. "I've known you for almost four years, and I haven't seen you drink it once."

"Obviously." Amusement edged into his snicker. "Because the first time I picked you up from a shift, you wouldn't stop complaining about it. If I remember correctly, you said—and this is a direct quote—the smell alone makes you want to *shrivel up and die.*"

Yes, perhaps working at a coffee shop hadn't been the best career choice.

I blinked up at Henry. "So you just stopped drinking it?"

"When you're around."

He said it like it was a given. Like anyone would

sacrifice part of their mornings for a college relationship that, statistically speaking, only had a 50 percent success rate to begin with.

"And you *really* like it?"

Henry shrugged. "It gets the job done."

I shouldn't have expected any other reason. With Henry, anything that got the job done was a good thing. After I forced another sip of battery acid down my throat, I blurted, "I'm sorry."

His eyes flicked to mine, brows drawing together. "Honestly, coffee is not even all that good for you." *How someone could think anything that tasted like this could be healthy was beyond me.* "So no need to be sorry."

But that's not what I meant.

"No, no." I waved him off. "For coming, I mean. I'm sorry for intruding like this."

We came to a stop at our gate, and for half a second, I was surprised to see a line moving in front of it. Then I remembered I was traveling with Henry, who'd probably planned for a perfectly timed arrival at the gate, even down to our coffee run.

The genuine smile on his lips turned into its forced equivalent at my words. "For the profile. Right?" He huffed. "It's not like you wanted to be here."

"And it's not like you wanted me to," I offered with a shrug, unsure which one of us was wrong. If anyone was at all.

Henry sighed, wanting to say something and doing nothing about it. Silence settled between us again. I smiled at the man checking my boarding pass and passport. Henry caught up with me and we walked onto the jet bridge.

"About that," he finally said, sounding unsure, a little nervous. Usually, Henry was neither of those. "It wasn't supposed to seem like—" He hesitated, then changed his mind. "You weren't the problem." He waved his boarding pass between us to make a point. "I just haven't been on a plane since my parents' accident. Like, I usually just drive everywhere or don't go. This is the first time in seven years that I'm not." Nervous chuckle. "And I wasn't expecting to have company. On such short notice."

The realization struck me like a ton of bricks, and I felt like an idiot. *How could I have missed putting that into the equation?*

Their crash hadn't been a commercial one that would've made the local news; they'd been in an inconspicuous private plane on its way to the Bahamas. Those went down all the time, and no one batted an eye. Only that it had been Felix Pressley and Naomi Yung on that flight, and so yeah, it didn't make local news. It went straight to an international media circus. When Henry and his sister were about fifteen years old.

"Oh my God," I muttered. "I didn't—I *should've* known that. You told me." He didn't meet my gaze when I looked up at him. "I'm sorry."

For forgetting and the fact that they'd died at all.

Henry's shoulder lifted in a gesture meant to convey that it was no big deal, but his smile didn't quite reach his eyes, and overall, he looked stiff. It was a big deal. *Of course it was.*

As we squeezed through the aisle of the plane in an even more uncomfortable silence, the fact that our seats weren't together somehow made the situation worse. Not only did I know the next sixty minutes were going to be hell for Henry, but there was nothing I could do to make it even a little more bearable.

I kept going when he shuffled into a row in the front, aware he wouldn't have any reassuring smiles beside him, no hand-squeezing or bad jokes to help him relax. The thought of this usually unbothered guy sitting in his seat, frantic and alone, made me ache. With him, for him.

So much so that the second I got to my aisle seat, I gave the nearest flight attendant an over-the-top smile and gently reached for her arm. She beamed back at me with that same customer-service expression. I couldn't help but wonder how early she'd gotten up to curl her hair so perfectly.

"What can I do for you?" she asked, voice probably a few pitches higher than usual.

I think Henry might've snagged a seat with extra legroom in the front of the plane, while I was stuck all the way back here. I pointed at him about twenty rows in front of me, his head peeking out above the blue seats.

"Do you see that guy?" I asked. "Light-brown hair, baseball cap, black hoodie. Kind of looks too large to be here?"

"Oh, yes," she said, eyes finally locking in on him. "Who'd miss someone like that? Talk of the town . . . well, plane." The correction left her with an airy laugh. When she turned back to me, she winced like she just realized she'd said that out loud. "Oh Christ. I'm so sorry. You're his girlfriend, aren't you?"

Girlfriend. I tried not to let that get to me.

Her eyes flicked down my frame, then back up to my face. "Of course you are. I just called your boyfriend the *talk of the plane—*" She cut herself off, sounded a little panicked. "I should tell Linda *not* to make a move. Oh God, I really am sorry. This is my first month, and I'm already—"

"It's alright." She seemed surprised by that. Even more so by the gentle smile on my lips.

"Thank God," she whispered to herself.

"I was just wondering." I didn't debunk her girlfriend theory. Denying it would've made my request *so* much weirder. "In case the seat next to him stays free, could I relocate?" We'd been one of the last passengers to get on, so my chances weren't awful.

A knowing look formed on her face, and she considered me for another second. "Ah," she said. "I see. Well, I think it's a seat with extra legroom." *Figured.* "So we'd have to charge you." Her face told me she really didn't want to, but I waved her off.

"Twenty-five dollars won't break the bank." It might, actually. College wasn't cheap, and I'd been picking up fewer shifts since the profile. Fewer as in zero.

"Fifty." She winced. I tried not to.

"No problem."

"Alright." Her tone adopted that airy lull again, and I

only realized she'd dropped her customer-service voice when she picked it up again. "If it stays free, it's yours."

*

It seemed not many people were willing to pay fifty dollars for extra legroom on an hour-long flight. I couldn't blame them. But ten minutes later, when the doors of the plane had closed, I moved from row twenty-eight into row six anyway.

Henry stared at me as if he'd seen a ghost.

"Thought you might need a . . . friend," I offered.

Friend.

I did not like that word. I liked it even less than *ex*, because it meant that funny feeling in my stomach when he smiled at me was very much one-sided.

The first time I called him a friend, he told me we weren't going to be friends at all.

"Friend." He repeated the word with a huff, then looked from the seat beside him up to me again. "I'd like that."

CHAPTER 22

Now

I woke up on Henry's shoulder, the corners of my mouth wet.

It's funny how life works sometimes. I'd been unable to get an ounce of rest last night and spent fifty dollars to metaphorically hold Henry's hand through his first flight, only to sleep through the whole thing. My drool had probably seeped into his hoodie.

I wouldn't know; I was too afraid to check.

To add to the humiliation, I woke up with a stomach so empty it felt as if I hadn't eaten in a week. Which made me realize I'd been so occupied with complaining about the black coffee, I'd forgotten about breakfast.

And as we stepped onto the jet bridge, I remembered—

"Fuck," I muttered under my breath, throwing a desperate glance across my shoulder. Henry stopped beside me.

Our flight attendant sported her best customer-service

smile, wishing each guest a good day and thanking them for flying with her airline. She was completely oblivious to the fact that I hadn't paid for that seat yet. "I forgot to—"

But Henry nudged me along gently. I turned to him, honestly a little frantic, because I hadn't paid, and that poor girl would probably lose her job because of *me*. His smile felt a little too easy, though. A little too knowing.

"Don't worry about it," he said, as if it were that easy. *They're going to fire her for this!* I wanted to scream. "I took care of it."

I deflated like an old balloon. "What do you mean?"

As in, he charmed his way into not paying? I could see it. He *had* been dubbed the talk of the plane.

"She came over with the machine like halfway through the flight. Since you were passed out"—he glanced my way, amusement glimmering in his green eyes—"and I didn't want to wake you, I just paid it."

I blinked up at him. Once, twice. "You were not supposed to do that."

I'd been the one who wanted to do *him* a favor. Not only had I slept through my supporting role; I hadn't even paid for the seat. Henry had essentially paid to be drooled on. One glance at his shoulder revealed the damp patch and confirmed my fear.

"It's nothing," Henry assured me. "Besides, Heather thought we were *sooooo* cute together." He didn't try to hide the teasing tone in his voice. In fact, it was on full display. Paired with a matching smirk and a cocked brow. "How could I not pay for my girlfriend's seat? When she wanted to sit next to me *so* badly?"

It wasn't just my little white lie being revealed that brought color to my cheeks, but the word *girlfriend* coming out of Henry's mouth. It reminded me of when that had been true, when he'd hold my hand and kiss my lips. My stomach dropped at the thought, and I groaned.

"Fuck off," I muttered, only half joking. "Here I was trying to do something nice for you . . ." I crossed my arms in front of my chest like I was five years old and hadn't gotten my way. "And this is the thanks I get?"

We continued through the airport. I stomped, Henry navigated. Outside the terminal, his eyes searched the parked cars. "What?" I huffed, and I wasn't proud of the tone in my voice. "Can't find your driver?"

Alright, yes, maybe I still wasn't over those fifty dollars and tried to compensate massively for the fact that I'd drooled on my ex-boyfriend.

His eyes sliced to mine at the remark, a puzzled glare in his expression.

"*They* got *us* a driver," he said slowly, amending my very unserious guess. He looked across his shoulder one last time before nodding in the same direction. "And he's right there."

Black SUV and a driver who looked like he came straight out of a movie. He stood on the curb beside the car, holding a sign in front of his round belly. On it: "Henry Pressley. Paula Castillo. New York Blue Eagles."

I tried to ignore the warm feeling in the pit of my

stomach at the way our names looked on a sign. Like they belonged together.

"You would've probably already seen him if you weren't so busy trying to argue." Henry smiled as he said the words, and it seemed nothing could get him to argue *back*. Nothing could rile him up enough to be mad. Not even my piss-poor attitude.

The driver offered to take my bag, then opened my door, and Henry exchanged a few words with the man in black once I'd crawled into the backseat. He joined me a minute later.

"Don't tell me what I'm trying to do," I snapped even before he could close his door.

"I'm not," he said. "But you know we wouldn't be having this conversation if you weren't hungry."

And the way he still knew me so well was . . . shocking. Kind of. Another part of me wasn't surprised at all, and it only irritated me further.

I whirled around in my seat with a fierce glare, ready to throw the next harsh words at him. Instead of the teasing gleam in his eyes I'd expected, Henry held a protein bar toward me with an eyebrow raised.

"What's this?" I asked like a dumbass. Like it didn't say on the packaging in bold capital letters.

Some of his brown hair fell into his face, tilting his head like he thought the same thing. "You're hungry." *Masterful deduction.*

"I'm vegan."

He turned the bar in his hand. "I know." And honestly,

he sounded a little exasperated at that point. I couldn't blame him, and anyway, I was only looking at the V-label in the corner of the protein bar.

Reluctantly, I took it out of his hand, and my stomach roared so loudly, the man in black behind the wheel, Andy, probably heard it.

"Have you been carrying this around for a year?" I asked, ripping the package. Honestly, I did not care if he had.

"No." He threw a pointed look my way. "I got used to having food around when we went out together, and it kind of stuck with me. I just adjusted from Oreos to . . . well." He gestured to the bar in my hand, one bite already missing.

"So," I hummed, spirits suddenly lifted after the second bite. Like the past twenty minutes hadn't happened at all. "Vegan pancakes. Vegan protein bars. Are you sure you haven't adjusted your diet?"

Henry barked a laugh, and I could really get used to that sound again. Leaning back in his seat, his shoulders sagging, he shook his head in amusement. "Just trying to up your daily intake from those ten grams of protein you mentioned," he joked.

That protein bar was gone quicker than I'd thought, and with it the mind-riddling, insanity-inducing hunger pains. By the time we approached the hotel, I almost felt like a human being again.

"Hey," Henry said, his voice gentle and quiet beside me. "About the flight." When I looked at him, he scratched the back of his neck, seemingly just to have something to do.

I'd done my best to ignore the fact that I'd basically left him alone with his fear of, or at least discomfort with flying, if only to avoid my guilty conscience.

"I really did switch seats to be there for you!" I blurted out before he could accuse me of being a horrible . . . friend and then tell me not to use what he'd revealed in the article. Which I wouldn't, obviously. "I'm sorry."

"You're sorry?" he asked, puzzled. "Why? What could have possibly been more reassuring than you, Paula?"

My breath caught in my throat, and it was hard work trying to hide it. *Friend, friend, friend*, I reminded myself.

"Bad jokes, statistics about how unlikely crashes are, reassuring hand squeezing! Just being awake during take-off and landing."

He huffed, almost laughed. "It just means you didn't have to see my sweaty palms and weak knees. Win-win." The thought only made my insides clench harder. "As for the reassuring hand squeezes."

I shouldn't have mentioned those out loud.

"The way you clung to my arm like it might detach from my body if you didn't . . ." He let the words linger between us on purpose. "Very reassuring. I think I might've even slept for a minute or two."

The smile on my face turned sheepish, solely to distract from the added color in my cheeks. "No!" I gasped. "That many?"

The car rolled to a stop before he could reply, and his driver opened Henry's door for us to step out right into the lobby of a hotel that looked like it offered a standard rate of my *rent.* "Ashwood" was carved into one of the columns outside, so it made a little more sense.

I went to grab my bag from the trunk, but Henry held me by the shoulder just long enough for me to notice the bellhop, who'd taken the task on himself. A minute later, our bags rolled past us without either of us lifting a finger.

Honestly, until now I hadn't been sure bellhops weren't just a thing in movies—had never stayed in hotels expensive enough for them to be real.

"You get used to it," Henry said, responding to the look on my face. While he slipped our *luggage man* a twenty-dollar tip, I tried to keep my mind from replaying his whispered words on repeat. Rough voice, amusement etched into the sound.

Mierda. I'm in so much trouble.

*

It never occurred to me that hotels with a nightly rate of over half a grand would be fully booked. Today, I'd learned that they *could be*—and ours was. Which meant our rooms were still being turned over, and we'd only be able to check in after 3:00 p.m.

Henry, of course, hadn't planned for time in our rooms anyway, and he seemed only half as distraught by the minor change of plans.

"No worries," he'd said to the receptionist. *Mandy.* He told me he'd planned to be at the stadium by 11:30 anyway, and I just grabbed my interview essentials before we were back in Andy's SUV.

I had no idea how Henry perfectly factored New York City traffic into his schedule, but we arrived on the dot.

"Your punctuality needs to be studied," I muttered in slight disbelief, slipping my phone back into my pocket when we got to the back entrance of the arena. The one reserved for players, friends, and family only.

"One of my many talents."

"Another one must be humility?"

"Precisely." He held the door open for me, which led into a hallway stretching in both directions. As soon as it fell shut behind us, a semi-familiar voice echoed off the white walls. *Marty.*

Henry seemed to have expected his manager. And unlike the last time, he did not seem opposed to his presence. He even sported a polite smile and initiated their back-pat-hug.

"Paula," Marty said by way of a greeting when he turned to me. The harsh light from the ceiling bounced off his bald head. "So good to see you decided to come." And the lingering glance at Henry told me how big of a deal this must've been.

For Marty, because his newest addition to the roster was supposed to sign his final contracts this weekend. Because he'd see Henry in the team colors and had me here to write a stellar profile that would hopefully sell to a bigger press. PR was more important than ever in the big sports leagues.

And for Henry, because this would be his home stadium for at least a year, and the idea was probably settling in now.

Confirming that he'd worked hard for what he'd wanted and had gotten it. That our breakup must've been worth it because, in a way, it had gotten him drafted by an MLS team. He'd made it.

"Team's out for camp," Marty continued, eyes flicking back to me. "So he's got the whole thing to himself. I'm sure you'll get some good stuff. Are you taking pictures?"

I shook my head, unsure. *Was I supposed to?*

"I was told they'd be provided."

"Perfect." Marty clapped his hands together in delight before one found itself on Henry's back and the other on my own. The Blue Eagles' manager nudged us around a corner that revealed the soccer pitch.

It smelled like freshly trimmed grass, dark green contrasting with the perfect white lines. I could see the blue seats of the stadium, all empty except for a single woman sitting in the front row.

"Hi!" Getting up, she held her hand out for me to shake, then Henry. "I'm Hallie." Her dark braids were tied into a high ponytail, and she wore casual jeans and a T-shirt that made it impossible to miss the camera around her neck.

"The Blue Eagles' photographer," Marty offered in explanation. "She's getting some shots of Henry for the website and everything today anyway. So, if you want, she can take some candid ones on the field too. Get them to you—"

Hallie cut him off. "Thank you, Marty!" she said cheerily. When what she seemed to want to say was more along the lines of *I can speak for myself, thank you very much*. She turned back to me. "I won't be in your hair for long at all. Twenty minutes tops. Then you've got him all to yourself."

Her attention flicked to Henry, who'd been treated like a second thought so far. By the smile on his face when he looked at me, he seemed content with that. "And you've got the pitch, of course," Hallie added.

I felt a little like I'd just been rolled over by a truckload full of information. So all I said was "That would be lovely, thank you" and hoped it sounded as polite as I'd intended it to.

CHAPTER 23

Now

The blue jersey looked good on him. Henry dribbled left and right, then broke into a sprint until he was still an impressive distance away from the goal. He delivered the ball into the net with a *whoosh* that echoed through the empty stadium, and my hands fell away from my keyboard to clap.

Again, the sound echoed.

He repeated the same drill a hundred times more. Dribble, sprint, score. Dribble, sprint, score. And my intention really had been to focus on writing, on the blank pages on my screen and how I could fill them.

But the sweatier he got, the harder it was. My eyes kept drifting to him, watching him stretch, and run, and use the hem of his jersey to wipe his forehead. Just the sliver of midsection that motion revealed had me squirming in my seat.

My gaze snapped back to him and, unfortunately, connected right with his.

"How's writing going?" he asked sheepishly, jogging the last few feet toward the would-be VIP section above the sideline, where I'd gotten comfortable.

To make up for the fact that it wasn't going great, and he was most likely the reason for it, I snickered. "Ask me again once you start doing something worth writing about."

Henry grabbed his water bottle with a laugh, then took a big gulp. I tried not to watch his Adam's apple bob. "I'm sorry," he said. "Am I boring you, Miss Castillo?"

"Terribly," I whined.

I watched my cursor blink. Because I wasn't quite sure how to say *Henry Parker Pressley looked so handsome when he played soccer* and phrase it in a way that didn't get me banned from every news house in the country.

"You're pretending to work again," Henry noted in amusement, and behind my screen, I grimaced at the accuracy. "Come here," he chirped, looking up at me with raised brows. He held his hand out. For me to take, presumably.

"What?" My eyes flicked to my screen again. "Why?" I wasn't ready to give up on my document's word-count goal just yet.

"Just come here, Paula."

"What for?"

Despite the annoyed tone in his voice, his lips spread into a wide grin. Exasperated and amused and beautiful.

"Don't make me come up there," he threatened. "I'm sweaty and gross."

I doubted it. Still, I closed my laptop slowly, the gesture a small win for him. "Tell me why," I said, standing up.

"Do you trust me?"

"No."

I slipped under the railing and dropped to the field regardless. Dread formed low in my belly when he grabbed a ball from the sideline, and we walked to the penalty spot.

"Kick it."

My head shot in his direction. "What?"

"If watching me is too boring," he said in a singsong voice, "you might as well do it yourself."

I shook my head so quickly, the stadium around me blurred for a moment. "Absolutely not."

Obviously, I'd kicked a ball before. Although soccer wasn't at the top of the Dominican Republic's favorite sports list, it was still popular enough. And with Dad forcing me to learn how to dribble when I was seven, it had been impossible to avoid scoring a goal here and there.

But that didn't mean I had to put that particular *untouched* skill set to the test now. In a twenty-five-thousand-seat stadium. With one of soccer's most anticipated new players only a few feet away.

"Paula," that same man whined at my side, nudging the ball right to my feet. "Come on. What do you have to lose?"

My pride and humility, among other things.

He interpreted my eyes narrowing as conviction, and he took a few steps back to give me space. "All yours," he said.

So . . . I lined up the shot, tried my best to get the angle right, and went for it. No time for overthinking.

I wish I could say there'd been too much force in my kick. That I hadn't angled my foot right and that was why the ball flew so sideways, it would be annoying to get it back.

Unfortunately, the ball hadn't even made it into the vicinity of the net. It stopped a good ten feet short, slowly running out of momentum.

"Well," Henry said, considering the ball, "no one can say you're too harsh with it."

I did not think before I hit his shoulder. Affectionally shoved him. But it felt like justice, and when he just laughed, I made it my mission to score that damn goal. The fact that he thought I couldn't was motivation enough.

I got the ball back. Placed it on the penalty spot. Lined up my shot, tried my best to get the angle right, and . . . then Henry came up behind me, and my entire focus was elsewhere.

Who cared about a ball when I could feel his body against mine?

His hand lingered on my shoulder so lightly, it was barely a touch at all. He waited, silently asking if it was okay, giving me enough time to move away if I wanted to. I did not.

"Let me show you," he offered. All the earlier amusement had disappeared from his tone, and although there was no one else between the thousands of seats around us, his voice was hushed.

As soon as I turned to him, the warmth of his body and the soothing sound of his voice made me realize it was a mistake. A mistake that left us standing about a hair's breadth away from one another.

I wasn't quite sure what to focus on first: the different shades of green in his eyes I'd slowly been forgetting or the residual pink in his cheeks from running around. The fact that he didn't smell like sweat at all but pinewood and citrus. And bad ideas.

"I think I can manage to kick a ball," I said—whispered, maybe?—because there was no room for bad ideas on this trip. Or any time after it. Right?

Something in his expression shifted. Determination and amusement in his gaze held mine for another one, two, three seconds before he shot forward, kicking the ball from where I'd lined it up perfectly. He ran until he was far enough.

"Henry!"

He snorted a laugh when he turned back to me, so maybe my glare wasn't quite as vicious as I thought. Or the guy who'd once spent so much time looking at me had learned to read me so well, he knew it wasn't real.

"If you're so sure you can kick a ball," he challenged, "get it first." He dribbled in place as if that would make the idea more enticing. If anything, it put me off the whole thing.

"Henry Parker Pressley," I said seriously, still standing where he'd left me. "You're about to do this for a living. I've never played a single proper soccer game. How is that fair?"

"I'll go easy on you, Charm," he mocked, taking a step away. His brows rose, and when I faked a start toward him,

Henry only hopped a few steps back. Quite leisurely. The ball was secured under his foot again. With a cocky smile, he said, "Be careful. The grass was watered this morning. It's slippery."

"Fuck you." The words burst out of me, but given how his laugh echoed through the arena, he seemed to love it.

I groaned, looking up at the blue spring sky. There was no way I'd win, or even get close to him, by playing fair. Fair was overrated anyway.

Without a moment to change my mind, I charged toward Henry, completely ignoring the ball at his feet and focusing all my strength on pushing him far enough away from it to get my chance. But our bodies became one entangled mess of limbs; my hands grabbed onto his shirt for support, and as I felt him falling, I realized a little too late that I was going down with him.

Rolling onto my back, I snorted laugh after laugh, and I only noticed that Henry was also cracking up when I briefly calmed down. When our gazes met, I wasn't quite sure if it was him or the adrenaline pumping through my veins that made my stomach turn.

Somewhere along that line, we'd stopped laughing. Henry smiled at me, and silence lingered.

"That's why I do it, by the way." His eyes didn't waver from mine. His breath fanned against my cheek; that's how close he was. "The adrenaline, the fun. The urge to win, even when nothing's at stake. That's why I love the game."

"Oh," I offered unhelpfully.

I couldn't imagine coming up with a better response

when all my willpower had gone into not looking at his lips. Right there, so close and kissable, I might combust.

"And that was a foul, by the way," he added as an afterthought, finally releasing me from my dire situation by getting up, then holding his hand out. "But because I'm a good sport, I'll help you anyway."

"Do not pull away," I threatened when I took it. He did not.

His hand wrapped around mine, tugging lightly and tightening once I was halfway there. I tried to ignore the tingling of my skin where it touched his and the empty feeling in my palm when he let go.

"I should—" I threw a glance at my laptop in the stands. "I'll have to write that down. The . . . you know." I gestured around wildly. "The 'adrenaline, fun, urge to win' bit."

I flew across the pitch like a mouse hunted by a stray cat. I may have even beaten Henry's five-minute-mile pace. And when I got to my seat, the first thing I did wasn't write his quote into my document but soundlessly squeal into the crook of my arm behind my laptop.

CHAPTER 24

Now

"Mr. and Mrs. Pressley, we've been waiting for you."

The sentence was so wrong, I didn't know why it felt so right.

Henry didn't correct the suited receptionist checking us in, so neither did I. "Your room's on the sixteenth floor, and your bags will be waiting for you." He handed us the key cards with a smile. "The minibar is complimentary, and there'll always be someone at reception should you need anything. Enjoy your stay!"

When we made our way through the marbled lobby and waited for the elevator, something struck me as odd.

"Did he just say *room*?" I asked, dumbfounded. "As in, *one* room? A single room?"

Alarm struck Henry's features when his head swiveled in my direction. He shook it quickly. "A twin then, surely."

*

Not a twin. His confidence had been profoundly misplaced. From the foot of it, we stared at the king-sized bed like it might split in half if we kept it up for long enough.

"Well." I blinked once, twice. "At least it's beautiful."

I think Henry might've winced, but I couldn't be sure because my eyes were still glued to the bed, and I couldn't shake the thought of both of us in it. He cleared his throat.

"You take it," he offered hastily, already moving to grab his suitcase by the door.

"And let you sleep on the floor?" I shook my head, following him across the room. "No way!"

He's the only reason I was here in the first place—the only reason I was in a room with high ceilings and tall windows revealing a view of the New York City skyline people dreamed of waking up to. The bathroom was so big, my entire room would fit in it.

"Imagine the aches you'd wake up with on the floor. Your body's worth millions—" I cringed. "That could've been worded better," I admitted. "But it's true."

His lips, once pressed into a tight line, curled into a smile. His face, which had been as unyielding as stone, softened.

"Thank you, Paula," he said smoothly. "I didn't know it was still worth that much to you."

"I didn't say *to me*!" I protested.

"It was insinuated, no?"

"No."

Henry pouted but couldn't hide the delight in realizing

he was at least halfway to the truth. He circled back to the actual conversation. “Not the floor, though,” he said, slipping back into our argument. “I’ll book another room. You get comfortable here, and I’ll come grab my bag once I’ve talked to reception.”

I would’ve liked to argue that (1) *I* should be the one booking another room—preferably in a different hotel, because this wouldn’t just break the bank, it would blow it into tiny pieces, never to be found again. And (2) he shouldn’t have to drop an extra $500 a night because of the inconvenience I was causing. Even if he could afford it.

But Henry was out the door before I’d managed to voice any of my concerns. With a loud groan, I let myself fall onto the duvet, legs dangling off the foot of the bed. *Great.* The mattress felt heavenly, adjusting to the shape and weight of my body as if it were made specifically for me. As soon as I’d made contact, I knew my own mattress would never compare, and I’d probably never sleep well on it again.

Despite the fact that I never wanted to get up, I did. I forced myself to take off my shoes, brushed my teeth, and wriggled out of my pants to crawl under the sheets in my hoodie. Just when I was getting comfortable, the door beeped, and Henry was back.

“That doesn’t look good,” I commented as soon as he trotted into the room, annoyance bunching up his brow. “What is it?”

He sighed, leaned against the wall, and crossed his arms in front of his chest. “Nothing,” he said, then reconsidered.

"Everything. I don't know. They're fully booked because of some conference, so I'll be trying my luck at one of the other hotels around here. If the penthouse wasn't under renovations right now, I'd just stay there . . ." He trailed off.

When he looked back at me, a small smile tugged at the corners of his lips. "You should sleep, though, Paula. It's getting late."

"Are you serious?"

Henry shrugged, then went on like he really thought I'd go along with it. "We've got an early start tomorrow. I'll be waiting for you in the lobby at seven." His eyes narrowed slightly. "*Sharp.*"

I couldn't help my laugh. "Don't be ridiculous."

"I'm not." His face contorted in irritation for the first time since we'd been forced back into each other's orbits, and it reminded me of the last time it had.

When he'd said *"We shouldn't do this,"* let me leave, and never looked back.

"We have to be at the stadium by eight. I need time to change, stretch. Then my lawyers will have to go over the contracts after—"

"No." My head shook enough to stop his rambling. "That's not what I meant." Gently, hesitantly, I peeled the blanket off the other side of the bed, beckoning him in. "Just . . . stay here."

I couldn't possibly be the reason for Henry Pressley wandering around New York looking for a hotel. He probably wouldn't find one anyway; there were signs for two different conferences in the lobby.

His eyes flicked up to mine, a million things in his gaze. None that I could interpret.

"Before I change my mind, Henry." Another minute, and I might have to. The longer I looked at him—his brown hair only half as neatly parted in the middle from a long day, the top buttons of the shirt he'd changed into after practice open—the worse the idea seemed.

He only took a single step farther into the room, giving an almost nonexistent nod before he said, "You do know I'll have to get ready for bed first, right?" The tension seemed to fall off him; I could see it. "Brush my teeth. Wash my face."

Looking at him, rolling my eyes only to be doing something that wasn't staring, I imagined the agony of his scent lingering in the sheets and the weight of his body on the mattress.

"If you must," I said at last, hoping he'd at least be changing into a shirt.

Which reminded me of another problem.

"Oh" slipped past my lips just before he closed the bathroom door behind him. His head poked back out of the frame, a puzzled look urging me to elaborate on the worrying sound. "I may have forgotten to pack something to sleep in." My gaze flicked to Henry's silver suitcase, then to my overnight bag. I had not been paying attention to what I'd been throwing into it yesterday, and apparently, that had left me without PJs.

Henry snickered. "Why am I not surprised?" With only a glance in the direction of his luggage, he nodded toward it. "Should be an HBU jersey in there. I packed one just in case."

"In case I forgot a shirt?" I wondered, almost laughed at the thought.

"In case I don't get the Blue Eagles' one."

He shut the door between us.

I thought about that statement when I pulled the red jersey out of his perfectly packed suitcase. Was there still a possibility that the Blue Eagles wouldn't take Henry on? The MLS draft had been months ago—I remembered it to the date because the day the results came out, I'd been heavily avoiding the internet and my need to Google which team (if any) had taken Henry. Maeve might've suspended my electronics that day.

He was scheduled to sign the last of his contracts tomorrow after practice. So if he didn't, or if they didn't let him, where would that leave Henry? Without a team? Without a pro career?

Sure, there were other ways to get into soccer on a professional level, but he hadn't planned for any of them. Had he?

I wasn't quite sure how long I'd been standing in the middle of the room, Henry's jersey bunched up between my hands. But it was long enough for him to finish in the bathroom and scare the shit out of me when he asked, very calmly, "What are you thinking about?"

"Mierda!" I cursed, more to myself, when I jumped and clutched my chest, still holding the jersey. "Don't sneak up on me like that." My hands back by my sides, I turned to shoot him a glare that evaporated swiftly.

His eyes ran down my frame the same second I remembered I still wasn't wearing pants.

Obviously, I wasn't. I'd already been in bed, waiting to turn off the lights after a day that had felt twenty-five hours long. So, no pants. In the middle of the room. With a hoodie that wasn't oversized enough to cover the important bits. Mortified, I fled behind the only door in the room. Slammed it shut a little too loudly, then hid in the bathroom.

Technically, yes, Henry had seen me with much less on. But that's when he was more than Henry, *friend*. Or Henry, *subject of my profile*.

I spent as much time as I could justify in the bathroom and only came out when he'd probably started to wonder if I'd flushed myself down the toilet.

That jersey covered up more than my hoodie had, but I rushed to my side of the bed without looking at him anyway. I didn't even notice his exposed chest, covers draped only across his legs.

He watched in amusement as I slipped under the covers we shared and stayed so close to the edge of the bed, I couldn't play it off as anything but intentional.

"We can build a pillow wall," he offered, entirely too amused by the situation. "If you want."

Did this not affect him at all? I felt stupid all of a sudden.

"What?" I waved his comment off as if I hadn't been two seconds away from suggesting it myself. I scooted farther onto the bed, maintaining steady eye contact with the red light coming from the TV on the opposite wall. "I used to share a twin with two of my cousins. I'm sure we can manage a king. Right?"

"Right," he agreed, and the gruff sound of his voice finally drew my eyes.

He'd turned away to cut the lights, and I had all of a second to marvel at his muscled shoulders and defined back before darkness enveloped us.

We both sank into the mattress. I turned the opposite way, toward the window with a perfect view of the city that never slept all lit up, and thought I'd probably join it tonight.

It felt awkwardly quiet. I could hear his breath beside me, which meant he could hear me breathing too. I felt every single one of his movements, every shrug and every repositioning of his arm. Which meant I stayed eerily still, and he probably noticed that too.

I tugged on the blanket just a little, adjusted my position, and screamed at my body to fall asleep and stay asleep until the alarm blared.

Henry had other ideas.

"I forgot you're a blanket hogger," he whispered into the dark. I could hear the amusement in his voice, the grin on his face.

"My only fault. I can admit to that."

He snorted with laughter, breaking the quiet that had only been disturbed by our breathing and whispered voices before. I wanted to glare at him, even though he might not notice, just to make a point.

But he was closer than I'd anticipated when I turned, and I forgot to glare.

"What?" I managed to hiss, voice still hushed as if there were a thousand other people in the room with us and I didn't want to wake them.

Henry was lying on his back, and I watched as his head turned to me slowly, almost cruelly, before his brow raised. "Your *only* fault, is it?"

"I don't know what you're trying to insinuate, Pressley."

"Oh, nothing. You're an angel, Paula Castillo. I'm sorry I suggested otherwise."

I huffed. "That's what I thought."

We'd been looking at each other through the darkness long enough for my vision to adjust. To see the way his eyes flickered over my face restlessly.

Henry's smile didn't fall, per se. It felt like the longer we got stuck on each other, the more his features and body relaxed. I only noticed his smile had gone when the corner of his lip twitched up again—just slightly, in that kind of sad, regretful way.

"Paula," he said in a low voice, and I wasn't sure if he meant to or if it just slipped out. He lifted his hand hesitantly, tucked the single curl that had escaped my bun back behind my ear. I don't think he had any kind of control over the gesture. In the same way, my eyes couldn't help occasionally flicking to his lips either.

His fingers brushed my cheek so lightly, I thought I might've imagined the touch. But the smooth skin of his hand felt too familiar, and the way his breath fanned against the spot felt too . . . real. I think I was holding my breath right up until he spoke.

"Just—"

Which was when I'd accidentally exhaled so loudly, he cut himself off. With a smile. "Do you still sleep like a starfish? Or have you learned to keep to your side of the bed?"

I barked a laugh I didn't mean to, then replaced the amused look on my face with a halfhearted scowl. "I wouldn't need to leave my side of the bed, *Henry*," I said matter-of-factly, "if you would just share the blanket better."

"*Share it better?*" He sounded offended by the accusation. Would've looked the part, too, if he'd been successful at keeping a smile off his face. "You already have two-thirds of it now! And we haven't even closed our eyes. I can't share any more of it without giving it up completely."

"Excuses." I sighed airily, shaking my head and feeling the urge to press my face into the pillow, if only to keep the wide grin off my face. I didn't.

*

I woke up with my head on top of Henry's arm, approximately four inches from his face.

The alarm that'd ripped me out of my sleep was already off. Normally, I'd turn around and close my eyes again, but his presence so close threw me off guard.

If Henry was wide awake, apparently so was I.

"Oh," I mumbled into his skin, feeling his muscles shift underneath me. His hand was in my hair. The way it used to be whenever he'd been about to give me a head massage that eventually moved to my neck, shoulders, back, and then lower again.

"Morning."

I don't think he was really aware of the fact that his fingers danced across my scalp. He was only looking at me, green eyes focused.

My focus was scattered.

"I thought this would be harder," he admitted, and maybe he *was* aware of his action, because he nodded toward his fingers twisted in my hair.

"What would?"

"Waking you up." He allowed a laugh. "Only took scratching your head and whispering your name a few times. Not much has changed, has it?"

My eyes narrowed in on his, and although it hurt, I put some distance between us to really look at him. "Ha-ha," I mocked. His hand fell from my hair, and he shifted on the mattress to face me completely. "Like the alarm wasn't enough to—"

"The alarm rang five minutes ago, Paula."

Oh.

So instead of shaking me awake, saying my name, and hoping I'd be up by the time he got out of the bathroom, he'd done what he used to do when I refused to wake up: gently woke me with his fingers in my hair, massaging my scalp, *whispering* my name.

I rolled onto my back, rubbed the sleep out of my eyes with a mandatory yawn. "Sorry."

Henry sat up to stretch in all possible directions. He gave me a look across his shoulder, and only when he stood, he said, "I didn't mind."

CHAPTER 25

Now

When I was with Henry, I stopped thinking. I stopped wondering where to go next, how to get there, and whether I'd be on time. I stopped worrying, generally. I'd always been able to rely on him for our plans.

Until now, I'd never seen a downside to it.

But standing back in our shared room after an entire day of lawyers, paperwork, and three different offices spread across Jersey and Manhattan, Henry asked what I'd be wearing tonight, and I had no idea what he was referring to.

Suddenly, I felt like I should've inquired about our weekend plans beforehand.

"For the gala," he explained. "The MLS preseason fundraiser?"

I blinked up at him like it was a bad joke. But he just stared back at me, not a glimmer of humor in his green eyes. "Paula," he repeated. I suspected I'd gone into some kind of shock, frozen in the middle of the room because...

A gala. The MLS preseason fundraiser, apparently. With other teams, other players, important managers, and more people with a lot of money. The press, probably. Eddie had thrown me into the shark tank without a word of warning. And without a bathing suit.

I'd prepared for office runs and stadium tours by packing my favorite pair of jeans and three different tops. A jacket in case it got cold. I did not pack a fancy dress, heels, or Mom's beautiful gold jewelry that she'd reluctantly parted with when I went to HBU.

"I don't—" I couldn't even say the words. "Eddie didn't—"

Watching the realization settle on Henry's face made my cheeks turn a blotched red I couldn't do anything about.

I shook my head. "I don't have to go." It was five. When did galas usually start? Seven? Eight? Not enough time to fix this mess any other way.

Henry paced up and down in front of the large windows overlooking Midtown. Just once.

"Not an option," he said curtly. When his gaze met mine, he'd come to a conclusion. "Give me a minute."

And by the time I wanted to ask for a reason (around three seconds later), his phone was already by his ear, and he began pacing again.

"I need you," Henry said in that no-nonsense way of his to some woman on the other end. "You remember the dress I made you run across half of SoHo for last year, right? The dark—yeah, the dark-green one." Henry's gaze found mine again, and he startled like he'd forgotten about my presence.

Or maybe I'd surprised him with the bewildered and confused look on my face. "Give me a second, Céline," he said into the phone, then, on his way to the door, he mouthed *Be right back* in my direction before he escaped through it.

Céline.

The name seemed familiar. Like maybe he'd mentioned it before or I'd come across it while analyzing every single one of the profiles he followed on Instagram during what was, admittedly, one of the lower points in my life. An inevitable stage of grief after any relationship, though.

So perhaps Céline was an old fling I'd found stalking his Instagram or a newer one he'd met after me. The thought shouldn't have stung, but it did, terribly.

Who else would he call about a dress? He probably wanted her to wear it so badly that he made her *run across half of SoHo* to get it. And now he wanted to do what? Make me wear it afterward?

The thought felt objectively wrong. And no matter how much I wanted to mingle with journalists and press people who might know about job openings that no one else did, I wasn't sure if I could wear one of his other girls' dresses to do so.

The door beeped, and Henry returned. I don't think I'd moved an inch in the time he was gone. I wasn't even sure if it had been one minute or five or ten.

"Sorry," he said as he leaned against the closed door. "It's all sorted. Just start getting ready, Céline will bring the—"

Céline.

I shook my head again. Quickly. "I don't need to go. Really," I stressed. I didn't want to explain how the only problem I had with a borrowed dress was who had worn it before. That he might've seen someone else in it, that it had probably fit them better, and that he'd taken it off them by the end of the night. "I don't even know if Céline and I are the same size."

Henry's brow furrowed in confusion. His jaw ticked, and his eyes narrowed. "I'm sorry," he said again, like he wasn't quite sure what he was apologizing for. "I assumed you'd want to go. With the press there, you can network a little. It's the only reason I RSVP'd after I knew you were coming. And—"

He pushed off the door toward me but paused a few feet away. I tried not to notice that I'd been hoping he'd come closer. "And I don't think I can do tonight without you."

The confession hung in the air, and I could imagine his reasons. "They'll all want to talk about your parents, won't they?"

"I'll be surprised if they find anything else to talk about."

Seeing the expression on his face was the reason I hadn't directly brought them up in any of our interviews yet. I didn't want him to see me the way he viewed any other reporter who had crossed that boundary in his teens—I couldn't stand the idea of disappointing him once their names slipped from my lips on the record.

I don't think I can do tonight without you.

"Alright," I agreed, and I could hear him exhale in relief. "What about the size issue, though?"

"What size issue?"

"How do you know Céline's dress will fit?"

"Céline's—?" Henry's eyes widened. "Oh," he said, like he finally understood my apprehension. "Oh no. I got that dress for you, Paula. Last year. When I decided to get over myself and invite you to that New Year's Eve party."

I blinked at him. I was under the impression Athalia had invited me. And only because her best friend was dating one of mine.

"Clearly, I couldn't get over myself *enough* to actually give it to you. So it's just been collecting dust here. Don't worry. I know you, and I know it fits."

*

An off-the-shoulder neckline. A subtle mermaid cut in a beautiful shade of emerald green that seemed almost black in low light. The dress fit like I'd had it tailored. Accented by a gold necklace right where the neckline of the dress plunged.

Turns out, Céline was Henry's PA. She'd delivered the dress, jewelry, and matching heels to the hotel.

Curls in an updo with a few front pieces loose and framing my face, my eyes flicked to Henry's in the mirror we were both standing in front of. Neither of us had said a word since I'd gotten out of the bathroom fully dressed. His suit had clearly been tailored, and I tried not to wonder whether his tie's dark-green accents were supposed to match his eyes or my dress.

"What?" I asked. "Are you going to tell me you forgot how pretty I am when I try?"

"I didn't." Henry's gaze fell down my reflection again, slowly and deliberately taking in every curve and dip of my body in his dress. The one he'd picked out long after we'd broken up. "I couldn't. And I don't think you ever had to *try* to be pretty."

I finally turned to face him, wishing his gaze lingering on my neckline wouldn't send heat straight up my spine. It would be easier if it felt insulting instead of flattering. I could draw a boundary and keep him on the other side of it. But I had always liked the way he looked at me. With love, adoration, and lust in his gaze.

"You need to stop flattering me, Henry," I said honestly.

"Why?"

Because you're my ex-boyfriend. Because we agreed to be friends and this conversation is more than friendly. Because it makes my heart stutter and I'm not sure how much of that I can take.

"Because." I wasn't planning on finishing the sentence, and he knew that.

Henry laughed, then held out his arm for me to take. "If you can't give me a reason to stop, I won't see the need to. Sorry, I don't make the rules," he said sheepishly. "Let's go, beautiful."

He'd briefly let go of me once we'd gotten in Andy's SUV, but by the time we'd made it to the venue, my arm had interlocked with his again, and we ascended the stairs together.

Henry hadn't let me move away since. I seemed to be the lifeline he clutched tighter whenever someone mentioned his father.

Five times so far.

My hand still rested on his arm when he was drawn away from one group into another, and perhaps at that point, I was using him as a lifeline instead. If only to avoid getting lost in the bustle of New York City's soccer scene.

I tried to take in as much of the evening as I could: stuccoed ceiling, massive half pillars in the walls, flower arrangements, chandeliers above us and the people below them. Soccer legends left and right, players and managers I'd never thought I'd meet. Henry spoke to them like he belonged.

"It's so dark, I can't see if there's a ring. Are you two married already?" an older man asked, gray hair thinning and an outdated bow tie around his neck. His tone was friendly and unassuming.

His question was not.

"Oh God." I winced, shaking my head adamantly. "No. God no. We're not—" I didn't know how to even begin explaining. Why, if we weren't together, had my arm been in Henry's for an hour? Why, if he was my ex-boyfriend, were we even here together at all?

My eyes flickered to Henry's for help, but he seemed,

for once, without answers. Which left the man to make assumptions. One that would follow us for the rest of the evening.

Amused, his gaze shifted back and forth between us before he patted Henry on the back. "Get on that soon, son. You'll be gone so much during the season; a ring will make sure she won't forget you." He winked and left.

Left me mortified and Henry speechless.

"I'm sorry," I whispered right away. "I should've said—I don't know why I didn't say anything."

I did know. But I had no idea how to explain that to him either.

Henry cleared his throat, eyes dancing across the room in thought. "Maybe it's easier this way?"

I turned toward him so fast that I almost lost my footing. My eyes widened a little because he wasn't really insinuating—"What way?"

"You know." He cleared his throat. Finally looked at me. "If we didn't have to explain you're my ex-girlfriend every time someone asks who you are. Or that you're writing a profile on me, and the only reason you're here is to meet other journalists."

I blinked up at him. "You want me to—"

"Pretend you're my girlfriend tonight. Or just don't deny it when someone assumes as much. They all are, anyway. Just keep doing what you're doing."

"Holding your arm?"

"Yes. Or my hand."

My heart skipped a beat at the thought. "What else

have I been doing that makes them assume you're my boyfriend?"

Henry's lip twitched, and he leaned against one of the stone pillars behind him. My hand was in his now; it had slipped from his biceps into his palm without my notice. "You do that thing. Where you look at me and drift off, and I can't focus on the conversation I'm having because I'm so busy trying to figure out what you're thinking. If you're thinking about me at all."

"I—" Didn't know what to say. Thanked God for the dim lights because the blush on my cheeks was devilish.

"You move closer when someone you don't know joins the conversation. I don't think you notice, but I do. Your hip brushes mine, or your chest presses into my arm, and I—" His eyes closed, like he was remembering exactly what that had felt like. The hand in mine twitched, pulled me closer—just enough for a single finger to trace along my waist, down to my hip. Where he lingered. "And I can't think of anything but the way you used to feel underneath me."

"*Henry,*" I gasped. The room was spinning.

"You also blush a lot. Whenever I squeeze your hand or look at you a little longer."

Or when he told me, in a room full of important business partners and future colleagues, that he was thinking about the way he'd fucked me.

"So just keep doing more of that, and no one will even ask if we're together."

I thought it would be harder, but once I focused on

acting like a girlfriend, I realized I already laughed at his jokes, listened to his stories intently, and squeezed his hand when someone mentioned Felix Pressley. I wasn't sure if I'd ever really stopped acting like Henry's girlfriend around him.

I knew that I did not want to.

Henry introduced me to a journalist he knew, followed by a photographer from a renowned sports journal who was responsible for the pictures in their soccer column. Between his third and fourth glasses of wine, the photographer let slip that their columnist might not make it another year.

Those were the only two conversations in which my hand had not been in Henry's.

When we got back to the hotel, it must've been past midnight. Henry hadn't let go of me in the backseat of the car or when we'd walked through the sparsely staffed lobby to the elevators. His hand was firmly in mine, like he knew the spell of the night was about to wear off.

Like he might not want it to.

Smiling, I nudged him into the elevator as soon as it opened. It reminded me of the way we used to get home from one of his games or when he picked me up from a shift at Daisy's, and I couldn't wait another second to be alone with him.

But we weren't supposed to be tearing clothes off each other once the elevator door closed behind us.

Henry looked at me like his thoughts had taken the same turn. Like he was remembering the way my legs wrapped around his waist and his head dipped between my breasts too.

Never mind that a hotel elevator wasn't really all that private to begin with.

I shook my head to snap out of it, let myself fall against one of the mirrored walls with a relieved sigh. My eyes closed, but I knew Henry had followed. I could smell the pine cologne and his citrus shampoo. The bad ideas always lingering in his vicinity.

"I'm sorry," he said, and it was almost a rasp. "I'm going to have to compliment you again."

Even though I'd told him to stop being so nice to me earlier, the high of a great night hadn't worn off yet, and it was making me reckless.

Opening my eyes, I wasn't surprised to see him in front of me. His gaze fell down my frame again, and he seemed more unapologetic when it lingered on my cleavage.

I was so distracted, I didn't even know whether we'd already pressed the button for our floor. I couldn't tell whether we were moving or if the elevator still stood in the lobby, only a closed door separating us from the staff.

"When I got this for you last year," Henry began, his finger gently trailing along the neckline, careful not to touch skin, "I wanted to see you on New Year's so badly, I thought if I took the burden of an outfit decision off you, you might come."

My lips tipped up teasingly, and I didn't know what compelled me to grab his tie. "You didn't even say hi to me that evening," I reminded him, playing with the fabric, loosening it around his neck. He did not object. "You're telling me you bought an entire outfit but couldn't say hello?"

Henry nodded. Usually the epitome of control and confidence, he blushed, then let me pull him closer by his tie. One slow step after the other. "Yes," he admitted. "I don't know if you've noticed, but you make me nervous, Paula."

"Do I?"

"Sometimes. When you look at me a little too long. When you accidentally touch me. More so when you deliberately touch me." His gaze trailed to his tie—and my hand still wrapped around it. "On New Year's Eve, I was nervous. And you looked so happy, I didn't want to ruin that."

Henry looked at me with those green eyes I'd recognize among a thousand other pairs, and I almost gave in. Almost forgot that he wasn't my boyfriend and that I shouldn't pull him even closer.

"Maybe it would've made me happier," I whispered. My eyes flicked to his lips, then back. "Maybe I was secretly waiting all night."

"Were you?" Without taking his eyes off me, he finally pressed the button for the sixteenth floor.

I nodded faintly, and Henry slipped one of the loose curls behind my ear. His hand lingered on my skin like it had last night. And despite the fact that we had been in the same bed, lights off, limbs almost touching, this felt more intimate.

I could write an entire article on the way his finger

curled around my chin and tilted it toward his own. I could spend paragraphs analyzing the barely noticeable tremble of his hand, his touch so delicate you'd think he was scared of breaking me.

But I wasn't, I remembered. Writing an article about how badly I wanted Henry Parker Pressley to kiss me. It was the exact opposite of my actual assignment.

Write a profile about him. Play the role of ex-girlfriend who didn't at all still care and actually kind of despised him.

Somewhere along the way, I'd forgotten. Started caring and stopped despising. "We shouldn't—" The words were barely a breath against his lips, no conviction behind them.

"I know." Henry nodded, pressed his forehead against mine. His hand slipped behind my neck, holding me like he was afraid I might run.

He didn't know I could barely move.

"I'm trying to be reasonable," he went on, taking a deep breath. "I thought I could handle it, but clearly—" He snickered, probably at the fact that this wasn't reasonable at all. The way we stood so close when we were friends. Interview partners. Journalist and subject.

"We can try, though," I suggested halfheartedly, hands still clinging to his tie between us. The urge to place them elsewhere was so strong that I had to physically restrain myself from doing so. Perhaps that's why my nails were digging into the fabric now. "To be reasonable, I mean. We can try, right?"

We had to.

For the sake of this profile. For the sake of my ability to write about him without thinking about the way he kissed or touched me. It would be hard enough now.

"We can try," Henry agreed right as the elevator doors opened with a sharp *ding.*

CHAPTER 26

Then

April: One year ago

Eddie had given me three months for the article. I'd never gotten as much time on anything else before, and it was solely because HBU had suggested the topic themselves, and they'd requested that I write it.

"Rare," Eddie had said. *"The top doesn't pitch things often."*

When they did, apparently it was this: "All Brains, No Polish: The Burden of Ivy Leagues."

Hall Beck University was one of the top schools in the country, but it wasn't an Ivy, and with this article, they were trying to compensate. For their lack of Ivy status, presumably.

"Henry." I didn't look up from my screen, but I could feel him turn away from the coursework on his desk and toward me, cross-legged on his bed. "You're smart and wealthy,"

I noted, only half aware of what was coming out of my mouth.

He snickered. "Why thank you." I could see him tilt his head in my periphery, but it wasn't enough to draw my full attention. "It takes a little more than some flattery to get me away from revisions, though," he joked, like I wasn't very aware of the fact that nothing could get him out of that chair tonight. Not for another half an hour, at 10:00 p.m. on the dot, when he'd go to bed.

I rolled my eyes, and they finally trailed away from the paragraph I finished reading.

Stray strands of brown hung into his face, and he must've driven his hand through his hair countless times for it to be as messy as it was. The loosely fitted T-shirt that was still snug around his arms drew my attention next. Gray sweatpants were such a rare sight, I couldn't help but love them.

Domestic, I thought. This version of him was so domestic that my heart swelled at the sight.

"My assessment was going somewhere," I huffed, but my glare wasn't genuine, and the warm smile on my lips gave that away. "You're smart and wealthy, Henry," I repeated, and now he couldn't help grinning either. "Why didn't you go to an Ivy?"

"Ah," he hummed. "The new article?"

I nodded, and he explained.

"HBU's soccer team is better than most Ivy teams. I knew Coach Hepburn. My sister." Henry thought for a moment, let his gaze wash over me, the way I sat on his bed in an old jersey with my hair in a messy ponytail and dark bags under my eyes. He got up.

In an unprecedented move, Henry Parker Pressley left his work on the desk and walked the two steps over to his bed. "And you were here," he said, then took my laptop and placed it on his nightstand. He ignored my protests, came so close that my breath hitched.

It still did that around him. After two and a half years, Henry still made me hold my breath and blush.

I shook my head inches from his. "You didn't know I'd be here," I reminded him, but my voice was hushed, and I didn't sound as amused as I had planned to.

"Intuition." He shrugged. Followed me when I leaned onto my elbows until he hovered above me. "Maybe I knew without really knowing. Maybe my heart followed yours, and yours followed mine. And now we're here."

"I almost went to Brown," I said.

"Then maybe I would've gone to Brown too." His eyes flickered across my face, restless, like he couldn't get enough of what he was seeing. "In every possible lifetime, I'm sure we'd still have met, Paula."

Suddenly, my article and research could wait. If Henry could abandon his work to be with me, surely I could do the same. It was so rare that I wondered how we would celebrate. Several things came to mind.

I giggled into his chest. Buried my face in it only long enough to feel the color in my cheeks start draining.

"Where's all this coming from?" And I wasn't sure if I was asking about the sweet words or the fact that he had deviated from his schedule to join me in bed. At a quarter to ten.

"I miss you," he sighed into my hair.

I didn't know why I was whispering. "I'm right here."

"I know." His forehead fell to mine. I could feel his breath against my lips, the unspoken words between us.

But I'm never really there. *You're here, but we rarely get moments like this. When was the last time we weren't both busy doing something else when we were together?*

Henry didn't say any of it. I didn't dare to either.

"Can I ask you something else?" I broke the silence because I couldn't take it—not knowing what he was thinking, whether his thoughts were leading him in the same direction.

Henry created a small gap between us, studying me for a moment, likely reading me like an open book. His lips twitched. "One more Ivy League question, Paula. And then we'll both turn our work brains off."

I laughed, nodded. "You're smart and wealthy," I repeated and finally managed to get a full smile out of him. The heavy air between us lifted, and I almost exhaled loudly with relief.

"We've established that."

"Do you think I could interview one of your smart friends who doesn't go to HBU?" Surely he knew enough people at Ivy Leagues to volunteer one of them. "Friends who maybe go to Harvard or Yale or Brown."

Henry kissed the tip of my nose, my left cheek, and then my right.

"Of course."

CHAPTER 27

Now

What happened in New York stayed in New York.

And Henry and I took our agreement from last night very seriously. No stray touches, no accidental brushing of fingers, hands, or hips.

We kept our distance until his hand slipped from the armrest between us to my leg thirty minutes into the flight. He had been asleep for twenty of those. I tensed, trying not to let my eyes drift from the document I was updating with the weekend's material, and pushed through the way his touch scorched through the fabric of my jeans.

Friends, I reminded myself. We'd slipped into old habits last night and shouldn't have. We both agreed we would try.

To forget. To stay away from each other.

From behind the wheel of his car, I could feel his gaze on me, just briefly. We'd almost made it back home.

"Thank you," he said, unprompted. My brow furrowed.

If anything, I should be the one thanking him. Right? Despite that hiccup last night, I'd gotten great material and even greater connections over the weekend. Stuff I'd never have without him.

"For what?"

He shrugged. "Coming with me?" It was a question more than anything else, and I wasn't quite sure if he knew the answer.

"You didn't even want me to come," I pointed out with a snicker, my head against the window as we rolled past street names I was starting to recognize.

"That's—" He hesitated, contemplated. For a second, I thought he might've been close to letting his guard down, to saying something without thinking thoroughly about it first. Unheard of! "Not true," he settled on. "It was nice, you know? Having you around. Even if you weren't supposed to be there." He frowned at that.

"Henry Parker Pressley!" I gasped, lips twitching despite myself. "Did you just admit that things can be good even if you haven't planned for them?"

He stopped the car next to the curb and threw me an exasperated look. "I'm being serious," he pressed, not looking the part. "I'm glad you came."

Henry got out of the car to jog around it, then opened my door. When I watched his smile grow, suspecting I was the reason for it, I couldn't help but think I'd made a good choice.

With the profile. With going to New York. With being *all in*—whatever that meant.

Those were the first good choices I'd made in a while. After a string of bad ones (or just one *really* bad one) that put me off ever making them again.

I came to a halt by the walkway to the house, beckoning him to hand me my stuff. Reluctantly, he let it slide to the ground by my feet. "The bag's really not heavy," I argued.

"Still."

My eyes rolled theatrically, but I smiled. "Thank you." Remembering his words in the car, I added, "I'm glad I came too."

And I really was. Not just because it's what had left us standing so close that I had to tilt my head up to meet his eyes. Something glistened in their green.

Henry huffed. He was aware that this was the moment he should turn around and get back in the car. Where I should wave goodbye and go inside.

Although I wasn't sure what I wanted instead, I knew that I *didn't* want to move. Didn't want to miss the proximity of his tall frame or the soft smell of citrus that the breeze blew my way.

Despite what we'd said last night, I didn't want him to leave. Maybe it was the way the sun played in his hair, the way he squinted against it, still smiling, and seemed like *my* Henry—just for a moment.

I diverted my eyes quickly. Henry cleared his throat like he didn't know what to do or say next either.

I looked around, trying desperately to find another anchor point that wasn't the six-foot-one soccer player still watching me. Our gardening had been lacking. The flowers beside the house were wilted, the bushes in front of the windows were bare, and three pairs of eyes stared back at me through the glass.

Wait, what?

My double take confirmed that yes, all three of my roommates were trying to hide behind a curtain and failed miserably at it. They didn't move even after I sent them a glare that should have made it obvious they'd been caught.

And now that my attention had latched onto them, Henry seemed curious to see what had caught it. He turned.

I couldn't have that.

I moved without thinking, and suddenly my arms were around his torso, my head was on his chest, and my eyes were so wide they might pop.

So much for keeping away from each other.

I turned his back toward the demon girls mid-hug.

Very awkward hug.

"Oh" escaped his mouth, and I was surprised to feel his arms around my shoulders anyway. "Are you *this* grateful?" he asked mockingly, then rested his head on mine. Being pressed against his chest, feeling his strong arms around my body, and being forced to inhale his scent made me feel like I was going to burst.

"I should've taken you away more often, then. Hm?" He muttered the words into my hair. I wasn't sure if he meant to say them, but Henry Parker Pressley always knew exactly what he was doing.

He was also my ex-boyfriend, and we weren't supposed to be this close. It felt impossible to stay away, though. Whenever

I thought of it—of him, away—my chest ached, and my stomach turned, and I realized I had missed him terribly. So much that I might start crying if I didn't get those memories of us being anything other than *friends* out of my head.

The way he'd play with my curls, wrapping each one around his finger after I'd washed them to make sure they set properly. The way he'd insisted I teach him Spanish and had become adorably flustered every time he pronounced a word wrong. The way he'd held me when I got homesick.

In all the ways a person could miss someone, I missed Henry. Which was absurd; I was *literally* in his arms. But that was ex-boyfriend/profile-subject/friend-Henry. Not boyfriend-Henry. Not pretend-boyfriend Henry from last night either.

That made me draw away from him so quickly that I almost stumbled over my own feet. "Sorry," I said quickly, clearing my throat and trying to keep it together until I made it into the confines of my own home.

Which was about ten seconds later, after I'd grabbed my bag from the sidewalk and sprinted into the house with nothing but a "See you!" shouted over my shoulder.

I pressed my body against the closed door as if it might open otherwise.

"That was one steamy hug," Riley whooped from where they'd watched the whole ordeal. And I really wanted to laugh at her comment.

What came out was more of a sob. Between tears, I could vaguely make out all three of my roommates jumping into motion. Riley made a beeline for me, while Maeve started after Henry, presumably to punch him. Which wasn't a great idea because he'd done nothing wrong except being a good boyfriend right up until he'd broken up with me. So much so that I still missed him a year after the fact.

I held her by her arm, shaking my head and trying to laugh through my tears to signal *It's not that serious!* But I must've looked ridiculous.

"Oh, honey," Maeve cooed, pulling me into a hug that only reminded me of Henry again. Another strange sob-laugh made it out of my throat. Still, I relaxed into her embrace and finally let go of the bag I'd still been holding.

"It's okay," she said. "You never really stopped missing him, did you?"

Her words punched me right in the gut, and instead of another earth-shattering cry, I groaned. So loudly I woke Pip on the couch, who glanced our way.

"Why?" I asked, desperate to get over him . . . or back with him. Whatever it took for this stupid feeling in my chest to lift.

"You loved him, Paula," Maeve said. "That doesn't just go away."

If I focused on her brown eyes for too long—the compassion and understanding and love in them—I might break into tears again. So I watched as Pip jumped off the throw pillow on the couch, leisurely wandered past the rest of the girls, and planted herself right by my feet. She looked up at me curiously, meowed terribly loudly, and then brushed along my legs until I picked her up.

One last tear escaped my eye, and Pip apparently found that very interesting. She tilted her head, eyes following the streak, and sniffed my face until I was almost offended by the insinuation. Her rough tongue licked my cheek. Once. Twice.

Cats did love their salt.

A shaky laugh escaped me, and I glanced at my roommates hesitantly. "Sorry," I said, honestly a little awkward. "I don't know where that came from."

Laila looked about two seconds away from crying herself if I couldn't get myself together. Riley's lips pulled up in an apologetic smile before giving me a little nod, as if to say *It's okay. You're good.*

And Maeve just gave me that sad, knowing smile when she stepped aside to gesture up the stairs. "We'll be with you in a minute, love," she said. "Girls' Night?"

Laila practically bloomed at the words. "Girls' Night?" she repeated, sharing a hopeful look with the rest of us. "I could really use one," she muttered to herself.

"What do *you* need it for?" Riley wondered.

"You know I hate when any of you are upset," she protested, her arms crossing in front of her chest like Riley should've known that. She did.

Pip was still in my arms when I nodded in agreement. "Girls' Night."

CHAPTER 28

Now

I had recovered from my moment of weakness. From the thought—*the fear*—that I might never truly get over Henry.

But in a few months, I'd never see him again. We'd graduate, he'd move to New York, and I'd be God knows where. The only time I could potentially run into him was when I'd turn on the TV or open Google and type in his name.

Until then, he was the subject of this profile—my *friend*. So what if I wanted to climb the man like a tree? I was old enough to keep my urges in check. I could admire him from afar.

Trying to keep a safe distance, I scheduled my next interview with his sister instead of him. I didn't think the two were particularly close—at least, they hadn't been in the past few years.

I had met Athalia a handful of times, but never because of Henry. The first time was at Daisy's, where she ordered a coffee and wasn't surprised to see her name on the to-go cup even though she hadn't given it to me. Then again, here and there, at one party or another, more or less intoxicated each time. By the fourth one, I wasn't quite sure whether she still didn't know me or just hadn't cared enough about the girl her twin brother was dating.

The last time I saw her was four months ago at the Pressleys' New Year's Eve party somewhere in the Hamptons. We'd spoken—mostly because her best friend Wren had started dating Laila. We'd been in each other's orbit for a while, never really crossing paths. It didn't keep her from greeting me like we'd been best friends for years.

"Paula!" Athalia cheered, her brown hair falling down her back in long waves, green eyes wide with surprise. Presumably because she hadn't asked who I was through the intercom, and I knew from Henry that she was as great at keeping track of her appointments as I was. So, not at all. "Come in." She shooed me into the loft across the street from Henry's.

"Sorry for abusing your doorbell." I slipped off my shoes and followed her into the living room, where she patted the spot beside her on the leather couch. "Just didn't want to run into . . . anyone," I explained as I sank into the cushions.

"*Anyone*, yes," Athalia said, mischief sprawling across her features in the same way it would across Henry's. Her green eyes trailed to the window. "If we're lucky, we might see *Anyone* peering through his windows," she said matter-of-factly, sending me an apologetic glance.

"How would he—?"

"Know?" she guessed. "I told him you're here. Sorry! It kind of just slipped out when he wouldn't shut up about my nonexistent life plan, and I threw *'Well, your girlfriend is in* my *plans for today'* at him." She winced. "Which just led him down this tangent of how and why you two aren't . . . you know." She stopped rambling. "Curious how he knew I was talking about you, though. Isn't it?"

"Oh," I offered unhelpfully. "Well." It *was* curious, but I couldn't say that to his sister. I cleared my throat, tried to subtly change the subject. "How are you guys?"

I'd asked Henry the same question a few weeks ago, but it felt like I might get a better answer out of his sister. Athalia was way chattier and much more likely to throw him under the bus.

She sighed, and her head fell back against the couch. "Better." Same as Henry had said. "In a weird turn of events I did not expect, dating Dylan actually rolled my relationship with Henry in the right direction. He hates him so much, he started to care about me! Can you believe that?"

"Totally." I snorted in amusement. Setting my phone between us, pen and paper in my lap, I couldn't even get half of the next question in before her eyes snapped open, connecting right with mine. She sat up, and I cut myself off.

"Wait, sorry. I don't want to interrupt, but I already have, so I might as well just—" She shifted in her seat, turned to me fully. "I gotta know this or I won't sleep tonight."

Although her eyes flicked to my recording phone, she didn't seem to care. "Did he end up apologizing?" she asked. "For being an oblivious asshole who can't grasp people's feelings if his life depended on it?"

I did not have a single clue what she was talking about.

Athalia elaborated with a knowing look. "Less cryptic, got it. Let me try again. For . . . not considering your feelings going into this, I mean. The profile, the interviews, the one-on-one time."

I immediately understood. Remembered the way he'd suddenly apologized for not considering it a few weeks back.

"Of course that didn't come from him." I sighed, head falling back like I should've known.

I really should have. Henry wasn't usually the empathic type.

"Of course not," she agreed proudly. "It took me an entire hour to explain it to him, then another hour of scowls because he realized I was right. Which . . . obviously?" Her nose twitched as if she couldn't believe he'd doubted her. "And sure," she sailed on, "he felt like an asshole after, but that's only because he is!"

I couldn't help but smile at how polar the twins were to each other and how much I liked it. How much I liked her. "I'm sorry. Usually I know how to shut the fuck up," she added, seeming to realize it herself.

"I feel like we were meant to meet like this a lot sooner."

The words just slipped out, so honest I surprised myself with them.

Athalia nodded grandly, her curtain bangs flying into her face. "I can't believe you were with Henry for over two years, and he never had the balls to introduce us." She sounded like she might actually take offense. "We haven't been all that close after, well, you know." Her easy smile dimmed. "But still. He should've introduced his sister to his girlfriend, right?"

"I always thought he might be—" For a moment, I hesitated. The next I thought, *Fuck it*. We were sharing. Bonding. I think. "You know. Might be embarrassed because I'm not this rich white girl with generational wealth. That maybe he just didn't want you to know—"

"Oh my God." Athalia shook her head. She wouldn't even let me finish the sentence. "You were never the problem, Paula! Trust me. Henry and I have been weird since the accident. We never talked. We never shared private things. The fact that you never met me probably meant he cared too much and didn't want me to mess things up." She snickered halfheartedly at her own words. "In some weird, fucked-up Henry way. Don't worry about that. *Please*."

The feeling in my stomach, spreading through my chest and perhaps into my cheeks, was unexpected. That worry must've sat heavier on my mind than I'd thought, so I was relieved. Relieved beyond words.

"He did talk about you," I offered. And her eyes widened like she really hadn't expected it. "Sometimes. I know you used to ride horses when you were younger. You hate roses because he accidentally pushed you into a bush full of them. He wouldn't have gone to HBU if you hadn't gotten in."

"Fuck." Athalia exhaled. Her face disappeared in her hands. "I can't believe there's an entire side to Henry I don't even know." Her hands dropped. "I mean, I *can* believe it. But still. It's—"

"Weird," I offered, and she nodded in agreement.

I wasn't quite sure where that left us. But with the second moment of silence between us, I took the opportunity to get back to the reason for my visit.

"Anyway," I began, "I do appreciate you doing this interview. If you're anything like your brother, I know you don't usually . . . like them."

"Hate them," Athalia corrected quickly. The sudden smile on her face didn't match the flat tone of her voice. "But don't worry. Anything for Henry, right?"

When I went to agree, I could sense another tangent coming at her next words. "Oh! Did you know?" she asked, like she wanted to repay me for what I'd told her about him. "For a solid few months, I actually thought you cheated on Henry. He did too!"

"What?"

Forget the interview for a moment. *What?!*

Athalia nodded grandly, brown hair flying. "I know!" she agreed, somehow seeming more outraged than I was. "And all because he saw you with McCa—*Dylan*. That's literally it."

Seeing as we were neighbors, I wouldn't be surprised

if he'd seen us together. And I might've vented to Dylan about our breakup, sure. He hated the guy almost as much as I pretended to.

"Talk about jumping to conclusions," I huffed, still putting the pieces together.

"Oh." Athalia laughed. "He's jumping alright." Her brows rose like she'd just remembered another big thing she needed to talk about *right now*. While the recording ticked on. "Whatever happened to that Jack guy?"

That took me by surprise. So much so that I drew back from her at the name. "When you said you and Henry are closer now, I didn't think you meant *this* close. Does he tell you everything?"

She waved the question off. "Only the things he can't go to anyone else with. Like you. Or the guys you're dating."

"I never dated—" I shook myself out of it. "He talked to you about that?"

The only answer was an unapologetic grin. Like there might be nothing better in the world than gossiping about your brother with his ex-girlfriend. Maybe there wasn't.

Unfortunately, I'd come to work. And I realized the only way I'd get anything useful out of her was an agreement.

A piece of his childhood from Athalia for a piece of Henry she might not know about. And round and round we went for an hour.

*

Later, when Maeve and I listened to the material like others might listen to a podcast, I was tempted to replay it all from the beginning just to make sure I hadn't missed any of the juicy details.

"God," the redhead sighed beside me, sprawling across my bed, eyes on the ceiling. "Athalia really is something. I'm a little jealous McCarthy took her off the market before I got the chance to."

Maeve had never dated anyone in the history of ever, but I liked to think she would've changed her ways for Athalia. "You guys would've been cute together."

"An absolute power couple," she agreed, nodding thoughtfully. "How far along are you with this, anyway?"

I assumed she meant the profile.

"I've talked to Henry plenty. Seen enough, probably." And it definitely wasn't just another way to postpone eventually seeing him again after New York. "I got the chance to talk to Coach Hepburn at the game the other day, and his friends after that. I should probably watch another one of his games from the stands, just to get a feel for him. On the field. Right?"

I preferred the idea of watching Henry from a distance, where we wouldn't have to interact. "Then I'll get to writing the first draft. Which would leave me with enough time to get some more stuff, should Eddie deem it . . . insufficient."

Maeve blinked at me, a little dumbfounded. "Did you just actually make a plan?" she asked as if the reality of it was impossible. "Like, in advance? Instead of doing and writing as you go?"

"That seems like a backhanded compliment," I deadpanned.

"Well—"

"Why does everyone think I'm incapable of getting my shit together?" I groaned like Maeve had accused me of that and it wasn't just what my own insecurities led me to believe.

She looked at me like she knew. "Paula." She rolled her eyes lightheartedly. "No one actually thinks that." She hesitated. "And even if they do. Who cares? You know how you work best, and if that's without a plan, chaotically doing whatever you want, whenever you want—" I shot her a glare I didn't mean. "Then so be it. As long as you get it done."

I wished I could believe in myself—my abilities and resilience—as much as other people did. Even Marty seemed impressed. *Excited*, even, about the prospect of *me* writing about one of *his* players. The thought still seemed odd.

Why, though? How come other people, some of whom I barely knew, had more faith in me than I did?

I was the one who ignored my parents' expectations and changed majors because I knew I'd be better at something else. *I'd* gotten article after article at the *Post*. I'd written for *The New York Times* as an undergrad student. I'd been there for all of that. I'd actually *done* it. But for some reason, I thought I might never be able to again.

And I decided something about that needed to change.

CHAPTER 29

Now

I don't think I'd ever dreaded watching a match before. But this time, I could barely get myself to the stands, terrified even though Henry had no idea I was there. I was supposed to watch him in his natural habitat, and no one acted naturally when they knew a journalist writing a profile on them was nearby.

So I'd rummaged through my accessories until I found the one baseball cap I never wore, threw on jeans and a tee, and went to the game.

With the season over, it was just another friendly, and the spring sun on our home field felt terribly summery. It was so close, I could smell it in the air, see it in the sky and the trees.

I couldn't wait.

In contrast to summers at home, which were too hot, itchy, and loud, summers on the East Coast felt warm, calm, and quiet. No cicadas outside your window keeping you up at night, and no cockroaches on the floor keeping you from getting out of bed in the morning. I massively preferred it.

Squinting against the spring sun, I watched Henry run onto the field. Judging by the way he sprinted to his position, I could tell he'd been itching to be put in.

Apparently, Coach had only deemed it necessary in the second half, when the score had already been 0–1 against us.

It wasn't ideal to write about a player who wasn't playing half the game you were watching. But as if he knew I was there—impossible, since I'd pulled my hat farther down over my features the moment he emerged from the bench—Henry made sure I had something to write about regardless.

The energy on the field shifted the second he touched the ball for the first time. Opponents didn't get as close to our box anymore; the game was mostly played on the other side of the field.

He was big for a soccer player, which made it easy to track him. For a defender, he was quite far from our goal, the ball always by his feet as he ran into the middle of the field—seemingly catching the Brinley Tigers off guard as he simply dribbled through their lineup. Right up until number 3 put a stop to it.

I was confused by the sight—a man taller and wider than even Henry running toward him and looking very intent on getting that ball away from his feet and their goal. Henry looked around to pass it the moment he noticed him.

The only number he had a free shot at was 7: Dylan McCarthy Williams.

For a moment, I honestly thought he'd rather give up the ball than assist Dylan with a goal. But that wasn't Henry—he was raised to do nothing *but* win. It was his thing.

Whatever rivalry the two had off the field, right then and there, with a ball between and the odds against them, you couldn't see any of it. They worked in perfect sync.

Henry smoothly passed the ball across the field, directly to Dylan, who sprinted toward the goal before he even secured the ball, then lined it up perfectly and didn't hesitate before firing it into the net.

With ten minutes to go, Dylan scored the equalizer to make it 1–1.

The relief and gratitude washed off Henry's face just seconds after the goal, and he glowered at the man like they hadn't just worked flawlessly together.

The game ended in a tie, and I was already crafting possible sentences about it by the time I followed the crowd out. Without my laptop, I was wildly typing into my notes app. Eyes glued to my phone, I focused on the structure of the profile and how I could seamlessly incorporate today's game into it. *Henry* this and *Henry* that—every second sentence started with his name.

Which was fine—and not creepy at all. This profile was about him, after all.

A hand on my shoulder startled me, and I looked up to find I was about five seconds away from running into a lamppost. I whirled around.

Henry. His tall frame blocked the setting sun behind him.

I couldn't say I was surprised.

His name was all over my life at the moment—literally, judging by the document on my laptop and the note in my phone. I couldn't avoid him forever.

"Knew that was you." His hand fell from my shoulder, and I hated the eerie cold it left behind.

I frowned up at him from below the blue baseball cap. "How?" I asked. "I'm incognito." I gestured to the hat, tapped it once. I had brown curls, not neon-pink hair. The back of my head wasn't unique enough to spot from a mile away *and* recognize.

"First of all," he began, his head tilting in amusement, "I don't know how great you think your disguise is, but you just look like Paula with a hat on to me. Second of all. That's *my* cap."

My eyes widened. As if he could read my thoughts, he snatched it off my head and turned the back toward me. It read "Parker."

"That's my name on it," he stated matter-of-factly.

My head shook. "That's not your name."

At least not legally. His full name was Henry Parker Pressley, and if it didn't say that on the hat, he couldn't prove it was his. There was probably a brand out there called Parker, right?

"Plus, I gave all your stuff back."

His eyes rolled at the technicality, widening the strap on the back and placing it on top of his head. It did look better on him.

"My aunt preferred my middle name," he said. "Which is why I hate my middle name and the reason I gave this to you. I told you that."

I tried to ignore the sliver of a memory in the back of my mind. I shook my head, fiercer this time. "Nope."

I grabbed for the hat, got on the tip of my toes to reach it, only to be stopped by Henry's hand. Around my wrist. Again.

I blinked up at him. "Doesn't ring a bell."

And I didn't mean to whisper the words. The air just felt thick, and that invisible string meant to keep us at a safe distance since our agreement in New York felt much thinner. It might snap.

I might.

I know I'd said I had enough self-control when it came to Henry. And I'd really been convinced I could keep my hands to myself, urges and wants and needs in check.

What I hadn't added to the equation was this.

The way his throat worked, the way he lowered our hands but didn't let go of my wrist. His touch made me *tingle.*

"Sorry," he said, but didn't draw back. His gaze flicked to my mouth, and he closed his eyes, squeezed them shut tightly, and exhaled loudly. "I'm really trying," he whispered, strained and desperate.

"Trying?"

"To stay away from you." His eyes batted open, connecting with mine. "To give you space. After New York."

"Are you?" My gaze flicked between us, the lack of

distance apparent. A touch of humor made it through the charged air between us. "This is the first time you see me, and you're not . . . away."

Not that I minded.

Henry huffed against my nose, minty scent still lingering from his toothpaste. "You *would* think this is the first time," he said cryptically. "I saw you four days ago. In the library, typing away. Twice yesterday, actually. At Daisy's in the morning, and then again on campus." The corner of his lip curled upward, affectionate and sweet. "But you've never been very aware of your surroundings, Charm."

I swallowed thickly, tried to blink whatever must've shown in my eyes away. "And you were always better at watching people," I agreed halfheartedly.

"Watching you," he amended.

Henry's tongue flicked across his lips, and he hesitated for a moment. His lazy grip around my wrist twitched just once, very quickly, before he let go.

"I made up this thing in my head where I told myself I needed to talk to you." The words slipped out, like he didn't know what else to say but didn't want the conversation to end.

"What reason did you come up with?"

It seemed we were both on autopilot at this point. Because if I had anything to do with it, if my *conscious* mind could get a word in, there wouldn't have been a flirty lull in my tone. I wouldn't have tilted my head, and my eyes wouldn't have trailed to his lips.

"Let me give you a ride home?" he asked.

Bad idea. But autopilot.

"Sure."

At least in the car, there was a console between us. Seat belts keeping us from jumping each other. Henry's undivided attention on the road instead of me.

*

"So, how's it going?" he asked as he rolled to a stop in front of my house. "With the profile, I mean. Have you started writing it?"

I shook my head. "No. About to, though. I think all that was missing was watching a game." Which led me to add, "Congrats, by the way."

"On not losing?" he asked, unconvinced.

I shrugged. "That too." I guessed? "And the assist."

Henry barked a laugh, unbuckling his seat belt. "McCarthy will never let it go." My eyes rolled as he went on. "He never stops gloating. He never gets over things—or lets *others* get over them. Paula," he pressed, serious, "he still thinks it's hilarious to be close to my sister whenever I enter a room they happen to be in."

"And you don't think he might just want to be close to her even when you're *not* around? Because he loves her?" I asked as he rounded the car.

"No." My door popped open, and it revealed a scowl on his face.

"Ay Dios mío, Henry." I groaned lightly, teasingly. I lost the seat belt and turned toward him. "Stop being a dickhead and start being happy for Athalia! She's in love with the guy!"

Henry, naturally, did not share that sentiment. His hand curled around the hood of the car, resting his head against it. "Who are you calling a dickhead, missy?" he challenged, an amused glare in his eyes. "Can't possibly be me, right?"

"And what if it is?"

We'd been joking a second ago, but the spring breeze had blown something else between us. A gust of tension, air filled with possibilities and bad ideas. Him closer to me.

"I haven't come up with a punishment yet," he said.

"No?" I wasn't quite sure what came over me when I added, "Do let me know once you have."

Something in his expression darkened, the teasing lines of his smile disappearing slowly. His brows drew together like he was about to kick into autopilot too. The way we had in New York when he'd confessed I made him nervous, then almost kissed me.

This felt similar. But I wasn't thinking about why we should be reasonable anymore. Instead, all I wanted to scream at him was *Kiss me! What's the big deal?*

We'd done it before. About a thousand times. We'd done so much more than share a harmless kiss in this car; there was no way one more could hurt.

Kiss me, kiss me, kiss me!

My gaze fell to his lips every .5 seconds. I couldn't help it. His attention wasn't wavering, though. Wasn't flickering between my lips and eyes wildly. It was fixed on the latter.

Like he was about to discover a new shade of brown in them.

"Paula," he rasped. And the string between us was about to snap again. *I* was about to snap again. I could feel it the same way I could feel the rough sound of his voice in the pit of my stomach. The way I could feel him all over when he wasn't touching any of me.

Like phantom pain. When you still felt your leg even after it had been brutally severed from the rest of your body. Maybe that's why I felt the ghost of his lingering kisses, his hands on my body, his fingers between my thighs—even if he wasn't touching me. Even if he hadn't since he'd been severed from the rest of my life.

"What?" When I finally answered, I couldn't get my voice above a whisper. My tongue flicked across my lips, and the motion drew his eyes to them for the first time.

He swallowed thickly when he looked back at me. "Please don't make me kiss you."

"Why?"

"Because I won't be able to stop," he said. "Because I won't want to."

I thought I might be seeing stars when I felt him draw closer. Felt myself inch toward him too.

"You—" I began, but my lips moved, and they brushed his, and it was a little too much. My breath stuttered in my throat, and Henry's forehead fell to mine, bringing some distance between our lips.

Just enough for them not to touch when I said, "You managed before. You were so . . . reasonable that night."

He'd been the one to draw away in the hotel. I didn't think I could have.

"And it almost killed me, Paula."

My head shook against his. Maybe to clear my thoughts, maybe because I had hoped the movement would accidentally let my lips brush his again. They didn't, and when disappointment settled in my stomach, I thought, *Fuck it.*

Let that string between us snap.

Fuck reasons. Fuck breakups. Just for today—for now.

I reached for his face, clumsy, needy, and said, "If you kiss me, you won't have to stop—"

So he did. Or I did.

I wasn't quite sure who finally did it. Only that his lips moved in sync with mine, and that the noise he'd made when they finally connected hadn't been in my head.

A sigh of relief, a groan, a plea.

The way he'd sounded a year ago whenever I'd trailed kisses down his neck, chest, stomach, hips—until he'd gotten impatient, and I'd finally wrapped my lips around him.

Only instead of whispering sweet, encouraging words and praise into my mouth or neck or hair like he always had, he was quiet. Like he didn't want to miss a single thing or risk any of his words interrupting what was happening.

My lips parted, our tongues reunited, and he interlaced his hand with mine on the seat. I could feel how much he wanted this just by the way he was holding tight—like he might spontaneously combust if he couldn't have me.

I thought I might too. So much so that when my name was yelled across our front yard, I'd been tempted to ignore it.

"Paula?" It came again—and pulled me back to the reality of the situation.

In my ex-boyfriend's car. His lips on mine. Him halfway on top of me. Us about three minutes from that point of no return. In the middle of an open street. With neighbors and nosy roommates around.

I froze at the same moment he did, but the space between us hardly existed. Henry looked behind me through the window on the driver's side that faced my house. He cursed, the sound low and intimate against me.

"The windows are tinted, right?" I whispered almost into his mouth. He nodded.

When he pulled back, it was the right thing to do, but it felt wrong beyond words. Worse once he straightened and appeared above the car again, revealing himself to whichever of my friends stood beyond it.

"Oh." And I could finally assign a face to the voice. "Henry. Didn't see you there," Riley said.

He cocked his head sideways, shooting the girl a look that implied she should've expected him. "It's my car," he explained.

"Good to see you too," she said, completely oblivious to the reason for his dismissive tone.

Which was her. Her and her cruel interruption.

I heard Riley's footsteps echo on the short walkway from the house, and before she could round the corner of Henry's car to find out just how close, how compromising, our position had been, I got out of my seat to meet her halfway.

Even if I'd tried, my last look at Henry couldn't have conveyed everything I had wanted it to.

I missed you above all else.

"Ah," Riley said when I finally jumped into view. "Thought that was you. We saw the car pull up through the window." She nodded toward said window behind her, coming to a halt. "So when so much time passed and you still didn't come in . . ."

Her eyes trailed to Henry behind me, and I knew she blamed him. Rightfully so, I guess. "Almost missed Taco Tuesday," she chided, some humor back in her tone.

Henry only thought it fitting to comment, "It's Sunday."

Which Riley and I both ignored.

"Sorry." I smiled as I caught up with her. "Wouldn't miss that for the world."

That was a lie. The reason I'd miss Taco Tuesday any day of the week—although the Sunday ones were my favorite—stood feet away, eyes probably on us. "Although I do miss Dominican food," I joked, lingering on the porch as Riley disappeared inside.

For a fickle second, I thought I shouldn't turn around. I could spare myself the embarrassment if Henry had already gotten back in the car, regretting our kiss.

But the attempt was useless.

He stood where I had left him. On the passenger side of his car, door still open, one hand on it, the other probably in his pocket. Eyes on me. Typical half smile on his lips that told me he wasn't regretting it at all.

CHAPTER 30

Now

PRESSLEY_PROFILE_V1.

I had stared at the blank page for hours with no movement except for the blinking cursor. That first draft was much harder now that every time I thought, read, or tried to write about Henry, all I could picture were his lips on mine. My fingers interlaced with his. The undeniable lust in every single breath we had shared.

Even though I knew it was the man on my mind and not the color of my walls that kept me from producing coherent sentences, I still opted for a change.

I'd been holed up in the *HBP* office for about a week since then.

With everyone else around me writing, I felt compelled to do the same. For almost a year, I'd been begging to be one of them. I wanted to type away until my fingers bled and my lips dried out because I'd forget to drink anything. I'd missed that.

The office also reminded me that I wanted to sit in one a few months from now and actually get paid to be there. This profile wasn't just about graduating with good grades or proving something to my parents once they inevitably found out about the whole thing. It was a way to restore my reputation and to hopefully write something so great, future employers wouldn't care about that hiccup in my record last year caused by a minor complaint from the source I had apparently misquoted.

Spending my entire week at the *Post* meant no accidental run-ins with Henry, and on top of that, I'd actually managed to produce a first draft. I was working through lunch, trying to make it into something more than half decent before my appointment with Eddie in thirty minutes.

That wasn't a lot of time, and it was stressing me out more than it would've a year ago. I was distracted, jumpy. I couldn't keep my legs still.

Alfie got up from his desk beside mine and strolled past me with a shrug. "Lunch," he said, and it was explanation enough. He didn't bother wasting his breath on an invitation he knew I would decline.

"And then there were two," Lacy said from four desks over, playful amusement in her perfect voice. She'd probably be a good singer if she gave it a try.

When I only answered with an uncomfortable laugh,

she spun her chair in my direction. "How's the profile going?"

I didn't expect to groan so openly. Judging by the look on her face, neither had she.

"Sorry." I tried to recover from my outburst. "It's just . . . I'm trying to fix this draft, and then someone asks a question or leaves the room, and I—" The ding of an incoming email cut me off, and I grandly gestured to my screen. "See!"

Lacy nodded as if she completely understood the feeling. As if she could truly grasp the stress I was putting myself under—the stress of my entire future being tied to one stupid profile about my ex-boyfriend, which could salvage the career that had been hanging by a thread since last year. It needed to be perfect.

So far, it was half decent.

"Just one of those days," Lacy said, giving me an encouraging smile. A shadow danced across her face. Her brow furrowed, her mouth twitched, and for a second, I imagined a tinge of jealousy in her tone when she said, "You'll manage, Paula. You always do."

"Thanks," I said a little gruffly.

We both turned back to our screens. While Lacy probably continued writing or researching or doing something else incredibly productive, I opened my emails.

<HALLIE.WEST@NYBE.COM> 1:36 PM

Got your pictures for the profile! I've attached the headshots as well as some candids, as discussed. Hope there's something useful between them and looking forward to reading this thing.

X, Hallie

"It's work related," I muttered in Lacy's general direction, just so she knew. I didn't know why I felt it was important that she did.

She gave me a confused thumbs-up in return, and my eyes returned to the screen. I scrolled through the attached pictures halfheartedly.

One of Henry frowning into the camera followed by one with his lips turning upward reluctantly. I was surprised to see a genuine smile in the next take and wondered what she'd said to elicit it. Either way, Hallie was skilled at what she did, because those smiles were rare.

I clicked through the folder distractedly until I got to the candids she mentioned, and—sneaky little woman! I hadn't even noticed her set up camp behind me. Judging by the angle of the pictures, she'd taken them from a few rows back.

Most of them were zoomed-in photos of Henry kicking, dribbling, shooting at the goal, and scoring. In another one, he stood in the middle of the empty field and looked up at the sky.

In hindsight, I wish that photo had been the last one in the folder, because when I clicked to the next, I stared back at my own face. His and mine as we stood by the penalty spot, the ball between us.

I frowned at it; he smiled at me.

I was reluctant to click through to the next one. But maybe I'd only ended up in her selection by accident, and she hadn't meant to take it, let alone send it to me?

No, unfortunately. I was on the next one too. Laughing up at Henry.

How hadn't we noticed her up there?

I winced as the next picture materialized on my screen. Henry and me. On the ground. It just didn't look like the vicious foul it had actually been. At all.

She'd captured the in-between: before he told me *"This is why I do it"* and after we laughed until my cheeks hurt. If Hallie's zoom had been just a little better, she probably would've captured my dilated pupils and the breath stuck in my throat.

Henry's face, though . . . her camera had been good enough to see everything written across it. He'd had his guard down for a little over a second, and Hallie had taken a picture of it.

This is how he looks at me?

My eyes continued trailing back to Henry, who was looking at me like he'd just found the center of the world.

Before I could convince myself that I was going mad—that there must've been a hundred other explanations for his expression—my phone vibrated against the wooden desk. I was hesitant to answer the unknown number but then remembered it *could* be work related. I got out of my chair with a pained sigh.

Lacy shot me an innocent smile from behind her screen as I passed. "Just not meant to be, huh?"

I grimaced on my way out, shutting the door behind me with more force than needed. *Not meant to be, huh?* I mocked her in my head, raising the phone to my ear. "Paula Castillo."

"Paula," the voice said by way of greeting.

I double-checked the screen at the familiarity of it.

"It's Henry." He confirmed my fear. "I got a new phone; you blocked my number a while back."

Maeve had. Months ago. After my second drunk call, right before deleting it.

I relaxed against the wall behind me. "You mean new phone *number*," I corrected him.

"Oh." The silence lingered from the other end, background noise the only thing making it through. "I could've done that. Yeah." It seemed he hadn't even considered the possibility. "Anyway, I need to see you—talk to you. I don't have much time, but it'll only take a minute. Can you spare that?"

I made up this thing in my head where I told myself I needed to talk to you.

The thought of what had happened after those words made my stomach flutter. A clear sign that I should stay away from him at all costs to avoid ending up in a situation where I'd have to depend on our shared self-control again. Neither of us seemed to have much of it.

"I'm at the *Post*, actually." And I didn't have much time because I had to be in Eddie's office with that first draft in fifteen minutes.

So when I saw Henry right as he came up the stairs, my stomach dropped the way it would at the top of a roller coaster right after the cart tips forward.

I heard the call disconnecting as Henry said, "Perfect."

He must've been at the gym because his hair was still damp from the shower he'd taken, and his muscles looked more defined than usual. I wasn't sure if that's how the science behind that worked or if maybe I was just *too* aware of every sliver of skin he was showing in the black tank top.

Whatever it was, my heart sank into my stomach, beating unsteadily at the memory of our last encounter. The image in front of me made it hard to forget when his hair had been equally wet, and he'd looked just as good. His lips had been just as pink, eyes just as green. The freckles around his nose were just as perfect.

Be reasonable, I tried to convince myself. But there was no point anymore. Not really.

"Hi," I breathed. He came to an abrupt halt a few inches away, like his body had wanted to come closer and he physically had to deny the subconscious request.

I looked up when his head tilted to the side, scanning the hallway as if he couldn't bring himself to look at me. Instead, his eyes flickered from door to door, and I wondered which one would lead to an empty room. For no reason at all. "What's up?"

"Can we talk?" he asked again, gaze finally snapping to mine. "Alone." *Technically, we were alone.* But he amended his words quickly. "Somewhere more private."

The last time we'd been in public, I almost climbed the man. To think what might have happened behind closed doors—

"Of course." Autopilot again. Otherwise, I wouldn't have sounded so obviously eager. I might not have said it at all. As if I hadn't already been too desperate, I added, "Follow me."

I guided us to the room where we'd had our first interview. It was the only one I could think of that was likely to be free. No one would willingly spend a sunny lunch break there, and I didn't want to risk delaying any time I might have alone with him by searching for another room.

So up the stairs, down the hall, and a right turn later, I opened the door. Empty.

Relief flooded every single one of my senses.

It had taken physical restraint to stay away from Henry after he'd kissed me. Multiple times, I'd been on the verge of marching over to his apartment. In a small office on our own, my body thrummed with every single desire I'd been trying to push away for a week.

Given how Henry stepped past me and into the room without an invitation, it seemed like he was feeling the same way. Eager. Desperate.

Please don't make me kiss you. Because I won't be able to stop. I won't want to.

My breath hitched at the thought, imagining his rough voice against my lips, my breasts, below my hips.

"Listen," he said, shaking his head like he was trying

to escape similar thoughts. "I tried. I *really* tried so hard not to read anything into last week—"

I didn't even feel bad for cutting him off. That string between us just snapped, violently lashing out in every direction. I might've been embarrassed if he'd been anyone else.

But he was Henry. My Henry. Wasn't he?

"Please just kiss me again," I begged.

In the second it took him to adjust to my request, I knew I was right to trust him with the pure honesty of my words. Because I could see the same desire on his face.

It was clear, with each of his heavy steps, that he wanted me too.

"What?" he asked from a hair's length away.

"Kiss me."

He did not hesitate. With everything that he was, Henry Parker Pressley kissed me again.

With one hand on my cheek and the other on my waist, he kissed me. With my hair in his face and my arms around his neck, he kissed me. With my body pressed between his and the door, he kissed me.

Desperately and longingly, as if he were trying to make up for the past week and the year before that all within just a few minutes.

Over and over and over again, he kissed me. Or maybe he never really stopped. My hands found themselves in his brown hair, grabbing, pulling, and earning me a soft groan from Henry that could make me come undone just by the implication. My hands fell from his hair to the waistband of his pants.

"Paula," he panted, and I only allowed his lips from mine for a second. "Darling, hey." The sound he drew out of me when he disconnected our lips was needy, whiny—half a broken moan. "Here?"

He looked around, not opposed, but unsure when his eyes found mine again.

"I don't care." My voice broke. "Anywhere."

His next kiss landed on my neck. He sucked and nibbled, coaxing hushed moans out of me as he held my thigh, pulled it against himself, only for his hand to move to my backside.

"You still taste the same," he groaned against my skin, voice hushed. "Feel the same, sound the same." His lips trailed up my neck. "It's like you're still mine."

I almost told him I was.

But my breath was too heavy to speak. And when our lips connected again, and another one of my moans got swallowed by his lips, I couldn't *think*, let alone speak.

"I couldn't stop thinking about you. After New York. After last week. I—" He groaned into my mouth, teeth digging into my lower lip softly. "I need you. I—" And it seemed he had more to say, but he gave up when my fingers began fumbling with his belt buckle.

His head fell back at the implication, hands driving up the back of my neck and into my hair. Belt open, he kissed me like he was rewarding me for finally getting it done.

Which made the generic ringtone blaring through the room so much worse.

I could feel him draw away, and I didn't like it.

"I'm sorry," he whispered, and he sounded like he meant it. "I'm sorry. I'm really sorry." Which was when he took a step back, and my body sagged against the door because my legs had turned into jelly. "Remember when I said I don't have much time?"

That reminded me of something awful: I really didn't either.

"How late is it?" I asked, panicking when I realized I probably wouldn't make it to Eddie's office in time.

"Two."

"Fuck." My hand ran down my hair, and I smoothed out my clothes in an attempt to look like I wasn't thirty seconds post–*heavy make out*. And sixty seconds pre–much more. "Fuck, fuck, fuck."

As I opened the door, I realized the phone was no longer ringing, which meant Henry had taken the call.

"Paula." When I turned around, Henry covered the microphone with his palm, holding the device a few inches from his face. "I'll call you."

CHAPTER 31

Then

May: Eleven months ago

Henry yawned beside me, nuzzling his face deeper into his pillow. I lowered my screen brightness to the minimum. It's probably why he was awake in the first place. "Is this still about Mark?"

Mark, Henry's friend who'd managed a full-ride scholarship to Harvard. Mark, the thin, blond European guy I'd interviewed today. Mark, whom I couldn't help but have a weird feeling about. I'd been trying to ignore it ever since I'd gotten back from Boston. So far, I had nothing, though.

"Yeah," I answered his question. "How did you say you guys knew each other again?" I honestly felt a little bad when he turned, with a stretch, onto his back to blink at me sleepily. Quickly, his eyes trailed over me, the way I sat against his headboard. He shrugged.

"Friend of a friend of a friend. I think," he added. "But

however pretentious it sounds, he's the only guy I could think of who's smart enough for an Ivy and not filthy rich. That's what you wanted, right?"

I nodded. "Because going to an Ivy probably isn't as much pressure when you've got a hefty trust fund to back up your academic achievements. Or lack thereof, I guess." It was an interesting angle.

The damaging effects of the stress of meeting expectations at Ivy League colleges across the country and how most people might be better off attending equally good schools without that added pressure. Hall Beck University, for example.

I was essentially writing a marketing letter on HBU's behalf. Just with more words, research, and time invested.

"And what about Mark?" Henry asked.

I wish I could pinpoint it, but I had no idea what it was about Mark that made my stomach turn.

He'd been kind, and he'd detailed every way going to Harvard would look great on his résumé but was damaging enough to his mental health and self-worth that it might not be worth it in the end.

I'd been unsure how willing students were going to be, so I was relieved Mark gave me those details. From describing arrogant professors to detailing a stunning lack of a safety net for students' mental health, Mark had given me everything I could've asked for. He'd also included personal anecdotes that had been so perfect, I knew which parts to quote as soon as they came out of his mouth.

It's like someone had personally sent Mark Lager to make my life easier. It seemed almost *too* perfect.

"I don't know," I sighed. "Something feels off. I've gone through his followers, his following. Tagged pictures. *Facebook* friends."

"And nothing?" Henry's hand emerged from beneath the covers to trail along my arm, up and down, gently, soothingly.

"Nothing," I said, ignoring the goose bumps his touch still sent across my skin. "Just his own GoFundMe link and posts on financial struggles."

"Then maybe," Henry began, sitting up to kiss my shoulder, neck, and cheek along the way, "there's nothing wrong with him. Hm?"

I finally looked away from Mark's Facebook page. The sight of Henry's smile was much more welcoming. "You've been checking for the past three hours, Charm. Do you really think you're still going to find something now?" His gaze flicked to the time on my laptop. "At one in the morning?"

Probably not, I thought. "But if I just—"

"You're being paranoid." His tone wasn't judgmental or cruel. It was the opposite, and I could tell it pained him deeply to be so blatantly honest. I appreciated it, though.

Perhaps it really was time to give it up and go to sleep.

"I'm sorry this is worrying you so much," he sighed, slipping his hand in mine and bringing it up to his lips. He kissed it once. "Maybe I shouldn't have suggested him. I don't know much about the guy, but he seemed fine whenever—"

"Don't be ridiculous." My head shook at the suggestion. "*Thank you.* For getting me anyone to talk to at all," I pressed. "My overthinking isn't your fault."

The fact that he thought it might be was what finally made me close my laptop and place it on the bedside table. When I turned back to Henry, I could only make out his general shape in the dark and the fact that he was holding his arms wide open for me to fall into.

Which I did. Without hesitation.

We scooted lower, heads accidentally landing on the same pillow. "You'll do great with this article," he muttered into my hair, then kissed the top of my head. "I can already tell it'll change things. It's going to be amazing."

"You haven't even read it," I reminded him.

"I don't need to," he said before his warm body and sweet nothings whispered me to sleep.

CHAPTER 32

Now

<E.SMITH@HALLBU.COM> 6:17 PM

Paula,

Thanks for coming in the other day. Looks okay for a first draft! I think something is missing, though. Can't quite put my finger on what. What do you think? Left some comments in the margins for you. Can you get back with the revised version next week?

Eddie

Looks okay.

I read the email twice. Then once more just to make

sure I'd gotten it right. Not good, perfect, exciting. Not even boring or awful. *Okay.*

What was a piece of writing if it didn't evoke *something* in its reader? Nothing was ever just okay.

Then: "Something is missing."

How could a fifteen-page deep dive be missing anything? And what was an editor for if not to be precise on what exactly was missing and how one might take a mediocre draft and make it shine?

I replied to say the following week wouldn't be a problem, then thought about all the ways it would be. Reading that draft and Eddie's comments another four times, Maeve found me cross-legged on my bed, blanket burrito wrapped around me, the only light coming from my screen.

I was past breakdown number two by then. And sent one or two texts to Henry.

Okay, ten messages to Henry. Maybe more. I'd lost count.

Maeve didn't flick on the light, thank God, but instead closed the door behind her and joined me on the bed. My cursor blinked on the page, and my unlocked phone displayed my chat with Henry. The text bubbles were all blue, and shamelessly, Maeve read them all.

"Before you say anything," I started, unable to care about the pathetic picture she'd walked in on, "they're all work related."

Maeve's hands shot up in surrender, dropping the phone back onto the bed.

She nudged my shoulder with hers. "I was only going to say he read them five minutes ago."

New development. The last time I checked, he hadn't even bothered opening them. When my eyes flicked to my best friend, they were probably bloodshot.

Really, I'd excused the unopened texts due to the time. It was past eleven by now, probably closer to midnight, and Henry still kept an early bedtime. *He's probably asleep*, I'd told myself.

Well, he wasn't.

Maeve gave me a pitying smile I knew I deserved. When she got up, she pulled me with her, and I landed on my feet with a loud groan.

"Have you eaten?" she asked unnecessarily. I'd been holed up in here since six, so take a wild guess.

My stomach answered for me. "But—" My gaze drifted back to the laptop, and Maeve had to literally push me out of my room, then shut the door behind us when we got into the hallway. The light was disorienting for a second.

"There's no point in staring at that draft a second longer, Paula," she said, maneuvering me down the stairs and delivering me onto the couch. She disappeared into the kitchen, emerging with a pizza box. "We got one for you. I don't know how good cold vegan cheese is, but here you go."

Pip climbed onto my lap and was about to curl up, already turning on the spot and kneading my legs, when she went stock-still.

Her tiny head shot in the direction of the entrance

just before the doorbell rang. It was so loud, she took it as her own personal sign to run up the stairs, paws clacking across the floor.

Maeve and I exchanged a look. I think we were both wondering if we were about to get brutally murdered.

"Did you forget to pay for the pizza?" I asked, unable to stop myself from taking a bite regardless.

"That was two hours ago. We obviously paid for the pizza," she whispered back before getting up. On her way to the door, she grabbed the empty vase as a potential weapon.

Henry used to make sure that vase held new bouquets once a week. So when we broke up—and the flowers stopped, obviously—we really did plan to just get them ourselves. It never happened, though.

Maeve raised it above her head, ready to swing. She grabbed the doorknob, twisted it, and forcefully pulled the door open.

"Oh." The vase lowered. So did the piece of pizza from my mouth. "Henry," she said, kind of in warning, as if I couldn't see him in our doorway. Mere feet away, hair disheveled, in oversized T-shirt and . . . sweatpants.

Domestic, I thought.

Henry's eyes followed the would-be weapon in Maeve's hand, a frown on his lips. "Is Paula—?" Which was when his gaze wandered into the house and connected with mine.

I wondered if he was thinking about our last encounter too. If he remembered he hadn't called when he said he would as well.

A scowl tugged on Maeve's lips when I got up. I felt too aware of every single one of my limbs as I crossed the room, like I was a step away from forgetting how to walk entirely. One look at my best friend and a reluctant nod from her later, she fled up the stairs to give us privacy.

Standing in front of Henry on the porch, I felt his warmth, smelled his minty toothpaste.

"Hi," I said so quietly that I might as well have whispered the word.

The way his lips pulled up and the worried frown on his face vanished reminded me of our last encounter.

I couldn't think of anything but him and his groans and the way he would've had me right then and there if we hadn't been interrupted. The way we could've picked up where we'd left off if he'd just—

"You didn't call." I tried to sound unbothered, cool and calm. I couldn't tell whether I'd succeeded.

Something in his expression twitched. Like the fact that instead of being asleep in his bed, midnight found him ten seconds away from an argument with his ex-girlfriend.

"I figured—" But he cut himself off, shook his head. His shoulders sagged. "I honestly don't know *what* I figured. I thought you might not want me to call. After we agreed this shouldn't happen. And then it did, twice." His brows pulled together like he had to physically restrain himself from rambling on. "I thought you might be regretting it."

"You've never been one to question your actions. Or lack thereof."

He took a step toward me, hesitant and slow. "That's

never the case when it comes to you. You make me nervous, remember?"

I swallowed. "Right now?"

I felt the door against my back and watched him take another step toward me. So close, my neck craned up to keep our eyes connected. "Yes," he said, barely breathing the word. "Very much so."

My lips twitched just once. "Why are you here, Henry?"

"You texted."

"And you didn't reply," I reminded him.

"Because I was on my way to you."

His words hung between us, and I tried desperately to grasp for a response that kept my cool mask of nonchalance in place. But I was a very chalant girl, and I couldn't help the soft smile on my lips when I asked again, "Why?"

The porch light above us flickered, and it seemed like Henry had just remembered his own reasons. His eyes darted across my face, noticing the redness in my eyes and the stress-induced circles under them.

He frowned. "You seemed about two minutes away from a breakdown."

"Oh." *Well* . . . "You're about two breakdowns too late for that."

He considered me for a long moment, and I could tell he was trying to find a way to fix whatever was wrong. Even if he didn't have details, and even if he hadn't yet come to terms with the fact that he couldn't fix everything—that there were things outside of his control.

"Fuck it," he muttered to himself before giving it a try anyway.

When Henry threw me across his shoulder, I yelped. Loudly. Then held on to his torso, upside down, like my life depended on it. Clutching and grasping until he opened a car door and slid me into the passenger seat.

"Wait here?"

And before I could respond, he kissed me. Again and again until I followed his lips when he tried to pull away. "I'll be right back. Don't move," he pleaded as if I might really disappear if he blinked one too many times. He waited for my nod, then closed my door, jogged back to the house, and vanished inside.

My body slumped into the black seat the second he was out of sight.

It was too easy with him. Forgiving and forgetting and letting him carry me off into the night like nothing had ever happened between us. I tried to remind myself to be cautious, to remember who he was and what he had been.

Ex-boyfriend.

Henry didn't give me enough time for the reminder to settle. Five minutes later, he was back with my phone and laptop balanced on top of the pizza box in one hand and one of Maeve's light-pink duffel bags in the other.

I wouldn't have known where to look for mine if he'd asked. He put the bag into the trunk without a word of explanation, then jumped behind the wheel.

Henry placed the electronics on the backseat and gave

me a kiss, put the box in my lap, and gave me a kiss. Then when he turned the key in the ignition, as if he couldn't help himself, he leaned across the console to give me another kiss.

"Where are we going?" I asked after a few minutes.

Henry's eyes shifted from the road for a fraction of a second to look at me, but the lack of a response was not deliberate. His brows pulled together. He scowled. "I don't know."

The words lingered.

"You don't . . . know?"

He seemed as surprised by the statement as I was. A little helpless too. In all the time I'd known the man beside me, not once had he . . . not known something. He always had a plan. And a backup plan for the plan. Sometimes another one just in case *that* failed too. And yet he'd shown up at my place unannounced to drive off into I-don't-knows.

"I came over because you seemed stressed. In the texts," he backtracked. "And then you were there, and you *looked* stressed too. So I said—" His brow furrowed.

"Fuck it," I offered, like he might've forgotten what had pushed him to literally carry me off into the night.

"Yes." His eyes jumped to mine. "Fuck it."

Fuck it, like his busy schedule hadn't always caused problems in our relationship. As if the fact that he couldn't be spontaneous, couldn't do things without planning them thoroughly and a month in advance hadn't been the fuel in . . . many of our fights.

I've been getting better at prioritizing.

I didn't ask for specifics. Just enjoyed his company, the music from the speakers, the *whoosh* when we passed other cars, and the pizza I devoured. I think I might've fallen asleep the moment I swallowed the last bite.

CHAPTER 33

Now

Something was different when I woke up. The music had switched to lazy, rhythmic beats instead of catchy lyrics, the pizza box was in the backseat, and Henry's hand rested on my leg. His fingers drew absent-minded circles on my thigh, dipping between them because he'd made the circle too big. Or maybe his hand was just too large to draw a small circle?

I blinked sleep away, watching him nod along to the music, his eyes on the road, which had turned from gray highway into a small street lined with beautifully cared-for front yards, white picket fences, and fancy houses. I stretched, sat up.

"You do have a destination in mind at this point, right?" I yawned, a little surprised we were still on the road at all. The clock of his car showed something past three in the morning.

His hand gave a small squeeze, but he kept his attention on the street. "Ah, she's awake," he said. "I do."

He seemed proud of the fact, like the lack of plan and control earlier had only made him think of one harder and faster now. "And you woke up just in time to see it in all its glory."

He turned into a long, winding driveway. "Oh." I searched for any kind of navigational system that would confirm Henry had taken a wrong turn, but he must've been driving by memory. "There's a house in our way," I said like an idiot, brain still half asleep.

It was so dark I couldn't make out the details of it. Only that it was large and beautifully ornamented. Columns holding a rounded balcony up above what should be the entrance. Stairs led to it from two sides, and flower beds were in the middle. It seemed . . . familiar for some reason.

Henry snorted at my assessment and shut off the engine. Silence grew between us until he said, "It's only been a few months since you were here, Paula."

And it clicked. *New Year's Eve.*

I had been here before—considerably drunker and with Maeve, Laila, and Riley in tow. The latter had been so excited about the invitation, she drove all the way from Hall Beck University to the location the Pressleys had rented in the Hamptons.

But it still didn't explain why we were here now. "You didn't actually rent out a house for us to stay in, did you?" I asked because it was the only plausible explanation for why we'd stopped in front of it in the middle of the night.

"Rented? It's mine."

My head snapped in his direction. Then back to the most gorgeous house I'd ever been in. With the rose bushes to the side of the property, the flowers in the big pots making it feel almost cozy, merging nature with the delicate work of humans.

"What?"

I knew Henry was rich. Everyone did, and he'd never been modest about it. But *this*. A house like *that*.

I remembered the large stairway in the entrance hall, leading to the first floor from two sides. I remembered the expensive floors and beautiful furniture. On New Year's Eve, there'd been an actual *bar*.

"My parents' summer house when we were young. They sold it just before—" He skipped the next part, but I knew. "It was supposed to be torn down last year, so what's left of my family bought it back. Started thinking about it almost exactly a year ago now, actually. I could barely focus on anything else back then." And like the sentimental tone had never existed at all, he added, "But I made it."

Exactly a year ago. Right before we'd broken up, then.

I realized how much I must've missed in the year we hadn't been together. He'd bought a house. He'd made up with his sister. He'd signed contracts and met people I'd never hear about.

I shook my head at the absurdity of my day. Four hours ago, I'd been close to breakdown number three, having passed on the idea of sleep to edit a draft that wouldn't have gotten anywhere tonight. Since then, I'd eaten, slept, and hadn't thought about the profile once, even though I'd spent the past few hours with my central subject.

Henry shrugged, unbuckling his seat belt to turn my way. "I come here sometimes when it all gets a little too much. When I need some peace and quiet to hear myself think again." His eyes drifted to the house. "Turns out I needed that a lot in the past few months."

I didn't know how he managed to word what I'd needed so perfectly. I'd always thought we were so different from each other, our struggles so wildly opposite that we could never relate on that level, and yet.

Dios mío, I remembered why I'd fallen for him. The way he understood me, looked at me like he could see right through me, read every single wish from my lips.

"Henry?" I asked, need barely disguised. When his gaze met mine, I thought that man would give me the entire world if I just asked for it. "Are you going to kiss me again?"

Three hours ago, there'd been no asking involved. No anticipation or curiosity about whether he would. Just his lips on mine like it was second nature. But watching his eyes widen, mouth opening and closing when he decided against whatever he'd wanted to say, I was glad I'd asked now.

Henry huffed, reaching across the console to unbuckle my seat belt. His hand brushed my hip, across the black leggings I wore, and although it was really just a sliver of a touch, my breath caught in my throat.

"Do you want me to?"

His hand slipped to my waist, the simplest of touches guiding me onto his lap.

Slipping into old patterns was so easy with him. When we were together like this, alone and without disruptions, it felt like nothing at all had changed between us.

One leg on either side of him, I nodded faintly. "While we're here—" I whispered, then cut myself off when I wasn't quite sure what I'd been about to say. "Just for this weekend, we can pretend nothing's changed. Right? Not think about being reasonable and just—" I took a deep breath. "Just be."

Henry traced a hand down the small of my back, watching me squirm beneath his touch and sigh at the contact. "Anything, Paula. Whatever you want."

When his fingers made their way back to my face, trailing across my neck in a way that made me arch into his touch, the smartwatch on his wrist vibrated against my skin.

I didn't want to look away, but the buzz drew my eyes to it anyway. On the screen, a notification read, "Looks like your heart rate is up! Record this workout?"

I was unable to keep a smile off my lips. "Is your heart beating fast?" I asked tauntingly, because I didn't know what else to say, and the thought was objectively sweet.

His eyes narrowed. In response, he took my hand, pressed it to his chest, and kissed me. I swear his heart skipped a beat when we did. I know mine did. "I told you," he said between breaths. "You make me nervous."

Henry had kissed me a lot in the past few days. Short and sweet, messy and longing. But never like this—slow and passionate. I savored every sweep of his tongue, both craving more and holding back.

His hands explored my curves like he was seeing—*feeling*—them for the first time. His lips did the same. From my neck to chest to shoulders, he kissed every exposed inch, took what he could get, and when that wasn't enough, needily tugged on my sweater, let his hands slip underneath.

"Fuck," he groaned against my lips the first time his fingertips grazed my bare skin. His hand slipped up my torso until he realized I wasn't wearing a bra, then groaned again.

The sound traveled right between my thighs. With his fingers carefully, delicately playing with my nipples, his head buried in the crook of my neck, and his hard cock against me, I couldn't take it.

My moan rang through the car. Heat and lust and a million other things played in the air between us, drove me to roll my hips against him, and made him finally snap.

He matched my sound, just darker and rougher, and willing to do something about what it insinuated.

"Hold on," he said. We were out of the car so quickly, I didn't even get out of his lap. He'd just collected me in his arms and got out.

My legs wrapped around him instinctively, and I couldn't help that my lips were back on his before we'd even made it to the staircase. He managed his way up, drawing away from my face only to see where he was going.

"I don't want to let go of you." And the thought seemed to trouble him deeply. "But the keys are in the potted plant behind you." I jumped off him, only to get us behind that door quicker.

Henry moved purposefully, grabbing the key and unlocking the massive hardwood door, and we were right back at it before it even closed behind us.

My sweater landed on the marbled floor, and he pushed me against the door before lifting me up. I was back in his arms, my legs wrapped around his waist the way they used to, and his tongue playing with my nipples.

I didn't have enough time to look around when he moved us from the foyer into the living room. I only cared about Henry, who gently set me down on . . . something. I pulled him down with me, and the couch beneath us was luck.

I wanted him so badly, I might've let him take me on the marble too.

Eyes roaming up my body, down and back up again, he might've been praying when he said, "Paula." The sound guttural, raw. "God, you're so beautiful like this."

And I wondered if he meant out of breath, needy, desperate, and wet. Because *that's* what I was.

"Ready and waiting." His finger trailed from my collar bones over my breasts, all the way down my torso, lingering by my hips before he slowly pushed my leggings and panties down my body. "Naked and blushing." Which is when his fingers brushed back up the inside of my thighs. Stopped right where I wanted him. "Needy and wet."

A whine parted my lips, and it all but confirmed his words. "Henry," I moaned . . . groaned? I wasn't sure how to differentiate between pleasure and frustration anymore. They'd merged into one, entangling further with every sweet nothing whispered into the darkness. "Fuck me." I blushed before I'd even said the words. "Please?"

His eyes flew up to mine, and the look lingered.

Something else between us snapped, and we were back in our rhythm of unpredictable predictability, where Henry pulled his shirt over his head and I fussed with his sweatpants, my hands trembling with need.

Until finally, *finally*, I pushed the gray fabric down his legs, and I saw that he still wore the same kind of boxer briefs, and I didn't know whether to smile because he was still *My Henry* or beg him to hurry up so I could feel him again.

A year was a long time.

But the anticipation in my chest was swamped by a wave of dread. "Do you have a condom?"

He paused, deflated. Our panting filled the otherwise quiet house. "In the car," he winced. "Maybe upstairs."

But upstairs was far, the car even farther. When I looked back at him, chest heaving above mine, eyes wide, pupils blown out as he searched my eyes, I thought I might not be able to wait for him to get dressed, run around, and then come back. Even thinking about it physically hurt.

He seemed to share the sentiment because he desperately threw in, "I haven't been with anyone else. Since you. If that helps."

"What?" I wanted to believe that, obviously. But it didn't seem plausible. Henry hadn't exactly been a prude when we'd met, and he certainly wouldn't have taken up celibacy once we'd broken up. Right?

"I couldn't—I mean." He shook his head. "I *could* have. But they just weren't . . . you." Our eyes connected. "And that's what I wanted—who I wanted. You."

I kissed him again. "If we don't get upstairs in the next twenty seconds—" I began, and before I'd even finished the sentence, I was back in Henry's arms, my legs wrapped around him.

I could feel him straining against his boxers. Every step he climbed made him push against my bare skin, groaning into my mouth or neck, and by the time we made it to his room, he seemed as needy as I'd been.

At least we'd leveled the playing field.

Once more, Henry lowered me. This time, it was onto a perfectly made bed, almost as comfortable as the one in New York had been. He lost his boxers somewhere between getting that condom out of the nightstand and joining me between the sheets.

Hovering on top of me, his hand slipped between my legs, and he touched me exactly the way I'd shown him I liked.

"I dreamed of this," he said. I could feel him hard against me again, his tip glistening. "For months, Paula." He slipped a finger inside, just to feel me for a second, and my moan was strangled—like a broken whine.

"In New York." He lined himself up, trailed a string of kisses from my neck to my breasts, then sat up. His eyes never left mine when he ripped the packaging open, and my heart dropped into the pit of my stomach when he rolled the condom over himself. "Wearing that jersey. My name on your back, and you were so close. Right there." He looked up at me. "The fact that I couldn't do anything about it was killing me."

My breath caught in my throat, his tip resting against my entrance. I felt him twitch, felt the groan bubbling in his throat.

"Then do something about it now."

And he did.

When Henry pushed inside me, I didn't know whether to focus on the euphoria of *finally* or the way he couldn't seem to keep himself upright or that unapologetic moan by my ear. If I should tell him to go faster or slower—because I wasn't sure if I wanted to savor every moment of this round or get to the next. If I only wanted him this way for the rest of my life or in a thousand other positions tonight.

I settled for not saying or thinking anything at all. Just flowing with the rhythm of his hips against mine and the feeling of him filling me so perfectly, snugly, that knot in my stomach tightened. Within a few minutes, I was ready to come apart for him.

He muttered a "Thank God" because with the pace he was holding, he couldn't be very far from release himself. His hand slipped to my clit again.

And I lost myself in the bliss of a perfect orgasm while he twitched inside of me, groaning and cursing and praying.

CHAPTER 34

Now

I should regret last night. Technically, I shouldn't still think about the things Henry had done to me and wish he would do them again.

And it should've been a big deal—sleeping with your ex-boyfriend, then waking up in the same bed.

It was!

I should be nervous and confused and, honestly, a little frantic. I was not. My head was clear and my mind sharp; maybe a good lay was all I'd needed for the fog around my brain to lift.

Because suddenly I knew what Eddie meant when he'd called the profile okay.

I was still in Henry's arms, cuddled against his chest, when it dawned on me. As I replayed my editor's feedback for the thousandth time, I realized what had been missing.

There were things I hadn't asked Henry much about

because I knew he wouldn't want to talk about them. His parents, for one. Then there were all the things I hadn't brought up because I was his ex-girlfriend, and asking about other girls, parties, and whatever else successful college athletes might be up to in their free time would've felt uncomfortable for him. Probably even more so for me.

But another boundary between us had been crossed last night, and it brought us closer to how things used to be—back when I would ask him whatever I wanted to ask without worrying about his reaction.

When my phone was recording our conversations, I wasn't just Henry's ex-girlfriend. I was Paula Castillo, unjustifiably shunned college journalist.

Henry stirred behind me, almost like he could tell I'd been thinking about him. "Paula, are you up?" he mumbled into my hair, arms slung around my body to pull me closer.

His voice, raspy from sleep and right by my ear, did things to me. All the clarity I'd gained in the past five minutes, about the profile and my writing, threatened to disappear with the way he'd said my name.

But wasn't that exactly what had gone wrong last year? When I'd prioritized Henry over and over until it came back to bite me in the ass? When I hadn't quadruple-checked my source—his friend—because Henry had been tired, and I'd been tired, and I'd never been great at resisting him.

"Can we just stay like this forever, Paula?" he asked.

"You don't have any other plans for today?"

Henry thought for a moment, then shook his head. An unprecedented answer.

Because Henry Parker Pressley always had a plan. Followed by a plan for the plan.

I smiled at the disruption of normalcy for a second. "I do," I said and laughed at the way his eyes widened mockingly when I turned toward him. "For both of us."

"Who would've thought," he said, then kissed my bare shoulder to hide his smile. "What do you have in store for us, Paula Castillo?"

"You still owe me answers to three deeply personal questions." From when he'd forced me onto the treadmill. "And there might've been a few I skipped before."

*

"If this is what it's like to be a full-time journalist . . ." I said with a contented sigh, leaning into the lounge chair and squeezing my eyes shut against the first warm rays of the year. Despite our rushed departure last night, he had packed me a bikini. Red and tiny. "Sign me up."

Henry, arms propped on the edge of the pool, snickered. "It's not." His clarification popped my momentary bubble of bliss. "Only when you're interviewing people as popular, rich, and nice to be around as I am."

"And humble," I added. "All four? That's rare."

Water sloshed against the edge of the pool. "Well, not everyone can be Henry Pressley."

Muscles in his arms strained as he heaved himself out of the water, revealing everything else he had to offer. The sun reflected in the drops clinging to every crevice, shifting as the light dancing across his body drew my attention to all kinds of places. Collarbones, forearms, fingers. My stomach tightened. He was dripping wet in nothing but a pair of swim shorts, and I—

Water. Cold and wet.

I squealed as I shoved Henry off me, but he continued shaking his wet hair in my direction, laughing loudly before planting himself on my lounge chair.

With a glare, I watched him grab my phone, unlock it (I should've probably changed my passcode after we'd broken up), and press record when he'd found his way into the voice memo app.

He placed the device on the small table between the loungers. "This is a professional interview, Miss Castillo," he said as if he wasn't wrapping his wet arms around me and pressing his wet torso and chest against my body, which had previously been warm and dry from the sun.

I groaned, unable to do or say anything else given the recording capturing everything. I grew accustomed to his cold, wet limbs quickly, though, and he seemed to love how warm mine were, so he scooped me up in his arms, lay back on the chair, and somehow positioned us so that we both fit perfectly. My head was on his chest, one leg draped over his lower body, and my arm was behind his neck.

"So, you do this often?" I asked, mindful of the recording. "Bring girls to Long Island and charm them with your . . . money?" I wish I could've delivered the question as stoically as I'd planned.

"I don't need money to charm girls." He paused, pretending to think. "Do I?" I felt him tilt his head, glancing at me. Meanwhile, I was so comfortable on his chest, I never wanted to leave.

"Depends on the girl," I conceded. He hadn't needed much to charm me. With words and a smile, I'd found myself in the same situation years ago. I remembered how it felt then, lying in his arms, moments away from falling for him. Maybe I'd never really gotten up.

That same pesky voice in my head chimed in again. I called her *Reason*, and she shouted the words in my head over and over again, reminding me that not much had changed between us.

Henry was still a busy man, and he'd be busier so very soon. His priority was still his career, and I was trying to focus on mine too. He'd broken up with me for a reason.

Despite all of that, I was still in his arms. Laughing and blushing and sighing contently. I shouldn't be, but detaching myself from him required willpower I knew I didn't have. Henry took up so much space in my life; he had his own gravitational pull. And I continued orbiting around him, unable to stop even if I'd wanted to.

Figuring out what was happening between us had to wait until I got what I'd needed for this profile.

"What about *this* girl?" He smoothed over my curls absentmindedly, and it brought me back.

When I looked up at him from my corner of his chest, the light reflecting in his green eyes made them sparkle. Like, *actually.*

"She . . ." I trailed off, eyes flicking to my recording phone. "Does not reveal her secrets that easily."

Henry rolled his eyes.

"*And*," I added, "this interview is not about her. So tell me, Mr. Pressley." His nose crinkled, but he did not laugh. I could tell he wanted to. "No parties? Alcohol flowing from fountains?" There had been on New Year's Eve. "Girls?"

Which had been one of those topics I'd steered clear of in our first round of interviews. But to write a good profile, I couldn't avoid questions I might not want answers to.

So, parties and girls.

"Well." He thought of his answer, affirmed it in his head with a nod. "We celebrated New Year's Eve here," he said. "Once. Before that, we'd always done it at one of the New York apartments. My sister and I always throw this bash on the 31st. So, that's a party," he assessed. "As for the girls . . ." I only noticed his gaze on me when I looked up at the lingering silence.

"Yes?"

He cleared his throat, eyes trailing off. "My parents met at college."

I nearly choked at the mention of them. I'd asked a few general questions about family, giving him room to talk about them if he wanted.

This was the first time he brought them up. On the record. I tried not to reveal how big of a deal it was to me, how much I appreciated his opening up for the sake of my career. I stayed very still on his chest and listened.

"I always thought I might get that. You know? High

school sweethearts seemed overrated. I didn't even know *myself* at sixteen, never mind getting to know someone else on a level like that." He waved the thought away, moved on. "I thought . . . well, I thought if there's one thing I wanted to do like they had, it wouldn't be soccer or business or whatever else they're known for." He let loose a breath. "I'd want it to be love. It sounds ridiculous, I know. But my parents were great at love. By far, they were best at that."

"And?" I pushed.

"And . . . I thought I had it. For a moment there, I really thought I did." I could feel his eyes on me, burning into my profile. I didn't return his look. "Then I realized that no matter how much I told myself I wasn't like them—that money and fame and career weren't more important than the rest of my life—when it came down to it, we were identical. Prioritized the wrong things, hurt the people we shouldn't have. Left them behind to fend for themselves."

My breath was shallow at the raw honesty in his voice, and when I sat up to look at him, I saw things in his gaze I never thought I would. Hurt, heartache, grief. They felt like a punch to the gut and made me hate what I had to do next.

I squeezed his hand tightly to let him know I was here, then squeezed it once more to let him know I'd stay too. If he would have me.

I'm sorry, I thought at him. As hard as I could. And I hoped he could read the apology on my face.

"You say your parents were great at love?" I repeated. I almost sighed in relief when he didn't seem offended by my question. When he just nodded like he'd been wondering when I'd ask about them. When I'd finally double down. "How so?"

And Henry was right. They seemed great at love.

Theirs was a handwritten-notes-without-occasion kind of love. Letters when they'd been apart for longer and dancing in dimly lit kitchens. ("Badly," Henry had emphasized with a smile on his lips.)

Flowers. Date nights. Trips.

"Their last trip," Henry started, and something in his face shifted. Mirroring his change in mood, clouds had drifted in, covering the sun. I'd shrugged into Henry's loose sweater halfway through the interview. He'd put on sweatpants. "Felix planned it as a very belated anniversary thing. The twentieth, I think. And he thought it'd be a nice addition to leave the kids at home, give Mom a break. Not that Athalia and I were very demanding children. We were happy with nanny-hopping. By the time we were fifteen, we'd gotten used to their absence more than their presence."

He got up, and for a second, I was scared that I had breathed the wrong way or stirred when I shouldn't have, and that signaled the end of his vulnerability.

But Henry held out his hand for me to take, with a smile so sad it almost broke me. "Let's get inside," he said, nodding up at the ever-graying sky. I followed, phone in hand and still recording.

"And you blame him?" I cleared my throat when the words came out as more of a croak. We made our way across the garden, back to the house. "Felix, I mean. Is that why you . . ." *Hate* seemed like a strong word for a deceased parent. "Aren't very fond of him?"

Henry gestured for me to step back into the living room, then followed and closed the French doors behind us. He shrugged. "I guess. *Yes*," he corrected. "Partly? That's what my therapist alludes to, anyway."

His pained expression was enough to make me grant him a break. To change the topic, go off the record and let him *be* for a while. At least until tonight, when I'd go for round two.

"Stephanie," I remembered his therapist's name out loud. "I should've gotten her on the record about you, then."

"I'm pretty sure that's a crime." And he seemed happier to talk about his therapist than the reason he had one in the first place.

"Tomato, tomahto," I said, waving him off. I was relieved to see his mood shifting, and making sure he could see, I ended the forty-two-minute-long recording.

Henry visibly relaxed, and I threw my phone onto the couch, right next to his. Which buzzed with a notification at the exact same time.

I didn't want to look.

Really.

My eyes shot to his face, actively suppressing the urge. Half because I didn't want to intrude on his privacy and half because I was kind of scared of what I might see if I did. He'd said there hadn't been other girls, sure. But that didn't mean he wasn't kissing them or texting them. It only meant he hadn't slept with any of them. Yet?

I lasted about three seconds, which was when my self-restraint ran out. A notification pinged at the bottom of his lock screen. I could make out the green icon, the flame emoji in the message, and—

"Don't read that!" he spluttered, basically jumping for his phone on the white couch.

Too late, though.

Duolingo
> Hey, Henry! Losing that 360-day streak would be a bummer. Get some Spanish in now!

Henry's ears had turned pink by the time he slipped his phone into the pocket of his sweats. "I'm gonna shower. The chlorine—" He tried to justify his quick exit, already making for the staircase he'd carried me up last night.

"Hey." My hand caught his just before he'd successfully fled the scene, and I could tell he was mortified when he turned back to me. "¿Has estado aprendiendo español?" I asked slowly. His eyes snapped to mine like he hadn't expected to understand my question.

Have you been learning Spanish?

"Un poquito." The pink spread from his neck and ears into his cheeks now, and he cringed at his own words, the pronunciation of them, and whatever else he was clearly overthinking. I wasn't paying attention to any of that.

"¿Para mí?"

"You." He nodded in affirmation. "And your parents." Henry thought for a moment, drew his wrist out of my grip to interlace our fingers. "And my ego, a little bit."

I recognized the fuzzy feeling in my stomach, the tender pull on my heart, and the way I couldn't stop smiling. I was just so, so happy.

Henry didn't share the sentiment, likely because he still had a terrible accent when he spoke, and he was doing something he hadn't been perfect at right away. But he was still trying after 360 days.

I drew him to me and walked us backward until I was leaning against the wall right by the bottom of the staircase. The smile on my lips was wide enough to coax one onto his too.

"Three hundred days?" I asked again, disbelief mixing with awe.

Henry gasped playfully. "And sixty!" he corrected. "How dare you bury my achievements like that!" He laughed, then kissed me.

Almost a year. And for ten months of that time, we hadn't even looked at each other, let alone spoken a word.

CHAPTER 35

Then

June: Ten months ago

I could feel Lacy's eyes on me. From the desk beside mine, her annoyance peaked whenever she heard another "Congratulations!" directed at me.

"All Brains, No Polish: The Burden of Ivy Leagues" had been a big deal for the *Hall Beck Post*. It inspired other writers to hope they might receive an assigned article from the board and editors to hope their work might finally be appreciated by their own school.

I handed in the final draft two weeks ago. After a few more minor corrections, it went to print in this week's issue.

An editor stopped by my desk to pat me on the back with celebratory words. When he was gone, Lacy's chair spun in my direction.

"Is there anything you can't do?" she asked with an unexpected smile on her lips. Fake, I figured.

Lacy and I had always been cordial with each other, but we both knew we weren't . . . fans. She had a great style and a great writing voice, which meant she always managed to get exactly those articles that I'd wanted. I'd been a little surprised not to see this one on her desk.

She probably had been too.

Lacy tilted her head and brushed her blond hair to one side. "*Seriously.* I mean, *The New York Times*, now this?" Still, her words seemed like praise, and I failed to spot the usual bitterness in her tone.

"Thank you" was all I managed to say, hoping to keep the conversation civil and our fake smiles in place until we turned back to our respective screens, ignoring each other like we had for most of the past three years. But—

"How was it?" Lacy asked. Her smile hadn't faltered; if anything, it had turned sly and knowing. Of what, I wasn't sure. "I can imagine it was hard to find someone willing to snitch on something they pay so much money for every year. Would they still be able to justify spending it once they realize it's *all brains and no polish*?" she pondered the question.

I had tried not to, and I hated that she knew exactly what I'd been struggling with—what I'd only overcome because I'd had Henry's help.

I took a deep breath. "Apparently. They said what we'd hoped they would. It all worked out in the end, didn't it?"

Lacy's dark brows lifted in sync with her smile. Like I'd finally taken the bait. And that I still wasn't sure of what killed me. "Yes," she agreed, nodding smugly. "They said what we wanted them to."

Another voice saved me from scrambling for a reply. "Paula?"

My gaze snapped to Eddie in the door right behind my screen. My smile turned genuine, but he didn't seem happy enough to congratulate me too. He forced a polite half smile and said, "Let's talk for a second."

Gesturing toward the hall, I followed him out. I could feel Lacy's blue eyes on me until I closed the door behind me.

Edward Smith went quiet as we walked to his office, past the rec room, media labs, and stray classrooms. He beckoned me inside, and I started worrying when he almost closed his door.

He sat behind his desk and gestured for me to take a seat opposite him. We just looked at each other, and the moment seemed to stretch endlessly, until he folded his hands on the table between us and his jaw twitched. His eyes narrowed.

I finally asked, "I'm sorry, what's—?" But he cut me off.

"You got sources on the record, right?" The question shot out of him like a bullet out of a loaded gun. "You quoted accurately, Paula?"

My brows pulled together. I didn't know why my heartbeat picked up. "Of course." My head shook in confusion. "Of course. Why—?"

"Someone complained. That you misquoted them. That they never said what you wrote. That—"

The ringing in my ears was louder than Eddie. My face fell. Something inside of me shattered.

What?

What?

What?

"Paula? Do you understand? I'm not talking about some whining after realizing what they did and regretting it. They didn't beg me to scratch their stuff out of the article. They went straight to the SPJ ethics committee and filed an anonymous complaint."

I knew it was Mark before Eddie told me who had accused me of lying and bad-faith journalism. Mark was the one who had left a permanent stain on my record.

I knew it was him because I'd had a feeling and ignored it. Because I'd told myself it would be fine a million times instead of figuring out where that feeling had come from.

"I'm looking into it, but now I'm in trouble with the school board because they're in trouble with Harvard." Eddie's hands ran across his face in frustration. "Paula, I don't know how I could let you write again."

"I thought they loved it," I croaked.

"They did. Until they found out you lied—"

"But I didn't!"

The timing was terrible. A week before, my laptop crashed, and I lost a bunch of audio files I hadn't backed up elsewhere. But even after what I'd deemed an accurate and damage-reducing account of the interview, Eddie's features didn't seem less distressed. He didn't seem more open to letting me stay at the paper. He seemed like he had made up his mind or, at the very least, like he couldn't change anything about the outcome.

"Paula," he sighed. "My hands are tied. Unless the source withdraws the complaint, or it's been without a doubt disproven . . . let this die down. Focus on your classes and assignments, forget about writing for the *Post* until they're not going to have my head for seeing your name in a paper again."

Which, apparently, would be 264 days later. When he'd decided to give me Henry's profile.

CHAPTER 36

Now

Maybe a change of scenery had been what I'd needed. Looking out into Henry's rose garden certainly made the whole process easier.

With all the new material from yesterday's final interviews, I'd reimagined the entire article. Three hours into the day, and I was looking at a completely different story.

I sighed. "I can feel you staring at me." I reluctantly looked away from the screen. Henry sat on the opposite couch. Instead of scrolling through his phone, his full attention was on me.

"Good." A smirk pulled at the corner of his lips. "My plan worked. Now you can come here." His arms spread, inviting me into his lap. I wished I could, but—

"I can't." I nodded to the screen. "I need to finish this."

We'd been in a similar situation before. Almost exactly a year ago. Where I had work to do and he'd asked me not to do it. Begged and pleaded until I'd given in. When I'd been trying to figure out what felt off about Mark, Henry had told me I was being paranoid.

And I had been. Even if I'd scoured the internet for another three hours that night, I wouldn't have found the thing that would cost me my reputation two weeks down the line. I still hadn't almost a year later.

But I'd never stopped blaming myself for closing that laptop regardless.

After our breakup, I blamed Henry too. I wasn't sure if it was fair, but it made me feel better, and Maeve said that's all that mattered.

A year later, my first project after the debacle, and I was once again working, writing, and researching in the presence of Henry, who could so easily distract me.

I promised myself a million times over that I wouldn't let it be the same again. I chanted the words in my head like my own personal mantra whenever I got a whiff of his cologne or he made a sound from across the room.

Not again. Not again. Not again.

Turned out that's harder when everything around you screamed Henry Pressley. When I could hear him make a call in the other room, move around the house, or tell me from the other end of it, *"I found some vegan places that deliver! What do you want, sushi or burgers?"*

Sushi, obviously.

But I'd powered through and made it to the end of that second draft by early evening. I'd be lying if I said getting back to Henry hadn't been one of the motivators making me work faster.

Lying in bed in his arms afterward felt like a reward of some kind.

"You know," he said, his fingers trailing along my back, "this isn't very *friends* of us."

The way my chest pressed against his abs. The way he held me. The way not even a piece of paper could fit between us.

Yeah, I thought. *It isn't really* friends *of us at all.*

I sighed, shrugged. "In the good way or the bad way?"

Henry shifted underneath me. "I can't imagine a world in which this would be bad." I could feel him contemplating. "What makes you say that?"

"Nothing." Many things, actually. "Just . . ." I hesitated.

To address the elephant in the room or not?

"Back then." I began. "What we had wasn't so bad. Was it?"

Henry sat up now, leaned against the headboard, and drew me up with him. His green eyes searched mine for just a trace of humor, but I couldn't find it in me to pretend for him.

"You're saying that like I'd think it was," he figured. I grabbed the first shirt I saw from the foot of the bed, and he followed my movements when I slid into it. It happened to be his. "Why?"

I couldn't believe he was asking me why I'd ever assume he thought our relationship had been bad. With a tone that almost seemed insulted by the insinuation.

"Maybe . . ." I couldn't help the flat delivery. "*Maybe* because you broke up with me."

I looked through the big windows that stretched from floor to ceiling, showcasing the entire garden with its pool and statues and roses. I scanned the desk and assessed our clothes scattered around the room. His sweatpants by the foot of the bed and my shirt in the doorway. I was looking anywhere but at him.

Henry laughed, the sound dry and devoid of humor. "If I remember correctly, you seemed just fine with that."

My head shot back in his direction. "You can't—" But I'd begun too loudly, too defensively. I tried again. "You can't seriously believe that."

"Why not?" he pressed. "A week later, Maeve brings me a cardboard box of my stuff, then demands one with yours. A month later, you've got my number blocked. And I don't hear from you again."

Because I had to! Because there was no way I could've seen you a week after we'd broken up. Because I'd been so tempted to call and text you, Maeve had to block your number for me.

I wanted to scream the words at him.

When I didn't, Henry added, "You never even asked. Why I did what I did." His tone grew stronger, fiercer, like we might actually get into a fight.

Between the white sheets, birds chirping, and the setting sun. With the trees ruffling in the breeze, on a beautiful spring evening, Henry and I were getting into a fight.

He should understand why I'd never asked, though.

The suggestion that I hadn't cared enough to want to know felt . . . rude more than anything else. Because he knew how much I cared. He knew I'd oriented my entire life around him, and I'd paid for that, in a way. I could hardly remember the night he broke up with me because the thought had been so painful. Even now, it still hurt.

We shouldn't do this.

"I know why you *did what you did*," I repeated his words. "I didn't need you to throw all your reasons back in my face. Are you kidding me? I didn't need to hear any of it!"

Henry shook his head. "I don't believe that."

"Oh my God. You're you, Henry!" The way he furrowed his brows only made it worse. Like he didn't get what *that* might have to do with it.

"You were exactly where you were meant to be, doing what you were supposed to do. I got in the way of that! Don't shake your head like that. I did! You didn't want to make time in your schedule. You didn't even want to *think* about making time! I was a distraction, so you cut me off like a useless limb. The way you do with everything else—"

His mouth opened, he wanted to say something, but I wasn't done. "You know the worst part? That I was actually happy for you, in a way. I hated you, but I was happy for you. You're doing what you're supposed to do!" I repeated. "You *know* what you're supposed to do. And you're lucky enough for it to be exactly the path you're supposed to take. On top of that, it's the one your parents wanted for you too. Literally the entire world wants you to do this, and I was so happy that at least you still got to do it. Without distractions."

"Right," he scoffed. He slipped out of bed so smoothly, I only noticed when he stood beside it, pulling on his pants. "It's what everyone else wants from me. Of course it is! But has anyone ever stopped to wonder if it's what *I* want? Just because Felix left a fucking legacy behind, because I happen to enjoy the one thing my father was known for, and because I happen to be really fucking good at it too, that's my life. Just decided for me! By papers and press—by anyone but me. My father's corpse has more control over the trajectory of my life than I do!"

He shook his head, ran a hand through his hair. "I've been trying to figure that out since the draft, and it almost made me lose everything I've worked for. If you hadn't been there, I'm not sure if I would've signed those contracts in New York—" He cocked his head sideways and snapped his mouth shut before, God forbid, something else came out of it that he hadn't planned for.

I think it was the first time Henry openly articulated how his dad's life and death impacted him. I wondered if he felt better when he stormed out of the room, got into the car, and drove off.

I groaned as my head fell into the pillows, then groaned louder when they smelled like him. *Fuck!*

Hadn't we been arguing about our breakup? Why *he'd* broken up with *me*?

What he'd said was true and tragic and explained the

ways of Henry Parker Pressley so perfectly. Explained why he thought he hated his dad and loved being in control.

But I wasn't in the mood to be understanding. I was mad. And I decided, without calling Maeve, texting our group chat, or doubting myself, that I was allowed to feel that way.

For the first time, I felt my emotions deeply enough not to question them.

CHAPTER 37

Then

June: Ten months ago

My world came to a halt for a second time the day of the article complaint. When there'd been exactly one person I'd wanted to talk to, and my boyfriend wasn't picking up the phone. My heart was still beating three times its usual speed as I rushed out of Eddie's office, leaving my bag by my desk and my jacket hanging over my chair when I raced down the stairs and out of the building.

I tried Henry a total of seven times and then finally gave up. He was clearly busy with something that took priority over my feelings. That was usually the case.

Soccer. School. Soccer again.

I'd shot him a text—or ten.

Ethics complaint. Mark. I'll never write again.

I wandered aimlessly across campus because I couldn't bear to face anyone. The thought of Laila seeing me like this—mascara streaking my face and cheeks that were a blotchy red—almost made me laugh, so going home was out of the question. The poor girl would have a heart attack. As I walked, I cycled between humiliation and rage, shame and fear before settling into numbness.

I eventually ended up at Henry's apartment. No one answered when I rang, and I couldn't find it in me to care about that either. It was like the life had been drained out of me.

Was this what it felt like to have your dreams destroyed? To have everything that had been just out of reach taken away completely?

I honestly wasn't sure how long I'd been sitting in front of the condo. Neighbors came and went. By the time the sun began to set, I was all out of pity tears.

"Paula?" Henry's voice rang through the haze of my mind. "Are you okay? What are you doing here?" He crouched in front of me before I could even attempt to get up. "I called you back a hundred times. They all went straight to voicemail."

My phone must've died somewhere between my tenth text and now. I wondered how awful I looked when I finally raised my head. Blinking, brow furrowing, I realized Henry didn't look much better.

Not like he'd cried ten rivers or questioned his entire future for the past five hours, but exhausted all the same. Shaken. Confused. Worried and unsure. At least one of those I could probably blame on my own state. The rest, though?

"Are you okay?" I asked, wiping at my eyes for the first time, hoping I might get some of the mascara under them. My gaze flickered across his disheveled hair, the worried frown, his hand curling around mine, knuckles . . . bruised? "What happened?"

"No big deal," he said. "Fell during practice and slid across the fake lawn." He mumbled his explanation and took me up to his apartment. His attention was on me, but he was clearly distracted by something else. I couldn't figure it out as we sat on his couch—his hands in my hair, gently pulling to ease some of the tension in my head—and I told him what had happened in more detail. His freshly bruised hand curled by his side at the first mention of Mark while the other continued massaging my scalp so softly you wouldn't guess he was angry. He listened, comforted me, and blamed himself for what happened. *I'm sorry. I shouldn't have introduced you. But you'll be fine, right?*

I hadn't really thought this mess was his fault, and I shook my head and told him that I wasn't sure if I *would* be fine.

Maybe that's why, twenty minutes later, he said, "We shouldn't do this."

He'd been gnawing on his bottom lip, a frown forming. He stood against the kitchen counter, hands in his hair. The whole thing was kind of a blur.

"What?"

Henry repeated his words, explained what he'd meant.

This isn't good for us. Distractions. A lot going on.

We should focus on our futures.

Which I'd always seen with him.

The more he spoke, the more distant it seemed. Like I was merely observing the situation without actually being a part of it. Completely checked out. Maybe that way, I figured, I'd wake up tomorrow able to convince myself I'd dreamed the whole thing.

I'd rub the sleep out of my eyes, get dressed, and tell Henry I'd had a nightmare. He'd kiss my forehead, call it ridiculous, and I'd believe him.

Apparently, it wasn't all that ridiculous, though.

His mouth continued to move, his tone soft and apologetic, his eyes watery. I think. I couldn't be sure, because, *again*, I'd checked out.

I was too tired to fight. Numb. Unfeeling. Not a trace of emotion in my voicc. I couldn't possibly have fought for another thing I cared about, only to lose. Not after doing the same with Eddie and failing at that too. So instead of trying to save it and potentially failing, I conserved the last bit of dignity I had by accepting that another constant in my life had just been ripped out from under me.

I refused Henry's offer to drive me home.

And my world came to a halt again, one last time, when I'd sent Maeve a brief explanatory text on my way home and—like she knew seeing them would tear me to pieces—by the time I'd arrived, she'd already ripped down the few pictures of Henry and me on our photo wall in the living room.

CHAPTER 38

Now

Henry hadn't come back. I'd fallen asleep way past midnight and woke up too early, unable to contain the worry settling in my stomach. I'd been tossing and turning all night.

You weren't supposed to drive on high emotions. But when I snuck onto the balcony, the sun had just risen, and Henry's SUV stood slap-bang in the middle of the driveway. I exhaled so loudly, it hushed the birds in a nearby tree.

"Scared I left you stranded in the middle of nowhere?"

My hand clutched at my chest. "*Jesus*," I gasped, startled by his voice. I cleared my throat. "Something like that." I didn't feel like mentioning I'd been scared for him more than anything.

He leaned against the doorframe, a cup of coffee in hand. Not black. "Now that would've been a great reason for a breakup," he said solemnly.

I tensed at the mention of our argument. Henry leisurely pushed off the wall, moved toward me. He didn't look at me as he placed his cup on the thick stone balustrade.

He sighed, and I stupidly said, "As great as yours must've been?"

On to round two, I thought.

His eyes stayed on the winding driveway and the trees that lined it, like ignoring me was the easiest thing in the world. But I knew he heard me.

"The things you mentioned last night," he began, "are not at all why I had to break up with you." He said it like he wished he hadn't.

I did too. And with a sense of dread, stomach plummeting, I realized it was going to be so much harder getting over him this time. Because he wasn't my boyfriend and I wasn't his girlfriend. I had no *right* to his heart, not a sliver of a claim. We were just Henry and Paula. Friends. Partners. *Exes.*

"You didn't have to—" I started, but Henry shook his head, gaze still on the driveway, morning sunlight on his skin.

"*I did,*" he stressed. "Even if you didn't like it, and I hated it. I had to."

I felt some of the anger from last night stir. "What is it, then?" Finally turned from the view to face him. "Why did you *have* to break my heart?"

"Paula—" he began, worry in his tone. My eyes were stinging, my vision was blurry, and a tear rolled down my cheek. I didn't care.

"*No.*" My head shook fiercely. "Go on. Look at me and say it. Tell me."

His throat worked, but no words came out. He just looked at me in silence. It drove me mad.

"Say something!" I demanded, loud voice wavering. "Because I deserve better? Because you're not good enough?" I mocked. "Surely you can come up with a better excuse—"

"God damn it, Paula!" His calm demeanor snapped, and he matched my tone. "Yes!" he roared. "That's exactly it. Congrats."

The cup, still sitting on the banister, had been forgotten when he reached for the stone. It fell to the ground with a loud, high-pitched *clink*, like it might've been porcelain. He only sighed, hand washing over his face.

"You have dreams. Aspirations. Goals and ambitions!" He said it like those were bad things, then clarified, "And I almost ruined that for you. I almost fucked up your entire future because I'm selfish." His voice *cracked*. "When you told me what happened with that article, I couldn't think of anything other than the fact that it was my fault. I'd blame myself for the rest of my life if you couldn't do what you wanted because *I* got in the way. Because I stood between you and your career. Don't you understand that?"

"Mark wasn't—"

I wanted to tell him that Mark hadn't *really* been his fault. Even though I'd been trying to make myself believe it for a year now, I knew it wasn't true. Henry couldn't have known what might come of the introduction. He'd only wanted to help me, even if it had backfired massively.

"It's not just about him," Henry cut me off. "It's about *everything.* You kept sacrificing over and over again. Don't you think I noticed how much you gave up just so we could see each other? I didn't want that for you, Paula. You do deserve better than that. You know that."

My eyes closed when I shook my head, huffing and puffing until I could get my next words out.

"You know," I said, sounding and feeling defeated, "when a man says you deserve better, he's usually right."

He rubbed his temple. "I know," he said, tone matching mine.

The silence that followed almost choked me. Neither the song of the birds nor the rays of sun on my skin could make me feel like I wasn't suffocating. Like that silence between us wouldn't swallow us whole. I managed to watch him carefully regardless. I saw how his brows twitched when he said "Fuck it" under his breath, only to dismiss the thought. Whatever thought.

"I just—" Hesitation again. His eyes flicked to mine, burning through me, eating me alive. "Jesus, Paula! I just can't do this."

"Do what?"

"I'm *trying* to let you go," he stressed. "I've *been* trying. Because you do deserve better." Frustrated, he pushed himself off the balustrade. "You deserve everything. Someone who has all the time in the world for you and doesn't have to schedule ten fucking minutes between practice and dinner to learn the language you grew up speaking. It's pathetic. Your cat doesn't even like me." He laughed dryly.

"Pip doesn't like any—"

His eyes slid back to me, and he straightened. "I just can't picture it," he confessed, the bite in his tone gone. "You with anyone else. I want to be the man you deserve, and I've been trying to figure out how for a while now."

"Henry," I breathed, nothing but a whisper coming from my lips. He stopped his pacing. Looked at me.

"Yeah?"

"I can't picture myself with anyone else either."

From the other side of the ornamented balcony, he looked at me for a long moment. His brows pinched, and his breath stuttered in his throat before he finally crossed the distance between us. Slow steps, heavy and echoing in my mind until he stopped so close, I had to look up to level our gaze.

His breath fanned against my nose, uneven. "That's not good," he whispered, tucking a curl behind my ear. His hand lingered, holding my chin tenderly. He was shaking. "That's really bad," he amended.

My eyes closed, and I felt him more intensely. Hovering above me, his knuckles brushing across my cheek like he couldn't help it. Pinewood and citrus lingered in the air, but more than that, it was the sweet note of coffee on his lips, the scent of the bodywash we'd both used yesterday. The bad ideas. Always those.

"Is it?" My eyes fluttered open. He didn't seem very sure anymore.

Henry only mumbled, "Mm-hmm." Paired it with a lazy nod. Came closer. "So bad," he said, "because it makes me want to be selfish again." He pressed his lips to the top of my head, taking a deep breath like it took him everything not to place them elsewhere. "It makes me want to take you," he said. "Have you in all the ways I can."

My heart rate tripled in my chest, an unsteady rhythm that could still be felt between my legs. Pulsing with need and desire and tragedy. *He could have me,* I thought. *In all the ways he'd wanted.*

"Is it—" My breath caught in my throat. "Is it still selfish when I want you to be?"

I did. I wanted him to be selfish enough to throw his reasons to hell.

"I guess it wouldn't be. No."

And it was sad—full of longing and anger—the way I kissed him. The way he held my face between his hands and pressed his body against mine like he was scared I might disappear if he didn't hold on tight enough.

He kissed me like he wanted to make up for the fact that he'd ever let me go.

"I don't know how—" He breathed into my skin, connected our lips again. "How was I able to walk away from this?" As he trailed a string of kisses along my neck, I wasn't quite sure how I'd survived a year without it. I arched my back against the balustrade with a barely audible moan.

It drove his hands under my—his?—shirt, which I'd fallen asleep in the night before. He stopped short of where I needed him most, froze against me completely as his fingers curled around my bare hip. "You're naked," he discovered.

"I thought you were gone."

He fell into motion again with a groan, let his fingers draw across my hip, over my stomach, between my thighs. Never touching me where I wanted him to. "So, you thought"—his grip tightened—"you'd walk around the house with nothing but my shirt on? And what? Kill me in the process?"

I was going to say that no, I just meant to check for his car, then jump back into bed. But he'd swiped his fingers between my wetness, and every thought was wiped from my brain.

"God," he hummed against me as my knees buckled, legs giving in. "This is what I do to you?"

In answer, I took him down to the terrace floor with me, not caring how cold or hard or uncomfortable it might be. I leaned against the foot of the banister, back against stone, and pulled Henry over me, legs on either side of him.

I shook my head in answer to his question. "No," I moaned, just as he sucked on my neck, then trailed to my breasts through the shirt.

Taking his hand in mine, the one continuously teasing my entrance, I said, "This is," before I pushed his finger into me. Moaning and marveling at the way *he* moaned.

"Paula," he said, hushed and needy. I thought he might say something else, but he didn't.

Just Paula. *Just me.*

Slowly, rhythmically, he pumped his fingers into me until his head disappeared under my shirt and his kisses trailed over my nipples, down to my stomach, between my thighs.

Wholly, eagerly, while my head fell against the stone and I moaned his name into the trees around us, he devoured me.

*

I must've fallen asleep again after we'd moved to his bedroom, because when I opened my eyes, enough time had passed to make the house smell. I would love to say amazing, like home-cooked meals and freshly prepared produce, but it just smelled. Perhaps like someone was *trying* to cook.

I slipped out of bed, fished some clothes out of the bag Henry had packed for me, and went to investigate.

When I got to the kitchen, before I'd even said anything, Henry turned away from where I'd appeared in the doorway. "Are you wearing more than just that shirt?" he asked, continuing to shield his eyes. "Because I'm busy over here, and I don't want to have to abandon my workstation. Which I would have to if you're—"

"I'm decent."

Henry sighed in relief, let his hands fall to his sides. "Couldn't say I'm not at least a little disappointed," he said regardless, with an amused tone, as he returned to his pot. My eyes were drawn to the contents of it, and I stopped short when I recognized it immediately.

Arroz de pajarito.

My gaze snapped back and forth between Henry and

the traditional dish he was preparing. Seeing him behind a stove was already unusual—you didn't really learn to take care of yourself when you grew up with nannies, cooks, and housekeepers doing it for you—but he was trying to make one of the few Dominican specialties that don't revolve around meat.

"What are you doing?" I asked because I didn't know what else to say.

"What does it look like I'm doing?"

Cooking, obviously. A meal I hadn't had in years and hadn't realized I'd craved for just as long. "I thought I'd feed you before you tear my head off on the way home. And I remembered you said you missed Dominican food." His eyes slid in my direction, a playful grin on his lips as he turned the stove off. "And surprise, surprise. You came just in time. It's like you have a sixth sense for these things."

Arroz de pajarito was an almost foolproof dish. Cook rice. Fry plantain. Combine the two and cook them together for another few minutes. "This would've been one of my many groveling attempts."

I assessed the food absentmindedly. "*One* of many?"

He laughed.

Henry had nailed the rice like any Dominican might—burnt to the bottom of the pot. But instead of ripe plantain, he'd accidentally opted for its green equivalent. Which meant it wasn't sweet and chewy but starchy and a little bland. It worked well in a variety of other dishes, but not necessarily in this one. It could've also done with a bit more seasoning.

All in all, it was . . . okay. But I couldn't care less because Henry had driven to the store, picked up groceries, and cooked a foreign meal for me.

So when we sat at the dining table fit for a group of twenty and he'd asked me how I liked it from the chair to my left . . . I lied. *Who wouldn't?*

"I love it." I took another big bite to demonstrate, and honestly, it really wasn't *that* bad. He gave me a disbelieving look despite my great performance. "Seriously," I stressed.

His frown grew, and he rolled his eyes. "I like it," he countered, unsure what to think of his own creation. "I do think it could be a little sweeter?" *It would've been if he'd picked the right plantain.* "Maybe if I added sugar next time?"

I audibly snorted at the suggestion. Just so beautifully American of him.

"No." I shook my head quickly. "Dios mío, no." It sounded worse the more time passed. "That's the plantain's fault, mi amor. I'll help you . . . *next time*."

The nickname slipped out so naturally, I couldn't even freak out because I only realized I'd said it when we were back in the car, and the memory replayed in my head just before I fell asleep.

CHAPTER 39

Now

I got back to my cat and my girls by late afternoon. As soon as their voices boomed through the open windows, arguing about the last *Love Island* rerun, I realized I'd missed them terribly, although it had only been two days. How would I survive not living with them once we graduated in a few months?

The thought stuck with me. Because right then, tragically, I remembered it wasn't a few months anymore. I'd gotten so used to saying *"Well, at least we still have a few months!"* that I'd forgotten time went on. It was no longer early March, with trees turning green and flowers blooming, but late April. The sun was high, sometimes burning, and we only had weeks until graduation.

Only weeks with the people I'd shared every aspect of my life with over the past four years.

Exams passed, projects graded. The only thing missing

was the article. There was nothing left to do but wait until we'd put on those robes, get handed our degrees, and go out into the world.

What a terrifying thought.

The piece on Henry would be released in the graduation-day issue, when graduates were more likely to get and keep an issue for the sake of it. And there was a gigantic difference between having it graded and read by professors and having it scrutinized by your peers. The latter was obviously much worse.

After editing, rewriting, then editing some more, I'd sent the draft to Eddie by the end of the week, as promised. And maybe I *could* have the best of both worlds, because I'd done it all while having incredible sex with Henry.

When Henry would text, I'd reply, "CAN'T YET. WRITING." He told me to make him look good and left it at that. Sometimes he ordered food to be sent to my place because he knew that when I was in the zone, I was *in the zone*. Forgetting to eat and drink or care for my basic needs until the flow of words ebbed.

He never demanded my time when I couldn't give it to him. In return, I'd go over to his place the moment I could.

Thankfully, I was too busy writing to worry about what all of this meant for our relationship. The Hamptons trip had obviously changed things between us, but we hadn't talked about any of it.

I wasn't worried when Eddie called me into his office either. I was confident I'd nailed that article. It was dynamic, deep, and accurate. I'd seen and written about a side of him not many people would ever experience. In my piece, he'd spoken about his parents and his childhood more candidly than ever before.

Eddie smiled at me when I got to the office, door open like always. "Paula," he said by way of greeting, walking around his desk. But my attention wasn't on him or the fact that he was closing the door behind me a little farther, leaving only a small crack open.

It was fully and entirely on the perfect blond blowout and the body attached to the hair. Lacy threw a glance across her shoulder and smiled. "Hey. Thought you might not make it in time."

Her backhanded comment was like a slap to the face, and I whirled to Eddie, watching him walk back behind his desk. He sat.

"What is this?"

He gestured to the second chair on the other side of his desk, and I followed the request. He cleared his throat.

"Lacy has"—he hesitated, shook his head—"asked to meet us. Both." His tone indicated he had no idea what for either. By his preliminary door closing, though, he expected it to be . . . unpleasant.

"Yes," she said. "Thank you." Her eyes slid to me when she spoke next. "I didn't want to go behind your back with this, Paula. It would've felt wrong not to have you here, I think." Innocence radiated in the blue of her eyes, her soft voice.

I tensed when she handed Eddie a brown envelope, and I interpreted the curl of her lips when he pulled pictures out of it to mean Lacy was really saying, *I wanted to see your face when I did this.*

"What am I looking at?" Eddie asked, eyes narrowing at the A4 print of a *very* familiar photo. My eyes snapped to Lacy.

"How—?" *How did you get those?* I wanted to ask. But it sounded so incriminating, I cut myself off. My eyes trailed back to Henry and me in the photo.

Had Hallie sold us out?

Even if she had, she wouldn't have known what she was selling us out *for.* She wouldn't have done anything wrong, technically. Just sold photos of the newest NYBE addition and a rumored girlfriend to the highest bidder. But somehow, she didn't seem like the type. Like she would've at least let me know.

Lacy cleared her throat. "I found these in my inbox, Ed. Coming from Paula, of all people. Maybe she wanted to forward them to Henry but copied me instead?" *I* knew she was lying. Did Eddie?

But when I frantically felt for my phone in my bag, logged into my school email, and clicked on my "Sent" folder, there it was.

An email with attachments sent to l.halloway@hallbu.com. It was dated two weeks ago, on the day my first draft was due. That deadline robbed me of so much sleep, it will probably be burned into my brain for the rest of my life.

Coincidentally, it was also the day Henry had called me, come to the office, and almost had me in that broom closet of an interview room. I'd left Lacy alone in the office, and I couldn't remember whether I'd locked my computer before I answered that call.

"And . . ." Eddie cocked his head, brows drawn together. "What are these supposed to . . . show me?" He shuffled through the prints, then placed them on his desk. The one where Henry and I lay on the field topped the stack. I cringed.

Lacy blinked one, two, three times before landing her killing blow. "That Paula fucks her subjects for information. I heard Riley say it in the office. I know Henry came to see Paula here too. And who knows what happened in New York?" *Nothing!* "I think the pictures speak for themselves, though."

I flinched at the harsh language and how unapologetically she threw the accusation out. All the circumstantial evidence, presented like this, seemed damning enough. Even Eddie, who wasn't shocked by much, drew back in his chair.

"That's coercion," Lacy said when neither of us spoke. I was still too stunned, and Eddie was probably trying to figure out the best way to respond. "Clearly," she pressed, eyes flickering between us. "And who knows how long she's been doing that? In what other situations has she used her body to get what she wants?"

When had I ever *gotten what I wanted?*

Last I remembered, I hadn't gotten a damn thing for an entire year, then got stuck with a project I did *not* want. I almost roared the words at her, but I stayed quiet.

"Those first external gigs, *The New York Times.* Then

the Ivy project." She trailed off. "They always seemed a little too good to be true, right? Who knows. Maybe she knew a friend of a friend of a friend who knew the editor in chief, and . . . you get my drift."

The breath I'd drawn in was so sharp, I couldn't speak. Lacy went on, "She uses her body to get what she wants, then to get them on the record with what she needs. Maybe that's why that source said she lied—"

"*Lacy*," Eddie finally snapped. "That's enough." His voice reverberated in the hallway and bounced off the walls. "Nothing about this piece is of your concern. Paula begged me to take her conflict of interest into account when I assigned it to her, and I couldn't. She called me the second her relationship to the subject changed, and there's still nothing I could've done. We decided to pivot from a traditional profile to a personal piece, but it doesn't matter because it. Doesn't. Concern. You."

"It does!" She matched his tone. Snappy and loud. Like she'd had enough too. "You're giving me reason after reason why I should've gotten this gig, Ed! You know I should've." Her chair scraped against the floor when she pushed it back, stood, and spread her hands on the mahogany desk. "I'm tired of losing shit to Paula *fucking* Castillo."

Eddie rose to meet her eyes. "I don't know what kind of jealous rivalry thing you two have going on. Frankly, I don't care." His eyes twitched into a glare. "But how on earth am I going to give you a project Paula was specifically requested for?"

"Oh, please." Her eyes rolled before flicking to me, only for a moment. "By who?"

"The subject of it, Lacy."

Their back-and-forth continued, but I checked out. My head roared, my stomach lurched, and my heart missed a beat, I think.

The subject of it.

Eddie's words echoed in my mind.

He was very sure he wanted this profile and everything else that comes with it.

It suddenly seemed so obvious. Like it had been staring me in the face for weeks and I'd just ignored anything that had hinted at the possibility ever since I'd gotten this project.

Because of Henry. Because he wanted me on it, and he'd made sure it would happen.

"What are *you* smiling about?" The sweet undertone that usually played in Lacy's voice was gone. Probably because this wasn't going the way she had imagined at all. Probably because Eddie's frown was directed at her, not me.

"Nothing," I said so calmly, I surprised myself. After her accusations, I thought I'd be ready to physically fight the woman, but my hand didn't even twitch. I had no desire to punch her in her beautiful, perfect face. Instead, I got up and asked, "What is your problem, Lacy?"

"Sorry?" she spat, eyes narrowing.

"What. Is. Your. Problem?"

"You are!" She huffed, the sound self-righteous as she

slung her messenger bag across her shoulder. "You are, Paula Castillo. With your beautiful hair and perfect writing and that awkwardly charming way that just magically opens doors for you! I mean, just look at you. Mark actively went against your record, said you didn't print what he said. And still! Like an annoying little cockroach, you're back! Writing the profile of the year on a man half the country will probably talk about soon."

I found it ironic. That Lacy was jealous of me when I'd been jealous of *her* since the moment I started at the *HBP*. Everything seemed to come easily for her—friends, projects, words. Effortlessly pretty and successful was *her* thing. Not mine.

But the news that I was talented and beautiful enough to be envied didn't make up for the fact that she'd just said my source's name. *That* source's name. Mark.

She must not have noticed the slipup yet. I think Eddie had.

I exchanged one look with him before turning to Lacy. "I keep my list of sources under lock and key," I said slowly. "Use alibis, delete emails." And I could see the exact moment it dawned on her. The moment in which Lacy Halloway realized she'd made a mistake. Said too much, too quickly, too passionately—and fucked up.

"Everyone knew it was Mark!" she said, frantically trying to fix the situation. Her eyes searched for help from our editor, who was grimly watching from the other side of the desk. He didn't offer any assistance.

"No one else knows that," he said, just as slowly and

carefully as I had. And he was right. *He* only knew because of my desperate attempts to convince him that I'd written exactly what Mark had told me—unsuccessfully. And the only reason Henry had known was that he'd suggested the man himself.

Lacy's bottom lip quivered, and in the seconds of silence that followed, she tried to contain it. None of us said a word. I, for one, didn't even breathe.

The situation was so delicate, the unsaid accusation hung in the air like thick smoke. And it would be the proverbial nail in the coffin of Lacy's bright career prospects. Because if she really did what we were all thinking—if she'd manipulated a source, bribed them or got them to lie on the record—just to stop my streak of good journalistic luck . . . hers was about to run out.

Lacy moved toward the door, and I was sure she'd leave without another word. But she paused in the doorway. She turned, eyes fixed on me, and said, "You should ask your boyfriend how I know about Mark Lager."

Only then, after wreaking havoc in my life once more and throwing the pieces I'd so meticulously sorted through in the past few weeks back into my face, did she leave.

Left me dumbfounded, confused, and angry at a man who was *not* my boyfriend.

The insinuation lingered between the two of us awkwardly. I was still frozen by Eddie's desk, and he tried to keep busy by sorting through the pictures of Henry and me. Pictures I didn't want to see right then—of us smiling and laughing and staring at each other.

As if he hadn't given Lacy my source. Her insinuation had been so obvious—

Eddie cleared his throat. "I'll get her back in here tomorrow," he said. "And I'll get that SPJ record of yours cleared, don't worry." His gaze shifted from the door to me. "But there's probably something you want to take care of now?"

Henry.

CHAPTER 40

Now

I'd ordered Henry to come to my place. I'd told him to wait in my room, and I definitely sounded angry enough because he'd done what I'd asked without a questioning word.

I was still angry when I stood in front of him exactly twenty-three minutes later. He was pacing up and down the room. Hands in the pockets of his jeans, dark blue button-down lazily tucked into them.

"Paula?" he asked, looking worried and confused.

I was confused too, but mine was more along the lines of *Why?* and *When?* and *How could you do this to me?*

I closed the door behind me and leaned against it with my hands pressed against my back, feeling defeated before the conversation (Argument? Potential fight?) had even started. My heart sank to the bottom of my stomach when I asked, "How do you know Lacy?"

Because on my very brisk walk here, I remembered he *had* known her. That she'd greeted him like they'd spoken before. Like they were acquainted, at least. Right after our first interview.

Henry's brow furrowed. "Who?"

"Blond hair. Blue eyes. *Hall Beck Post*," I listed. "Hates me," I added, snickering. "Ring any bells?"

His eyes trailed through the room, and the way they drifted to the upper-left corner of his vision told me he was trying to remember. Trying to jog his memory. It was worse, somehow, that he had forgotten something that had almost cost me my career.

His gaze jumped back to mine. "Halloway. Right?" he finally asked in confirmation. "Yeah, of course. Your friend from—" Henry cut himself off at the same time as it dawned on me.

When I realized my mistake in sync with Henry realizing his.

"Did you say *hates* you?" he asked.

I cursed under my breath. My head fell back against the door with a groan. "I never told you, did I?"

"No." He stepped toward me but still kept a good distance between us. "Last year, a few days before you interviewed Mark," he began, "I thought you gave her my number. She reached out and said she was supposed to set up the interview, but you forgot to give her the details. You were so busy she didn't want to bother you, so I—" Henry worked to remember. "What did she do?"

"Fucked me over," I figured. "Paid Mark to say exactly

what I'd want him to say in the interview, only to go against what we printed after. Essentially getting me a registered complaint at the SPJ—Society of Professional Journalists," I explained at his questioning glance. I snorted at how obvious it seemed now. "Jesus, how would Mark even *know* to go to the SPJ? Why would he care *so* much about ethics in journalism—the man studies business, for God's sake! There's nothing ethical about—" *Stop*, I told myself. I was still in a room with a business major. "No offense," I said and cringed.

"None taken." Henry shrugged, but it did not seem like an explanation of the situation had made him feel much better. "Fuck, Paula," he groaned, burying his face in his hands. "If I'd known . . . *Fuck*," he repeated. "That bastard wouldn't have just been running around with a black eye for a few weeks. It's one thing to get my girlfriend on the SPJ register; it's entirely another to get her on there on purpose. To meet you with the intent of fucking you over—"

But I was still stuck on his words. "A black eye?"

Henry snapped his head in my direction, like he just realized he hadn't been holding an internal monologue but was very openly saying what he was thinking. No filter, just Henry. Who blinked at me, perplexed and a little apologetic.

"I'm sorry," he sighed, running a hand over his face in . . . defeat? I'd never seen that emotion on him, so I couldn't be sure. "When I saw your texts about what happened last year, I saw red. I'd just gotten out of a strategy meeting, and when you didn't answer the phone, I saw . . . redder, I guess. I figured you were with Maeve, so I got in the car. I wasn't quite sure what I was doing, honestly. Next thing I knew, I was at Harvard, though." Henry took a deep breath, and his eyes returned to mine across the room. "A two-hour drive, and I was still so angry. With myself, mostly, but so much more with Mark." He started in my direction, then stopped himself. "I swear I meant to talk to him. Ask what the fuck happened. My fist just, uh, slipped. Accidentally."

My breath came in ragged bursts at the new information, loud and heavy as I put the pieces together. "Slipped," I repeated. "Against his face?"

"Yes."

"Why?"

He finally overcame what had felt like miles between us to stand right in front of me, the intensity of a thousand suns in his eyes. "Because he hurt you, Paula."

Because he hurt me. Henry Parker Pressley had lost his bearings, driven to Boston, and punched a guy in the face because he'd hurt me, apparently. Without the plan to do so and without writing it into his calendar first. He'd done it purely on instinct.

Probably the same way he'd taken me to the Hamptons on instinct. Because I'd been stressed, and I'd looked like death, and he'd wanted to fix that. Giving Mark Lager a black eye hadn't fixed much last year, but it had probably felt pretty fucking great.

I looked up at him, mere inches away, not quite sure

what would come out of my mouth until it did. Barely a whisper. "*You* hurt me, Henry."

Just a few hours after he'd punched someone for the same offense.

His brows furrowed, the crease between them deepening with worry, guilt, and a thousand other emotions before he looked away, as if the reminder was a slap in the face anyway.

"I know," he forced out, then repeated the admission as it sank in. "I know. And I'm so fucking sorry, Paula. I felt guilty, confused, and . . . honestly, a little scared. I wasn't sure if Mark would go to the press over what I did, and I just . . . I thought we'd both be better off without my newfound love of making rash decisions. I put *your* future in jeopardy, then mine, and it just felt like I lost control over . . . everything." He shook his head, trailing off. "I am sorry, though. Really. For hurting you. For letting Lacy screw you over. I should've told you she asked about him—"

I grasped for his hand between us, and the words died on Henry's lips. "I—" he *stuttered*, and it took him about two seconds before both of his hands clasped around mine, holding on so tightly he might've been content with never letting go again. "This whole thing could've been so easily avoided if I'd just remembered to tell you about Lacy."

And I guess it could have been.

If I'd told Henry more about my life and he'd been less busy with his, this whole thing *would* have been avoided. Our breakup probably would've been too.

But there was nothing we could do about that now.

The anger I'd felt earlier—when I wasn't sure how well the two knew each other and why my boyfriend had told my nemesis about my sources—died. The lingering resentment over our breakup did too.

And I was only left with Henry. My hand in his, my body pulled against his chest, and the feeling of his racing heart beneath my touch. My eyes stung, and my heart was beating just as fast, in sync with his.

"I'm sorry," he whispered against my nose, as earnestly as every single one of his other apologies. When one hand left mine and his thumb swiped across my cheek, I realized I hadn't been keeping my emotions at bay as well as I'd thought. Just a few stray tears, but enough for worry to crease his brows again. "I'm not worth a single one of these, Paula. Please don't—"

I shook my head, fast enough for his hand to fall from my face and for my vision to blur for a moment. But I wasn't sure if the motion had cut him off or if it had been my strangled breath that sounded dangerously close to a sob.

"I forgive you, Henry."

My words hung between us for one, two, three seconds before relief spread across Henry's face, and he exhaled so loudly, it overcame the roaring in my ears.

It felt monumental. Like we might be about to get over everything that had come between us.

The article. Mark Lager. Lacy's accusation.

And, my God, if I wasn't just as relieved about it as he seemed. "I mean . . . you *are* still groveling, right?"

I didn't know how well the joke landed with tears

streaking my face and another sob—perhaps one of relief?—bubbling in my throat, but here we were.

His green eyes batted open a little wider, and his lips parted in surprise, replacing the tense frown. "You're not mad?"

"I've spent so much time being mad at you." My arms locked behind his neck, and his hands instinctively found themselves on my hips. "I don't think I could pretend for another minute."

He hugged me close. My nose pressed into his chest, pinewood and citrus taking over my senses.

But it no longer felt like a bad idea.

"So . . . groveling, hm?" he hummed into my hair. "Any specific requests?"

I tore my face away from his chest to look up at him. The insinuation, the mischief in his eyes, and the way his hand slipped below my shirt to caress the bare skin beneath it told me he certainly had something in mind.

And he was very willing to make up for whatever he still blamed himself for.

Who was I to object?

"I always thought the point of groveling was that the . . . grovel*er* had to figure out how by himself." But my tongue flicked across my lips, and my body betrayed me when I leaned into his touch, eyes threatening to close once his fingers danced across my back in featherlight patterns.

Henry's lips twitched. "Good thing that in my head, I replayed all those things you liked almost every night."

He pulled me with him until his legs hit my bed, and he sat. Looked up at me through heavy eyes. My hands were in his hair. I didn't know how they got there. "Good thing that I never forgot what you begged and pleaded for. The way you sounded. No matter how hard I tried."

His hands slipped to the waistband of my jeans. Our eyes locked as he undid the button and moved to the zipper. Didn't pull, just lingered. "Isn't it?"

And I meant to agree. Nod vigorously until he wriggled me out of my jeans and showed me exactly how much he remembered. Showed me that there was much more than what he'd shown in the Hamptons. And the times after that. But something in the back pocket of my jeans vibrated, then started ringing.

Henry slipped my phone out, probably to throw it across the room. I groaned when I saw the caller ID, though. Unhelpfully, he said, "It's your dad."

Which meant if I didn't pick up that phone in the next five seconds, my family would probably call the local police station all the way from the Dominican Republic to claim I was missing, had been kidnapped, or was lying in a ditch somewhere.

"Don't get any funny ideas," I warned, pointing a finger at Henry, whose hands lingered by my zipper. He raised both innocently, and I threw myself onto my bed. Henry followed and closed my button again before keeping his hands to himself.

For ten minutes, my parents filled me in on the latest gossip about various cousins, aunts, and old family friends.

"Sí" and "No" and gasps flew back and forth. Finally, they dropped the bomb.

"We're coming to America!" They said in unison, accents thick. "To see you finish school."

Henry must've heard them even with my phone pressed tightly against my ear because he smiled like he knew how much this meant to me. The last time my parents had been to campus was four years ago, the very day I met Henry.

"Will you be wearing one of those blue sacks?" Mom asked, put off by the thought.

My cheeks were beginning to hurt from smiling. "Yes."

"Do you *have* to?"

"Mami!" I protested and could hear her laugh on the other end of the line. Some rustling followed, and then my dad's voice rang through the phone again.

"Paula, it's me again," he said unnecessarily. "We have to go—" Again, some rustling, then a distant "Ay! Claro que sí, María. Es cara!"

He complained about how expensive phone calls to the US were for another minute—one that would cost him two hundred pesos, about three dollars.

"Lo siento, I'm back," he said, sounding like he had the phone back by his face. "We're so proud of you, cariño. Our little businesswoman. Adiós!" In the background, I could hear Mom shout a "Nos vemos!" before they hung up.

My smile dropped.

Businesswoman!

I'd been so focused on this article and my *journalism dream*, I'd forgotten my parents still thought I was doing something else entirely. Their daughter was about to get a business degree from HBU. I'd given them no reason to suspect otherwise.

"Hey—" Henry obviously noticed my change in mood and put two and two together. He squeezed my shoulder and brushed a curl behind my ear very sweetly. But that wasn't what I needed. I couldn't do this with just Henry.

A second later, I called my best friend's name so loudly, he flinched. I winced, throwing an apologetic look his way before Maeve burst into the room like she'd been on call.

"What's wrong?" she asked, brown eyes narrowing.

"My parents are coming for graduation."

She smiled at first, but I could pinpoint the exact moment she got it. Everything in her expression fell. She muttered a "Fuck." Sat on the foot of my bed cross legged.

We tried coming up with a plan. Mapped out the best ways to keep the lie going and explain why it said "Journalism" instead of "Business" on my degree. Lying was the only solution, after all.

I couldn't just come out and tell them *By the way, I've been lying to you for the past four years! You were paying a lot of money for a completely different degree! I'm a journalist now, surprise!* Instead, I planned to graduate, hopefully snag a job in journalism quickly, then tell them I was going to get business experience in a newsroom. Or something like that.

"Or . . . you know," Maeve said. "You could just tell them the truth."

I shook my head quickly, forcefully. "I can't." I let my

head fall onto Henry's shoulder in defeat. He hadn't said a single word yet.

"Paula," Maeve whined, drawing my thoughts away from him. She looked and sounded like she'd been talking to a wall for the past thirty minutes. She kind of had. "You'll have to tell them eventually! Might as well do it now?"

"Rip it off like a Band-Aid." Henry nodded in agreement. I lifted my head off his shoulder, betrayed.

"Thank you, Henry!" Maeve swept her hand in his direction. It was good to know she was aware of his presence; she hadn't otherwise made that known.

At my glare, he gave me a long look.

Maeve snickered. "Your boyfriend's right."

And the knowing smirk told me she'd only called him that to tease and taunt and embarrass me. Maybe so I'd agree to tell the truth, which would get her away from Henry faster.

Before I could protest loudly, then die of mortification, I felt Henry's hand in mine. Really, he only let it brush over my skin, but it was enough to keep my mouth shut.

Even Maeve seemed surprised. A small win in my book.

"Rip it off like a Band-Aid," she repeated then. "Plus. He has no choice but to agree with me."

"She's right." Henry nodded grandly.

"Will you two do nothing but agree with each other today?" I groaned, exasperated.

Maeve ignored my outburst. "No one wants their girl's best friend to hate them. Right, Henry?"

Her eyes narrowed as she doubled down, and this time

it felt more like a test. Like she said it not to annoy me but to see his reaction. She was acting like a parent trying to figure out their daughter's significant other's intentions before the two headed off to prom.

Henry's lips split into a deep grin, and I realized he was just as aware of the fact.

"Maeve," he said, leaning forward enough to poke her shoulder. She swayed slightly. "You could never hate me."

"Do that again and we'll see about that, Pressley."

Whether she meant the poke or the breakup, I didn't know.

Either way, Henry's expression turned serious, solemn. "I wouldn't dream of it."

Which . . . was nice. And terrifying.

Although we'd been enjoying each other's company beyond the physical—though that too—we'd never spoken of the Hamptons again. Of his confession. Of mine. Of the fact that no matter how much I wanted to be with him, our circumstances had hardly changed.

I'd forgiven him just half an hour ago, yes, but he was off to play in the big leagues soon, and I'd be doing . . . God knows what. Forgiveness was one thing, but balancing time, priorities, and schedules wasn't an issue we'd leave behind in college.

I paled at the reminder of conversations I needed to have, my color draining enough for Maeve to slip off my bed. "You guys should talk." It made me want to murder *and* thank her. "And just so you actually do, I'm leaving this door open."

"Question." Maeve was almost out the door when Henry piped up one more time. She glanced across her shoulder, a brow quirked. "You don't seem . . . surprised by me. That I'm here."

It wasn't a question, but she answered anyway. "I'm not," she said, smirking. "I know you've been at it like rabbits for . . . a while. Since the Hamptons, probably." At Henry's surprise, she elaborated, "Paula always has this glow around her when you're involved." And she left.

Right then, the only *glow* on my face was bright red.

"Aw," Henry cooed. "You glow!"

"Shut up."

"I will literally never let this go," he said, gloating in that way of his. Wide-eyed and happy, he couldn't get the grin off his face, and he could not keep his eyes off me.

How could I not spend every second of my waking life wanting to kiss him?

"Door! Open!" Maeve shouted from downstairs, as if she knew what we were about to do . . . and not do. "Talk! Now!" she added.

I sighed, letting my head fall back into the pillow. "I hate that girl," I whispered affectionately.

"Well." Henry mirrored me, laying his head on the same pillow and looking up at the ceiling with me. "She loves you."

He felt for my hand on top of the covers, intertwined a single finger with one of mine. I could feel the unspoken words on his lips. The moment was so tangible and the template so perfect, I think I was holding my breath, waiting for him to say something like *I do too*, or *Maeve and I have that in common*, or *I happen to know what that's like.*

"Talk about what?" he asked instead.

Disappointment settled in my stomach.

"You're the man with the plan," I said. "Tell me, what does your schedule look like after graduation?" *Do I still fit in there? Or is it already bursting with appointments and responsibilities?* "What's in your calendar on May 20th?"

The day after we'd officially graduated. When he'd move to New York and settle into his new life as a pro soccer player. He'd have more money, more fame, and more responsibilities but less time for any relationships that weren't professional ones. Less time for me.

In one of our many interviews, he'd told me the week after graduation would probably be the busiest of his life. Team introductions, interviews, business dinners.

"Oh," he offered unhelpfully.

"Yeah." My head turned, and I noticed his eyes had been on me for a while.

"So? What's it say?"

I couldn't pretend I wasn't the least bit curious despite the fact that it would set my biggest fear into stone. We were not meant to be.

The air was thick with the weight of the unsaid. Although he hadn't given an answer, I could imagine what it was. His life was about to fundamentally change. I didn't fit in his busy schedule or his New York life. God, who could afford to live in New York?

And why was I thinking about moving to New York?

"I can't tell you," he finally whispered, looking . . . mortified? The confused frown on my lips urged him to say, "It's embarrassing."

"Embarrassing?" It was the last word I expected to hear. *Private, full, none of your business*—all things I'd been bracing for. But *embarrassing*?

Henry nodded. "Very much so."

"Maeve just told you I glow when you're around," I reminded him. "I'm sure it's not worse than that."

He shook his head, but at least it was with a smile this time. "It's not the same," he said. "That's cute! My schedule on May 20th is . . . serial killer–esque."

"Tell me," I said in a singsong voice.

Henry groaned, turned back to look up at the ceiling so he could avoid eye contact.

I reached for him. My hand lingered against his cheek before I guided his head back in my direction, and our eyes met once more. My fingers continued their way along his jaw, trailed across his cheeks, and I watched as he became really still, like he didn't want to miss any of my touch by accidentally breathing too hard or moving too much.

His eyes fluttered shut, and my hand disappeared into his hair. He sighed, more content than I'd seen him in . . . a while. Ever? I think I could watch him for the rest of my life without getting bored.

"Please?" I asked, voice soft.

Henry's eyes stayed shut. "Just you." He barely spoke

the words; he breathed them, and I read his lips. "Just your name. On May 20th."

My breath caught in my throat. He hadn't opened his eyes.

"Henry." I couldn't interpret the way I'd said his name either. I'd never sounded the way I just had. "Surely you have to get to New York that day. Settle in?"

"I'll do it the next."

The words stretched between us. And I didn't know what *he* was thinking, but I wasn't. Thinking. At all.

There was this loud, thunderous booming in my head, and it might've been my heartbeat. I didn't know what I would say until it came out of my mouth.

But I guess we had to address the elephant in the room at some point. This seemed as good a time as any.

"And"—I swallowed—"has anything else changed? Since last year?"

"Everything." He seemed sure. But I shook my head.

"You'll be busier than ever after you graduate," I reminded him, but it was halfhearted. My brain tried to come up with reasons why this was a bad idea while my heart felt as big as my entire chest.

Henry shook his head, still sure. "It'll only be soccer after graduation. No more exams to study for, no more papers to write. It'll be soccer and you."

But—"You'll move to New York. You'll be traveling for games. You'll be away a lot."

"And I'll be with you whenever I'm not. Wherever you decide to go. You won't have to fit into my schedule; I will fit into yours."

"You seem to have thought about this a lot," I said.

"All the time," he agreed. "Every day."

"So you have a solution to every single problem I bring up?"

"I've got two, Paula. Three, for some."

And I believed him. The fact that he'd cleared his schedule on what was supposed to be his busiest day showed that. That he'd made time instead of expecting me to.

I took a deep breath. "You still owe me those deeply personal questions."

I hadn't used them in the interviews. Everything I'd asked, he'd given up willingly. Without the need for an ace (or three) up my sleeve. I could only think to use all of them on one question now.

"I do," he agreed.

"So—"

"No," Henry said, laughing and wincing, then closing his eyes like he couldn't bear to look at me. I waited. When he finally opened his eyes, the embarrassment and sheepishness had been replaced by what I knew of him. Mischief. Humor. Adoration. "That's the answer to your question. I do. I love you. I honestly don't think I ever really stopped."

Stomach turning, cheeks heating.

"That's what you were going to ask, right?"

It had been. I tried to play it cool, but I was obviously failing.

"I was actually wondering about your favorite breakfast food?" I smiled, cheeks hurting, deciding to climb on top of him and straddle his lap.

I looked at Henry and thought, *This man loves me.*

He loves me.

He *loves* me.

He loves *me*.

Again.

"I take it back!" he scoffed.

He did not take it back. Instead, his hands moved to my waist, and his eyes sparkled the way I thought they only did when he talked about soccer. But he looked at me that same way now, and I wondered if it had ever really been about the sport or just the fact that it was me he was telling about it.

I smiled at my thoughts, at him, at everything else in this world that was beautiful because I loved him too. Of course I did. And I told him with a kiss, and my hands in his hair, and then my words. "I love you," I repeated, over and over.

Which was when my cat hissed from the hallway. That was another reason the door was usually closed when Henry was around. I rolled off him with a huff.

When he sat up against the headboard, he maintained steady eye contact with Pip. She continued to hiss, but her back wasn't arched the way it usually was in his presence.

"We're going to have to do something about Pip, though."

And he sounded scared at the prospect.

CHAPTER 41

Now

It was graduation day, I still hadn't told my parents about my degree, and I had about six more hours before I had to figure out what to do about it.

On top of that, the *Hall Beck Post* issue with Henry's piece had just dropped. All morning, I'd run around campus and the office and my house like a frightened chicken until Maeve had finally confined me to the bathroom because with all my nerves, I'd forgotten to shower.

My hair was still damp when we arrived at the auditorium, which was gradually filling up. Parents chatted excitedly with their children after months or years apart, siblings played around, bored students stared at their phones, and exactly one person sat in the front row, holding an issue of the *Hall Beck Post*.

My stomach still dropped sometimes when I saw Henry unexpectedly. Like when we ran into each other at Daisy's or when he opened the door to his apartment wearing only a towel around his waist.

I walked to the front of the hall, probably a little sheepishly, and sat next to him. "Riveting read, I hear."

Henry held his hand up, eyes scanning the last paragraph before finally looking over. "This Pressley fella," he said, tone mocking. "What a guy, huh?"

"I was told he's a little full of himself."

"Funny," he huffed. "I heard he's humble as can be."

I snickered, letting my head fall on his shoulder with a loud exhale. "So, you like it?" I asked, and there was no point in hiding the desperation in my question. I needed this to be good; otherwise, I might as well throw myself into more debt for that business degree after all.

Henry nodded in agreement, smoothing a hand over my head. And then, like he'd been having a completely different conversation in his head, he said, "You didn't print it."

He was holding the paper in his hands. I could see some of Hallie's candids on the page and the paragraphs I'd meticulously crafted. So it definitely had been printed.

"What?"

"Those things I said." He swallowed, still looking at the stage in front of us. "About . . . Felix. The contract I almost didn't sign. Don't try to deny it; I know you realized." My mouth closed again.

My tone softened. "I printed some of it," I pointed out.

"Not the parts I wouldn't have wanted you to. The parts I started talking to Stephanie about. Like . . . Dad." Stephanie, I remembered, was his therapist.

Those things had been off the record. No self-respecting journalist would put them in an article like this. An article that was supposed to strengthen his standing in his industry and my ability in mine. Best case, this was supposed to attract more teams and players who wanted me to write about them.

So Henry could tell his story when he wanted to, if he ever did. Maybe when he won his first cup with the Blue Eagles and mouthed *This is for you, Dad* into a live camera. We'd see.

"Where's your sister?" I asked, changing the topic to clear the air. The air did not feel cleared when Henry groaned at the reminder, then fell back in his chair.

"I'm hiding," he joked. "She thought it would be a great idea to join forces with McCarthy's family—my aunt and uncle did too, obviously." Glancing my way, he added, "And I would rather not hear another person gushing about his commencement speech."

"He's doing the commencement?" I should've toned down the curiosity in my voice. Henry sent me another glare.

"Of course he is."

I snickered, nudged his shoulder with mine. "Did *you* want to do it?"

"No."

What's the problem, then? I wanted to ask, but he cut me off before I could. "Where are your parents?"

The parents who didn't know about my degree yet.

I swallowed my laugh and winced instead. The

twenty-pound boulder of dread plummeted to the pit of my stomach.

"Late," I offered. "Judging by the flight updates, they'll probably get here right in the middle of the ceremony. Or after, if I'm lucky."

That way, at least they couldn't hear "Paula Fernanda Castillo, B.A. Journalism" blasting through the microphone. Which . . . was at least one crisis averted. Only a hundred more to go.

"In that case," Henry offered, "you'll only have to lie about what you do for the rest of your life. Easy enough."

The plan was to find a job at a small paper and work my way up the ladder there, which would be decidedly easier than doing it at one of the big five. I had three job interviews lined up for local papers—one in New York, two in Boston. And one of them would have to bite. Right?

I'd tell my parents once I got a shiny new job. With a title, health insurance, and a stack of business cards, maybe I wouldn't get that *chancla* to the head I'd been dreading since changing majors.

"Lying forever is *not* the plan," I said. "And you know it."

Henry stood, smiling. I followed his lead. "Because you've always been so great at planning, I'll leave you to it." He kissed me, short and sweet. The way a boyfriend might kiss his girlfriend. "I'm hoping McCarthy has taken off by now. Went to rehearse his grand speech or something." Henry rolled his eyes theatrically when he left.

I watched until he made his way out of the auditorium.

*

I hadn't been sure if I'd wanted my parents' flight to make up for lost time or circle the airport once more before it landed. But when they burst through the doors with the commencement ceremony in full swing and my name not yet called, I knew.

My heart skipped a beat and my legs wobbled. Their presence—Mom's wide smile when she realized they'd made it in time and every single emotion I could spot on Dad's face from a distance—meant that everything I'd kept from them for the past four years was about to come to light.

And still, I was glad to see them. Tears-in-my-eyes glad. Suppressing-a-sob glad.

We hadn't been in the same room for a long time. Since I'd said goodbye to them at the airport, hugged them tightly, and promised to make them proud.

The name before mine was called.

The student just ahead of me shook the HBU president's hand, got her degree, and walked off the other side of the stage. After polite clapping and a single cheer, the room quieted down again. I felt a little dizzy.

Knowing that this was the moment I'd worked toward for so long, that this was what I'd deceived my parents for. A major change, a lying source, a jealous cowriter, and a mended broken heart later, I was about to graduate.

"Paula Fernanda Castillo" blasted through the speakers. I could hear Maeve cheer from somewhere behind me. Henry was near her, probably clapping too. Dylan and

Caden hollered from somewhere in the crowd of graduated students, and I almost felt proud. Then I remembered my parents at the back of the auditorium.

Despite my Jell-O legs, I moved. Took one step, then another onto the stage. Crossed to the middle of it. "Bachelor of Arts. Journalism."

My eyes closed as I shook the school president's hand, not wanting to see Mom's proud smile falling or Dad's forehead wrinkling in confusion. Once they realized the announcement hadn't been a mistake, I didn't know if I could still look them in the eyes at all.

I was ushered off the stage to the much smaller pool of students with their degrees already in hand. I held mine tightly—probably wrinkled it with *how* tightly. But it was my only anchor now.

The entire commencement ceremony lasted nearly two hours. I cheered as my friends stepped onto the stage. Caden had gone before me, but Laila eventually followed, then Dylan and Riley. When Maeve crossed and gave me a wink, I almost started crying. When Henry walked after his sister, I couldn't believe we'd found a way back to each other.

None of that made me forget what was waiting on the other side. When the last person took hold of their degree, I wished the commencement would stretch a little longer.

My parents were the first to leave that hall, and I sent a helpless glance across the many students around me, trying to find—

"Looking for someone?"

I could pick his voice out of a million samples if I had to. Leaned into his body behind me before turning around.

"You," I said.

Henry slung his arm around my waist, leaned his head on top of mine. "Where are they?" he asked, knowing about the decision I had to make now.

To tell them or to lie more. To spill the truth or blame it on a mistake.

I looked back at Henry for some kind of guidance. Remember? Making decisions was not my strong suit. But he didn't push me toward the exit to follow my parents and tell the truth, nor did he reach for my hand to pull me into a quiet place to talk about how to make the lie more believable.

He just looked at me with his green eyes and said, without a word coming out of his mouth, that it was my choice. He wouldn't judge whether I turned around and told them or faked a laugh and said I had no clue why my diploma was misprinted.

"Will you come with me?"

I hoped his presence would lighten the blow.

CHAPTER 42

Now

My parents both held high school diplomas. That's where they'd met. They never went to college because by the time they turned eighteen, Dad's parents had died, and he'd taken over their little restaurant by the beach. Mom waitressed until the place made enough to hire help, and Dad promised María Castillo she'd never have to wait tables again in her life. She thanked tourism for the business it brought every day. They got married, he took her name, and a few years later . . . there I was.

They'd been putting money into my college fund since before I was born and as I grew up in the sand, by the water. Dad never had a problem making *me* wait tables. *"You're working your way to America, Paulita,"* he'd said before I'd even known what the United States was.

That I'd gone to college here had been his dream more than my own, I think. Twenty-two years later, I stood in front of him like the manifestation of it, only for everything to be kind of fake.

Mom was furious. I didn't blame her.

She was so angry, she'd forgotten all about fitting in, shouting about trust and secrets in Spanish. Although our spot behind the library was more secluded, her anger still drew a few curious glances.

That wasn't what I was worried about, though.

It was the way they looked at that degree now. Their eyes skimmed over the words again and again. Probably ignoring my perfect transcript, because I could tell they weren't focused on my grades. They were looking at the classes I'd taken.

Again, I didn't blame them.

Instead of tax law, econ, and statistics classes, I'd taken creative writing, media law, and reporting workshops. Every single course reminding them of the fact that I'd taken their hard-earned dollars and thrown them at a degree they probably deemed unnecessary, stupid, and a waste of time.

Well, maybe. I'd been holding on to Henry's hand for dear life to keep myself from thinking about that.

Dad placed a hand on Mom's shoulder, gently squeezing it. He looked up at me, and I couldn't believe there was anything resembling a smile on his face. "So my little girl is going to be a writer?" he asked. "Like Leonardo Nin?"

I blinked like hell to keep the tears away. "No, Papi," I muttered, shaking my head lightly.

Nothing like Leonardo Nin, who wrote poems and fiction in books that were scattered all over the place I'd grown up in. Courtesy of Juan Castillo.

"More like . . ." I thought for a moment. "Like Rachel Nichols, Emily Longeretta. Edith Zimmerman."

Dad nodded like he actually knew who they were when he obviously had no idea. "Alright," he said, but Mom still looked tense under his touch. "Like Rachel Nichols."

I could tell it was all a bit much for him—seeing me again, then adjusting to the fact that I hadn't told them everything about my life while I was away. Most of all, going over my mother's head.

He cleared his throat, held on to Mom's shoulder a little tighter, massaged the spot I knew she'd always been tense in, and took out his phone. An old little thing, but it had internet. So he searched for Rachel Nichols, looked at pictures, read some of her Wikipedia page, then held the phone out for Mom to do the same.

"It looks like she makes good money, mi vida. No?" he whispered, close to her ear. I could see some of the tension rolling off her as her shoulders relaxed. Her face softened. I let go of a breath I must've been holding for so long, it was loud enough for Henry to give my hand an encouraging squeeze.

I'd forgotten he was still holding it.

"And this is what you want?" she asked.

I nodded. I thought I might squeal if I opened my mouth.

"It is done now. So." And she shrugged.

I never really thought about what their reaction might be. About the fact that, really, they couldn't do much but accept their—*my*—fate. They loved me too much to disown me.

"I always thought you'd be a little too soft for negotiating, anyway."

Exactly what I wanted to hear.

I rushed into their arms with such force, my parents stumbled several steps back. I mumbled so many versions of "Thank you" and "Sorry" into their necks that I couldn't remember them all when I let go, with the biggest smile on my face since making up with Henry.

They seemed to remember the man behind me at the same moment I did.

"So, you're still here," Mom said, giving him a once-over.

Which was weird for two reasons. I did not expect my parents to remember Henry, the stranger I'd forced into pretending to be my friend in order to stay at HBU all those years ago. I'd also never mentioned him again—certainly not as a boyfriend.

I knew my dad would've emptied his entire account to get on the next flight up here and cross-examine the unlucky guy.

"I didn't tell you—"

"Oh, please." Mom waved me off. "You were halfway to married when you introduced us." She was so sure of the fact, I didn't have the heart to tell her we'd known each other for all of five seconds back then. Plus, there was no need to reveal two lies in one sitting.

Dad's eyes slid from Henry back to me. "¿Estás segura de que es uno de los buenos?"

Are you sure he's one of the good ones?

I could feel Henry shift beside me as he took a step toward them. He held his hand out for my dad to shake, and said in choppy, imperfect Spanish, "I try to be."

And although he butchered the pronunciation, Dad took his hand, smiled, and said in imperfect, choppy English, "Good. Or I will kill you."

Even though Dad didn't laugh before, during, or after the delivery, Henry didn't seem phased.

"I'd hope so, sir."

Henry invited us to join his family for lunch, which—he begrudgingly told me when we led the way there—had been taken over by the McCarthys. Again.

On the way there, Marty had texted Henry, and Eddie had texted me. Three separate times, all about the profile.

> *Sports Illustrated* wants it.
> *The New York Times* wants it.
> Call me when you get the chance.

I would, right after I had lunch with the people I loved most. We had a lot of catching up to do.

After skimming his texts, Henry silenced his phone, kissed me, and whispered against my lips, "I have the most talented girlfriend in the world, don't I?"

I huffed a laugh, my heart doubling in size. "Girlfriend, is it?"

"Wait." His eyes widened when he blushed. "We're back on, right? You *are* my girlfriend?"

I don't know if you noticed, Paula, but you make me nervous. This was one of those moments, I think.

I snickered, glanced at Henry as we walked to the restaurant just a few feet in front of my parents, hands interlaced. "You know what they say." I smiled up at him, nudging his shoulder with mine. "Second time's the charm. Or something like that."

EPILOGUE

Later

July

"Give me a second," I blurted into the phone, trying to cut off the voice on the other end. "I'm almost—can we talk about this when I'm home? I can't take notes—*No*, I can't take notes. I'm in the elevator—"

I slid through the doors as soon as they opened on the twentieth floor, trying to wrestle the keys out of my tote, phone clutched between my ear and shoulder. "Marty!" I said. "Please wait five seconds until I can sit at my desk and write this down, will you?"

Somehow, I managed to get into the apartment with one hand, let my bag slide to the ground, and threw the keys on top of it as I closed the door with my foot. "Yes," I exhaled, crossing the entrance into the living room. The plan had been to get into the study—to my laptop and pens and paper—as fast as possible. If only to get Marty,

Henry's manager and *my* boss, to stop throwing ideas at me that I couldn't write down somewhere.

I stopped in my tracks when my eyes were drawn to the white sofa in the middle of Henry's living room. It probably cost a fortune and was definitely designed by someone whose name people oohed and aahed at.

Henry did not sit on it. He sat on the floor, leaning against the back with his long legs extended and a packet of cat treats that must've fallen out of his hand. His eyes were closed, neck craning in a way that would probably leave him with aches for days.

He wore one of his new jerseys in the Blue Eagles' signature color.

Number 7, Pressley. Same as his dad.

To his side, Pip had curled up with a single treat still hanging out of her mouth. She, too, was fast asleep. I was surprised my tumultuous arrival hadn't startled them both awake.

"Paula?" I straightened at the reminder of Marty on the line. "You still there?"

"Yes." I lowered my voice and gave the two a final glance before I tiptoed into the office. "Will you repeat what you need me to know for Lee's profile, please?" I grabbed my notebook, sank into the chair, and rolled the few remaining inches to the desk, which had a perfect view of the Upper East Side. "I can write now."

"Oh," Marty huffed. "No, don't worry about it. My assistant has all of that. She'll email you ASAP."

I suppressed a groan. *He couldn't have said that before I sprinted an entire block to get here?*

"How's the profile coming along, though?" he continued casually, as if he hadn't bombarded my phone and email with the same question.

Josh Lee was my third Blue Eagles profile, and as the team's star player—he had the longest contract, the highest pay, and the most media attention—it was understandable that Marty was . . . interested. Involved. More involved than with the others.

"Good. As the one before. And the one before *that*."

"Good," he mirrored. "Great. Listen, we've been thinking. There'll be quite a few away games in the coming months."

Like it wasn't a constant on my mind. They'd be hopping from city to city to play for the MLS Cup in December soon, hopefully winning it. By then, five months would've passed with me back in New York, watching and watering Henry's plants. Glancing to my right, I noted two of them on his bookshelf.

We didn't officially live together. I had my own place thanks to my freelancing, which included three profiles for the Blue Eagles' print magazine, a collector's item they released a few times a year. It was small and shabby, and I definitely saw a cockroach dash across the floor one morning. But it was mine.

So when Henry had offered his much grander penthouse for the time he was away, I'd declined. He'd already taken care of my student loans—who'd say no to that?—and I didn't ever want him to feel like I was using him.

But he'd begged and pleaded and schemed until one

day, I'd walked into his apartment, and an entire jungle stared back at me. Every room had gotten a lot greener.

"Can you take care of my plants, Charm?" he'd asked. "They're on a very meticulous schedule, so someone would need to water them Monday to Sunday, and—wait, in that case . . . you could just stay here, I guess?"

Plant duty it was.

"And with all these away games"—Marty's words snapped me out of my thoughts, and I nodded dutifully, even if he couldn't see me—"we concluded it would be great to have an in-house journalist. Who can really get to know the guys and write about them. Their wins and losses and strengths—maybe not their weaknesses," he thought out loud.

Immediately, my entire body buzzed at the prospect. I'd gotten up halfway through his words, paced the office until he was done talking.

It sounded perfect. Too good to be true.

I didn't think before I accepted. I thanked Marty over and over again, and we'd decided to meet next week to talk shop, and salary, and all the things you wouldn't necessarily want to discuss on a Friday evening.

When I got back to the living room, Henry was no longer on the floor. I felt him behind me a second before he slung his arms around me. "When did you get home?"

Home.

"Just now." I turned in his grip, smiled up at him. "How did the bonding go?" My head nodded to where Pip still slept on the floor. The scattered cat treats were cleaned up and put away.

Henry grimaced. "Not great," he admitted. "Apparently better after I fell asleep. Maybe she thought I was dead?"

I snorted at the image, but I couldn't disagree. She probably did think she'd finally won.

"I just spoke to Marty," I told him.

Whatever suspicions I had of Henry's involvement in the idea evaporated when his brows creased and his head tilted in worry. "What about? Is the Lee profile going alright?" Voice lower, he added, "Do you need me to talk to him?"

I beckoned Henry to the couch with me, rolled my eyes, and laughed as I shook my head. "Nothing like that. Marty offered me a job."

And with every word, every detail, Henry's eyes got wider. His smile bigger. "And?" he asked, trying not to sound too eager and failing. "Are you going to take it?"

He didn't know I already had. How could I not—on the road, I knew I'd have great access to my subjects . . . and my boyfriend. It was a win-win in every sense.

Henry agreed wholeheartedly. Kissed me into the pillows of his couch until he'd lost his shirt and mine was unbuttoned and he muttered I-love-yous into my bare skin.

"But what about the plants?" I asked, irony lacing my voice when I looked back up at him.

He shook his head, absentmindedly lost his fingers between my curls. "They'll be gone by the end of the week." He didn't even blink. "I only rented them so you'd agree to get out of that hellhole you call an apartment. At least while mine was empty anyway."

My head shook in disbelief and adoration and everything else I felt for Henry. "You always get what you want, don't you?"

He considered me for a long moment and said, as if he wasn't talking about his contract or the big apartment, the money, and the fame, "Yes."

EXCLUSIVE BONUS CHAPTER

There's nothing like a hot July day in the Dominican Republic. Or a hot March, September, December . . . *listen*, it's called the land of perpetual summer for a reason. I'd never been a big fan of the stifling heat, the incessant sweat clinging to every crevice of my body, but at least I was used to it. Henry, on the other hand . . .

"Paula!" he cried. His cheeks were redder than after the most demanding game of his career last week. His hair was damp, curling at the nape, and he was panting. "How much longer?"

We'd been out of the car for three minutes.

I skipped up to Henry for my bag, wanting to lighten some of the burden placed on him by the humidity and damn-near-ninety-degree heat. "Five minutes." Cars weren't allowed all the way up to La Palapa. "Feels more like two—hey!"

Bag previously dangling by his side, he swung it over his shoulder with a glare so cruel, the only reason it didn't land was the exhaustion behind those green eyes. "Don't you dare touch those bags, Charm."

But the delivery was all off too.

I rolled my eyes before I watched him set off across the sandy path—my bag hanging from one shoulder, my tote from the other, and my second sun hat on top of his head—his posture as close to slouching as Henry Pressley would allow. My heart swelled at the sight.

Nonetheless, I felt the need to comment, "You're clearly struggling."

Which he didn't like at all and made known with a gasp. "I'm a professional athlete," he argued, offended. "One of the highest-valued players in my field."

"I know."

"The Blue Eagles just won the MLS Cup."

"I was there," I reminded.

"I would've hoped you could trust me with a few bags, Paula." But he heaved his next breath, then immediately cursed himself for it.

Henry was used to relentless cardio drills, vigorous strength training, and adrenaline pumping through his chest with each step he ran. He *was* a top athlete. He *did* win the championship. But Caribbean heat hit different, and he was starting to realize that.

Not out loud, but the scowl on his face told me regardless.

After knowing him for so long—and now *months* without walls and masks and whatever else he'd tried to hold on to the first time around—it was easy to read him. Every twitch on his face, tone of his voice, and shift of his body had become familiar.

Whenever it was as apparent as it was now, I felt a little like Maeve. Or Dad whispering "Cuidado" across the dinner table before Mom had even said anything—knowing by her tells alone that I'd just revealed something I shouldn't have.

Henry was definitely giving me *cuidado* energy now. *Careful*, it said. *One more word, and he might snap.*

And what was I put on this earth for, if not to humble Henry?

"You know I love you, but your cheeks are the color of the HBU logo, mi amor. I can just take—"

"Don't." He did snap it, but as lovingly as he could. "If your dad sees you arrive with your own bag in hand, I'll never hear the end of it."

"We're only here for a week," I reminded, still beckoning him to give me my bag. Just to make it worse, I stopped.

"It wouldn't change anything if we were here for a *day*." But his eyes closed when he turned back to me, and he couldn't be too mad about my stop—and the fact that we'd be away from any kind of air conditioning for longer because of it—when he really seemed to have needed that break.

With the sun high in the sky, the complete absence of wind, and the hum of cicadas in the bushes around us, Henry was wavering. The heat was starting to get to *me*, and I'd grown up with it. I couldn't imagine what it was doing to him.

"He won't care. He's not like that," I said. Henry's eyes trailed to my outstretched hand as I went on, "He raised a strong, independent woman. Remember?"

And I think Henry knew I was lying when he handed the bag over.

*

"Would you like Paula to carry those bottles to the table, or will you be able to, Henry?"

"Dad!" If he was doing one thing, it was making Henry regret ever even considering giving me that bag.

With a heavy sigh, Henry got up, and not even my apologetic smile made his lips twitch. Like he knew exactly that every remark he'd gotten in the past few days was my fault.

"Coming, sir," he shouted back, making sure Dad could hear him all the way in the kitchen inside. "Anything else?"

A beat of silence before Dad's voice echoed through the restaurant again: "We did need a shelf put up. But Paula does know how to use a drill, so . . ."

With one more teasingly cruel glance and a mouthed *I told you*, Henry disappeared through the beaded curtain into the restaurant.

The same curtain I'd played peekaboo in growing up. Where I'd gotten my curls tangled up so badly, they had to be cut out and where my cousin and I ran into each other with so much force, she broke her nose at the ripe age of seven.

La Palapa held most of my significant childhood memories—from my first steps on the old wooden decking to getting my acceptance letter to Hall Beck University at the exact table I was sitting at now, in the corner, with a perfect view of the rest of my parents' restaurant.

Over the half wall, I could see Henry at the bar, holding two bottles of water in one hand and wiping his forehead with the other, despite the AC inside, which made the Dominican flag behind the counter flutter. Outside, heavy ausubo columns were spaced out evenly along the deck, tables with a perfect view of the ocean usually full after six. It was only two and never all that busy during the hottest hours of the day. After school, I'd do my homework at one of those empty tables. As a recovering picky eater, I'd have one of the two dishes I liked on the menu and would only be forced to go home when the tables were starting to fill up and I was keeping potential paying customers from, well, turning into them.

Seeing Henry in the middle of all those childhood memories was . . . weird. Good. Perfect. So nice, I didn't know what to do with the smile on my face or the gratitude in my heart for having found my way back to him. For taking that leap of faith, forgiving him, and letting him show me all over again how sorry he was and how he'd never be stupid enough to let me go again (his words, not mine).

With a sigh and a smile still so wide it hurt, my eyes drifted to my phone, which was vibrating with another reminder of how blessed I truly was. Having a man who loved me, parents who were able to look past their daughter lying to them for years on end, and a job so perfect, it seemed made for me.

Now that the Blue Eagles had won the championship—visibility, players' desirability, and media inquiries higher than ever—the only thing standing between me and a well-deserved break was a final piece about their performance this season and some quotes from the guys for that. The text notification on my screen was a friendly reminder that Henry's was the last postseason interview I still needed to conduct.

"What are you smiling at?" I recognized his voice, the way he pressed his lips to the top of my head, hand curling around my shoulder and—fuck! The ice-cold bottle of water currently pressed against my neck was *not* familiar.

Henry laughed while I screeched like a roach had just crawled across my face, jumping to my feet. Mom popped her head through the beaded curtain to check if I was alright, then deemed her support unnecessary when she saw us.

Me, gasping, cursing, wildly throwing my hands around and not making impact with what I would've loved to be his chest or arms or shoulders. Him, watching and laughing and eventually slinging his arms around my torso in an effort to keep me from seriously injuring myself or others. Once I finally managed to hit his back in what felt like a little bit of justice, I did.

The way I eventually relaxed into his touch felt natural at this point, and I let myself be swept away by the gentle, stoic presence he usually was (when he wasn't threatening me with cold water bottles).

"Hm?" he asked, amusement still in his tone. "Smiling at anything in particular?"

"Not anymore," I grumbled against his chest, but pulled him back once he tried to put some distance between us regardless. With a content huff, he let me. His gaze followed my nod toward my phone, still on the table. "Lee just texted about our postseason interview. He's freaking out."

"About saying too much?"

"He just talks without ever considering what's coming out of his mouth," I agreed. "Probably shouldn't talk more shit about the guy he fouled so hard, he got a red for it."

"Seems reasonable."

"You'd think!" I let my head fall into the crook of my neck, eyes connecting right with Henry's. Crinkles formed around them, sunlight reflecting in their green and making them sparkle. That same way they always did when he told me about soccer.

I wondered if I looked at him that way too whenever I told him about the things that made me happy. My friends, writing, him.

With a kiss to my nose, he let me slump back into my chair and got into his. "You should've never carried that bag three days ago, by the way."

My head shot toward my parents behind the bar again, wondering what they were so giddy about back there, before I turned to Henry again with a groan. "Still?"

"Still." He took a sip of his water, and I don't think the

relieved sigh after was intentional. "Juan asked if I expect you to get on one knee when—"

His eyes widened. Somehow, he choked on his words, not the water he'd already swallowed.

All I could do was smile. Blush. Damn near giggle when I pressed, "When?"

"When," he repeated, "I mean, if . . . Whenever. You know?"

"Do I?" *Yes.* I hadn't stopped thinking about what Henry's ring on my finger might feel like since that old man at the gala in New York had suggested it. And Henry hadn't even been my boyfriend at the time.

It had been less than a year since then, and thinking about marriage, kids, a future all grown up . . . it should've felt too early. It should've made me panic and spiral, but that had never been the case. It always just left that deep sense of longing behind. Of peace and security and a whispered *One day.*

Henry, probably sputtering for the first time in his life, found no way out of his slipup. Of admitting that he'd been thinking about it too, and it wasn't freaking him out as much as he'd expected it to either. He took another sip of his water, blushing and shaking his head. "Weren't there some questions you wanted to ask me?"

And without waiting for my reply, because I was still too amused by the picture of calm, confident Henry *stuttering*, he unlocked my phone himself, found the right app, and pressed start on the recording of what would be our last interview as boyfriend and girlfriend.

Two weeks later, blushing and stuttering all the same, he asked me to marry him.

And the reason my parents had been losing their minds behind the bar was because he'd asked both of them for permission.

ACKNOWLEDGMENTS

From the moment I mentioned Henry's ex-girlfriend in the first draft of *Lessons in Faking*, I knew that they would get their own book. I remember finishing Dylan and Athalia's story and being more excited about the fact that I could finally bring Paula and Henry to life (sorry!). Figuring them out was so easy, and I loved every second of writing their awkward tension and big feelings.

Still, there are so many people who helped me get them to where they are today, and I am forever grateful. A big, big, big thank-you to my editor, Katharina. That we managed two books in, like, half a year is pure insanity, but I loved every second of it. To the rest of team LYX—Steffi, Andrea, Jeannine—and everyone else I had the pleasure of working with: Thank you for making my books pretty, believing in me, and generally being the best publisher one could ask for.

Dad, thank you for being Juan Castillo's blueprint. I hope I did you (and all the aunts, uncles, and cousins) justice. Te amo.

To my agent, Ulf, thank you for taking a chance on me last year, and thank you for your continuous support since then. In the same breath: Thank you, Jonas, for connecting us in the first place. I don't know where I'd be without either of you.

To Manju, Annphie, and Clara, my own personal Maeve-Riley-Laila support trio, thank you for literally everything. Book related or not.

Naturally, writing a second-chance romance made me a little nostalgic and sentimental. Linda and Lau: Sorry for all the times you tried to keep me from texting my ex. And thank you for all the times you successfully kept me from texting my ex. If anyone read this book and is thinking *Hey, maybe I should reach out to my ex*, feel free to make use of my friends' advice and don't. You deserve better, and you will find it.

Last but not least, thank you. I'm so blessed to be writing these stories and even more blessed to have people reading them. Whether you enjoyed this or not, thank you for giving my stories and characters a chance. I'll be forever grateful.

ABOUT THE AUTHOR

Selina Mae is a writer of romance and reader of (you guessed it!) romance and has been compensating for her lack of meet-cutes by writing them into her rom-coms. When she's not writing, you will find her rereading her comfort books or crying at happy endings.

Keep reading for an excerpt from

Caden

I'd always thought of Valentina Rhodes as this whimsical, perfect figment of my imagination. Don't get me wrong, I knew she was real, and I was about . . . 90 percent sure that what had happened between us had been real too, but the second I'd laid eyes on her four months ago, she'd seemed a little impossible.

Her cherry-red hair, big brown eyes, round, rosy cheeks. The way she'd timidly sipped on her drink, smiled at me from across the bar—and the fact that she'd clearly had no idea that the way she walked and talked and danced had affected me so wholly.

That when she'd asked, after an hour of talking in some secluded corner of the party we'd been at, *"Are we leaving together, Callahan?"* I'd nearly combusted. And that sometimes, when I'd had a particularly bad day, I'd replay the way she'd said my name.

But because I hadn't heard from her since, I'd convinced myself I must've conjured her up. Ten percent of me, at least, believed I had imagined the whole thing.

Until now.

Four months later, a little past midnight too—but without a smile on her lips. Without that palpable tension between us, the need for more than flirty nothings exchanged in a loud college bar radiating off her. Because I was in her room, and judging by the scowl on her face, she had not expected me here.

In my defense: When Mike had warned me that I'd be sharing a room with one of his friends, the last person I'd expected to walk through the door was Valentina. Then again, when I'd walked through that door of our shared room a few hours earlier, the last thing I'd expected to find there was a bunk bed.

I'd been thinking about her a lot since we'd first (and last) seen each other four months ago, and still nothing could've prepared me for the visceral reaction I had when our eyes reconnected for the first time.

Like something had been unleashed, a sense of awareness that flooded through me. Reminded me of every single perfect thing about her—and why I hadn't been able to stop thinking about her. She'd been breathtaking then, in my mind, where I'd redrawn her from memory more often than I'd like to admit, but she'd still exceeded expectations. Somehow.

"What . . . ?" Her eyebrows drew together, as if she wasn't quite sure how to react to my presence. Fair enough, honestly. A (somewhat) strange man in my bed wouldn't exactly elicit a different response from me.

Valentina blinked rapidly, round eyes narrowing as she

searched for the right words. Going by what I'd learned about her in those few hours months ago, I expected a *What are you doing here?* Maybe a *What is happening?*

Clearly, I did not know her half as well as I'd liked to.

"What the fuck?" The words basically flew out of her mouth, and at least she seemed a little surprised by them as well. Then she caught herself—planted one hand on her hip while the other pointed an accusatory finger at me. "*What the fuck* are you doing here?"

CONTENT WARNING

(AND SPOILER WARNING!)

This book contains potentially triggering content. This includes

Mention of parents' deaths, plane crash, loss, grief